THE MAN WHO NEARLY HAD IT ALL

Geoff Daplyn

First published 2022

Publishing partner: Paragon Publishing, Rothersthorpe

© Geoff Daplyn 2022

ISBN 978-1-78222-978-0

Book design, layout and production management by Into Print
www.intoprint.net
01604 832149

By the same author

The Sniper, the Shopkeeper and Sami

Authors Note

THIS NOVEL IS a fictional account of what might have taken place behind the scenes in the bloody break-up of Yugoslavia. I have attempted to weave my characters into the events from Tito's death to the Dayton Agreement. Key events are followed as faithfully as the story would allow.

The few historical figures that are crucial to this story are given words and actions which I believe are credible in the light of their characters, and are mixed with their own words whether of speeches or conversations that were recalled by witnesses as accurately as records of the time show.

In all historical events, I recognise that there is always more than one viewpoint, especially those which are still within living memory. But in re-living these particular ones, my hope is that the terrible atrocities committed will never be forgotten, although I have to doubt whether that will be sufficient to stop them ever happening again.

As I write, Russia is shelling Ukraine in an ominous repeat not only of Syria but of Sarajevo, Srebrenica and many other places that have already been forgotten by the international community.

Characters

Significant historical characters:

Josip Broz Tito	President of Yugoslavia
Slobodan Milosevic (M)	President of Serbia
Mira Markovic	Wife to Milosevic
Franjo Tudjman	President of Croatia
Alijce Izetbegovic	President of Bosnia & Herzegovina
Radavan Karadzic	Leader of Bosnian Serbs
Ratko Mladic	General in Serbian Army
George H Bush	President of the United States
James Baker	Secretary of State of the US
John Major	UK Prime Minister

Main fictional characters:

Andrej Djuric	Adjutant to Tito and co-conspirator
Borislav Kovac	Senior Intelligence Officer and co-conspirator
Bojan	Treasury Civil Servant and co-conspirator
Petar	General in JNA and co-conspirator
Smolov	Russian advisor to M
Ivana	Personal assistant to Tito and girlfriend of Djuric.
Dragan	Treasury civil servant in Montenegro (Titograd/Podgorica)
Andries de Ryke	Corporal in DutchBat III UN force in Srebrenica.
Stefan Lukic	Son of Lukic family in Sarajevo and Lieutenant under Ratko Mladic

Other characters in Sarajevo, Kijevo, Zagreb, Srebrenica and other towns help to tell the story in those specific places.

SOCIALIST FEDERAL REPUBLIC OF YUGOSLAVIA
AS OF JANUARI 1991

Chapter 1 — Netherlands 2022

"WHAT DID YOU do in the war Daddy?"

Erik was home from his school in Haran, a small town situated in the north-eastern part of the Netherlands with Groningen the nearest city. Haran had developed into a typical commuter belt serving its larger neighbour, with many houses set back from the road indicating a degree of wealth that Erik and his family weren't privy to. The long drives, neatly manicured hedges and lawns and electronic gates all served both to stimulate jealousy and motivate those wishing to be upwardly mobile.

The de Ryke family lived in an eighties semi-detached house complete with a timber façade distinguishing it from the brick façade on the left and the tiled one on the right. These developers certainly knew how to differentiate their houses. It was a relatively quiet estate with neighbours keeping themselves to themselves except on April 26th and 27th when everyone celebrated King's Day or Koningsdag. On the 26th the men took charge of decking out the streets in last year's orange bunting while the women sorted the food. The braver ones later would join together singing the national anthem, the Wilhelmus. After the bunting was taken down, the place reverted to its normal introverted state.

Erik was sitting at the family table doing the homework his teacher at the primary school had set for the weekend. He liked school even relishing homework unlike most of his friends who preferred to be outside playing football. This weekend, he and his friends had to interview their fathers about their childhood, their jobs etc. and write up the conversation with anything else to fill up two pages of A4.

Just a ten year old, but quite dogged in the quest for answers to his important questions. He had been given a task and was determined to do it. So he tried again.

"What did you do in the war Daddy?"

There was no doubting that his father had heard him, but Erik had developed the knack of annoying his father with his persistent questioning causing his father to try to protect himself behind his newspaper. He peered around the corner of his De Telegraaph, ruing the day it changed from broad sheet to tabloid making it much more difficult to keep Erik at bay. He saw his son's head down, busy writing.

"Good," he murmured to himself, "Perhaps I can get some peace."

Funnily enough, he was just reading about children 'on the spectrum', whatever that meant, and what irritating habits they developed. He started wondering whether his son had this 'disease' and if so, where on earth he had got it from. It wasn't from him, or his wife, as far as he knew.

The lady of the house came out of the kitchen when she heard her son repeat the question. She knew how persistent he could be, remembering those earlier years when all he seemed to say when she asked him to do things was, "Why?" "Why?" "Why?" She tried to further protect her husband by diverting her son's attention, knowing failure was almost inevitable.

"Have you finished your homework yet?" she asked. Wrong question.

"This IS my homework," the boy replied. Defeated, she retreated to the kitchen and continued to make the evening meal. Erik turned his attention back to his father who remained unmoved in his armchair behind his paper, now reading the sports section.

Mr Andries de Ryke was a sales executive for a Dutch photocopying company and had experienced a tiring and wasted day. Not only had the morning seen rain pouring down with some ferocity but he had lined up two appointments with potential customers, one of which he knew would cause some considerable dampness to whatever business suit he decided to wear as he trudged several hundred yards from car park to reception. Looking at the weather, he fervently wished he had just gone into the office but he needed to add to his weekly tally of calls in preparation for the afternoon team meeting when the sales manager would go over everyone's activity for the week. Calls, suspects, prospects, proposals and forecasts would all be forensically examined in front of the whole team. His manager would have no qualms about setting one team member against another in a bizarre effort to build his team into one which would win him a national prize. This year the prize was a week cruising the Greek Islands.

He had no expectation of doing any business as a result of these calls but also no intention of giving his manager any opportunity to criticise. He would be ready. He always was. That was one of his strengths. His instinct was to look ahead and anticipate what might challenge him. After surviving another week in the sales business, he had come home early to relax and have a quiet evening with his wife.

"What did you do in the war Daddy?"

The forty-five year old breathed a heavy sigh behind his paper and gradually lowered it. He was quite a tall man, just over six feet two and weighing about fourteen stone. Quite slim for his height, but surprisingly muscular. With a mop of blondish hair, he still retained that boyish look that seemed to attract women. It certainly helped him close deals when he was negotiating with the ladies, but he also had that ability to look serious and businesslike when dealing with the male of the species.

Erik had his head down concentrating on his writing and didn't notice his father's partial response but just as the paper was going back up came the now familiar question.

"What did you do in the war Daddy?" This time the question had a little more urgency and vehemence. The pen came down and Erik looked around at his father with a child's no-nonsense gaze.

"I wasn't old enough to be in the war, Erik. Why don't you ask your grandfather? He will be here for Sunday lunch." Mr de Ryke was hoping that would end the matter. Mr de Ryke senior hadn't really been in the war having been born in 1948, a baby-boomer but he knew a lot about the war and would be delighted to talk endlessly to Erik.

Mrs de Ryke had come into the living room with plates and cutlery for the dining table in the corner. She had heard her husband's response.

"That's a good idea," she said, hoping against hope to give her husband some cover.

"But you were," insisted the ten year old. Erik's father put down his newspaper and turned to his son.

"What are you talking about?"

"But you were in the army," repeated Erik.

"Yes," came the tired reply. "I was in the Dutch army twenty years ago, but I was never in the war. That was your grandfather."

"But there's a photo of you on the wall in a blue helmet with some other men with guns," maintained Erik.

Mr de Ryke looked across the room at his wife, Elka, who shrugged her shoulders. This was not going away quickly, he thought, so better face it head on and then we can get on with the meal.

"Where is all this coming from?" he asked Erik.

"My teacher says that many Dutch men served in a war with the United Nations."

"Yes Erik, but we weren't fighting a war. I signed up for the army when I was twenty-five because I wanted to serve my country. My army platoon was sent to many different places."

Erik was not to be put off by so general an answer.

"So which countries did you go to?"

Erik, thought his mother, would make an excellent investigator. He wasn't going to miss a thing and she now knew where this was going, but also knew that her husband would procrastinate as long as he could trying, probably in vain to divert the boy's attention. It was not something he talked about.

"Was that where you got the blue helmet?"

"Yes, troops serving with the UN wear blue helmets so everyone knows they are not combatants."

"Does that mean they wouldn't shoot at you?" Erik wanted to get it all just right.

"Yes."

His father pulled up his paper, hoping that was the end. His mother hid her smile knowing that Erik was not going to give up that easily.

"But did they sometimes shoot at you?"

"Sometimes."

"Which was the worst place you went to?"

At that juncture Elka de Ryke announced that the evening meal was ready and began to bring hot food from the kitchen to the table.

"Erik, please put your books away."

He duly removed his books from the dining table and settled down to eat with his parents. With his mouth full, he repeated his question.

"Which was the worst place?" Elka de Ryke was about to chastise her son for eating with his mouth full, but her husband signalled that he would answer this one question.

"Erik, this is the last question. We were peacekeepers in a place called Bosnia."

"And did you keep the peace?"

Father and mother looked at each other.

"Well, we tried," his father said.

Chapter 2 — Belgrade 1979

HE WAS IN a good mood. Ivana made him happy and last night she had made an extra effort. It wasn't every night and the gaps were getting longer. There was some deep knowledge within her that told her that it wouldn't go on for much longer. This she had hinted to Djuric with whom she also spent some time. She had been with this VIP ostensibly as housekeeper for a few years longer than she had anticipated, but she was loyal to the Party and ready to do whatever was required.

Although he would sleep well for a few hours afterwards, he would almost always crawl out of bed in the early hours to relieve himself amid much shuffling and bathroom noise. She had trained herself to sleep lightly and be ready to respond to his needs afterwards but more often than not he would not come back to bed for a couple of hours. She would hear him shouting and cursing in the office next door as he worked on his papers. Then he might return to bed or just crash out on a large sofa located in the corner snoring until Ivana would have to wake him at 7am.

None of this was possible at his home though. That would never do. So he would often live at his suite at Party headquarters through the week and go home for weekends. His wife, even though a lot younger than he was, probably knew the score but as he was in his eighties, she decided that turning a blind eye was the appropriate course of action. It wasn't the first affair by any means and maybe not the last. She knew that he loved her but, more to the point, she didn't want to be arrested under some pretence since she enjoyed quite a luxurious lifestyle, provided she didn't embarrass him by also playing away. Quite a simple arrangement really.

Tonight Ivana had noticed that he had been away from his bed for just three hours and come back to his warm bed until the urge of nature took over once again.

"I need to take a piss," he said to Ivana having woken up, using the language that he had grown up with. He was still a man of the proletariat and, with that announcement, he slowly swung his legs over the side of the bed, tentatively stood up holding on to the headboard and moved his legs up and down to make sure they would carry him successfully. She lifted herself on her elbows and looked at him with some concern as he wobbled towards the bathroom. Not for the first time, she observed the colour of his blotched legs and wondered how long he was going to be able to walk unaided.

"Be careful, darling," she called. He muttered something in reply which she didn't quite catch. After loud and prolonged groaning, he reappeared.

"Get up," he ordered testily. "Help me get dressed. I've a meeting in thirty minutes. Can't keep the buggers waiting."

Sometimes he had meetings in his suite and sometimes in the boardroom next door, depending on who it was and what he wanted to accomplish. This time he would have it in his private office within the suite. His visitors would be waiting nervously in the boardroom watched over by a large security man guarding the door between the two areas. While Ivana did the necessary in the living quarters, he moved into his office and sat behind his desk. These days he would never allow his men, nor the public at large, to see him standing or walking. Much too risky. He pressed the buzzer to allow his visitors entrance.

Djuric and Kovac entered together and stood before the desk. Djuric was his adjutant and also had a couple of rooms in the building where he lived. He was on hand night and day while Kovac, his intelligence man, lived on the other side of the city and came only when he was summoned which he had been today. They were sworn on pain of death to serve their master faithfully, not that they had much choice. Both had been hand picked by the Boss for no-one turned him down. That was just not done for understandable reasons.

"So," the President started, eyeing them both. "What's going on? What are the rumours? Who's planning what?"

Kovac coughed gently. Why did the bastard have such eyes? They were dark and heavy, never seeming to blink and never giving anything away. His body may not have been in its prime but there was no doubting his mind was as sharp as ever. He looked at everyone suspecting any could be capable of becoming untrustworthy.

Kovac chose his words carefully and gave his brief report. "Rumours abound, of course. They always do. I'm keeping a close eye on M though, but nothing concrete to report yet."

The Boss knew to whom they were referring and waved his hand. "Don't worry about him. He's just a bureaucrat." He lapsed into silence, his eyebrows twitching as he eyed his two lackeys. They kept quiet. The President's moods were quite unpredictable, probably deliberately so but whatever the mood, the man exuded power. Although not tall, he had the broad shoulders of a working man and large hands to match. Undoubtedly, the mere fact of his physical presence caused fear amongst Party officials and few if any would dare to contradict him. If anyone came near they would be subject to prolonged silent scrutiny until they backed down. His control had to be absolute.

Djuric and Kovac looked at each other rather uneasily. He started.

"I shall be going into hospital shortly," he began in a rather conciliatory fashion, "and I want it to be kept quiet..... from everyone. Djuric, you will contact the hospital in Slovenia and brief everyone there to secrecy on pain of death. You will also accompany me in my car. Kovac, you will spread some diversionary rumours among Party members. That's all."

Both men left the room and the President hauled himself up and into his living quarters. Ten minutes later he buzzed the door open again and a man referred to only as Grgur entered while Ivana was cleaning up. They eyed each other; he with some greedy eyes and she with complete distaste. Both men went into the office whilst Ivana left through the back entrance. She would be back later probably to find him slouched down in an easy chair and trying to massage his legs. He knew his time could be short and he had a lot to do securing his legacy. He wasn't afraid of dying. After all, as a true Communist, he didn't believe in any life after death..... but you never knew. He tried to dismiss such dark thoughts. Yes he had done some bad things but it had all been in the service of his country. Surely that was acceptable.... acceptable to whom though?

He had been brought up as a Roman Catholic as all good Croats had and it was difficult in times of weakness not to relapse into Catholic theology. On the one hand with his conversion to Marxism, he despised a church which refused to acknowledge its only authority was that which it had given itself.

But on the other, maybe there was some truth somewhere in it? No. Of course not. He remembered that unique arrogance that priests had, thinking that they always knew the answer to everything, and everyone should be in awe of them and their little rituals. What conceit!

He laughed quietly to himself as he recalled how communists had infiltrated the church back in the thirties. Apparently over a thousand communist men had become priests in order to destroy catholicism from within. Who was it? What was his name? Ah yes, it was Dodd who had prophesied that in the future, 'you will not recognise the Catholic Church'.

Chapter 3 — Slovenia

A MOTORCADE OF three blacked-out Mercedes carefully made its way to the Medical Centre in Ljubljana, the capital city of Slovenia, in January 1980. It was only a twenty mile journey and the roads were quite empty with the remnants of the most recent snow on their side of the road pushed into the other, the snow plough seeming to have forgotten to make the return trip. Josef Broz Tito was in the large middle car smiling grimly to himself. He knew his adjutant's work when he saw it. Occasionally the wind would blow a rush of snow from the trees above the road on to the cars and the wipers would energetically move back and forth in an effort to clear windscreens. Snow was piling tenuously on the branches and twigs of the beech trees which shadowed the road.

He was cold, very cold, despite having twice ordered the heater to be on full and despite the two other occupants almost roasting. He enjoyed riding in the Merc but continued to feel the chill. It always gave him a reminder of how far he had come, how much he had achieved and how much he was above his siblings. He alternately grunted and sighed with the pleasure at the ride and the pain in his legs but there was no doubting that he could feel the pain beginning to seriously outweigh the pleasure. Nothing seemed to be able to touch it. He had ordered every kind of pill and treatment, standard or experimental, but nothing worked. He knew what it was, of course, but consistently refused to do what the quacks wanted.

"I will not agree, under any circumstances, to having my leg amputated. That's an order." Tito was used to exercising power. He didn't usually have to say anything twice but, perhaps for the first time in his life he was scared, an experience he hadn't had in a long, long time. And he didn't like it. To cover his unease, he had raised his voice more than usual which had the opposite effect than that he intended on those around him. There was a time when the merest flicker of his eye or his hand would cause fear, but not now. Instead of them being in his hands, he was now in theirs.

Djuric said nothing. He had served faithfully for some years; well, there was no alternative to serving faithfully, especially to this man. But he didn't have to like him. He wondered how Ivana kept going, doing what she did every night. "That must be really sacrificial," he thought. He liked her in spite of what she did for the old man. Yes, he liked her a lot. Perhaps when the old man was gone, he might...... His thoughts were interrupted by the patient who, with even more vehemence, repeated his demand adding, "And if I'm sedated, you will take charge and ensure that the doctors do nothing against my wishes."

This time Djuric stiffened. He wasn't thinking he had any responsibility in this situation other than a modicum of security. He certainly didn't want this particular burden on his shoulders but perhaps he'd better signal his obedience with a brief, "Certainly, Mr President." The driver and the adjutant exchanged glances in the car's mirror. There was a look of, 'Thank God I'm not in your shoes,' from the driver. The adjutant looked away. He didn't want to come between the President and his doctors. Way above his pay grade and besides, he had other plans.

The President had suffered from diabetes for years and had largely ignored his health conditions as men often do, only reluctantly giving into his wife who insisted he was entitled to the best Yugoslavia had to offer, after all he was the President. But in his world, it wasn't presidential to be afflicted in such a way. He didn't want anyone to know his weaknesses. Vulnerability was the result of weakness meaning potential loss of power, and he wasn't about to give power to anyone else. No, they would have to wrestle him for it. Over many years, the condition had progressed and he began to experience the impact of bad circulation in his legs. For the past few months he had taken to sitting for his public appearances as much as he could. He didn't want to fall over or trip causing either alarm amongst the masses or opportunity for his enemies, or both. However, most insiders and some outsiders knew exactly what the diagnosis was and how it was likely to develop.

The motorcade was met by the hospital administrator and senior medical personnel at the entrance. The President insisted on clambering out of the back seat of the car and walking in just to demonstrate to everyone that there was nothing wrong with his leg. Djuric, his adjutant followed at a respectful distance casually looking around for any possible threats. He expected none since hardly anyone was supposed to know that the President was here. By 2pm his master had settled having tried to enjoy a light lunch but, although he was good at hiding his stress from everyone else, inside he had to admit to himself he was nervous. A Martha Brau beer, specially imported from Germany, was offered contrary to hospital procedure which he enjoyed rather more. At 3pm he was gently awakened from his siesta by an attractive nurse who had been primed by Djuric to expect some rude words to be forthcoming, A pretty girl usually brought out the best in him and this was no exception. Tito was presidential, smiled at her and said he was ready for his doctors to attend him.

He had been born into a large peasant family who lived near Zagreb, the capital of Croatia, the seventh of fifteen children. He had been apprenticed to a locksmith in 1907 completing his training in 1910. But after working as an itinerant metalworker in various Austro-Hungarian regions, he was drafted into the Austro-Hungarian army in 1913 and, serendipitously, was sent as a sergeant to the war against Serbia in 1914. However, that didn't last long before he was transferred to the Russian front in early 1915 where he was seriously wounded and captured by the Russians in April 1915. After a long hospitalisation he was sent to a prisoner of war camp where he was profoundly influenced by Bolshevik propaganda.

By 1920 he had become a Communist party organiser in Yugoslavia, which at this time was a monarchy, later being elected General Secretary of the Party. During World War Two after the Nazi invasion, he led the Yugoslav guerilla movement called the Partisans against the Germans and at the conclusion of the war had become the chief architect of the Socialist Federal Republic of Yugoslavia.

Now the President's power was hanging by a thread. While his doctors were discussing how to approach him, who should take the lead and the inevitable flack, Djuric remained in the corridor outside the suite speaking very quietly on the telephone to someone in Belgrade. A number had been dialled and a voice on the other end was answering.

"Well, is he dead yet?"

Djuric responded "No, but I'm guessing that his leg will be amputated soon enough." There was a grunt at the other end and the line was cut.

A posse of doctors swept past him and entered the suite where Tito was resting. They came to a halt around the settee on which the President was seated. They looked at each other.

"Well, what have you got to say for yourselves? Don't stand there mute." Tito was not someone to be kept waiting, by anyone. The senior medical man took the lead.

"Mr President, sir. We rather expected you to be in bed."

"Well, I'm not."

"Sir," started the same man.

"Well spit it out, man. What is it?"

The senior man swallowed and tried to continue. "Sir, your diabetes is causing an arterial embolism in your left leg. We need to assess the situation, Mr President .....er, it would be better if you were in bed, then you could be comfortable as we examine your leg."

"Ummm. Have my adjutant come in. You are dismissed."

The doctors moved quickly out of the room to be replaced by Djuric.

"Bunch of fools," grunted the President, as he moved into the bedroom. Once settled, doctors were once again called in and they crowded around the President's leg to undertake a 'hands-on' examination. The medics muttered among themselves briefly and, as soon as the examination was completed, the President was thanked and they left the room bowing liberally.

In the conference that followed the best medics that Yugoslavia had to offer decided they needed to undertake an angiogram of the leg. It was unanimously agreed that this would give them a complete picture of the blood vessels and arteries together with evidence, should they need it, that some surgery would be required. The result of the procedure was hardly a revelation to them; the femoral artery and Achilles tendon artery were severely clogged.

The next procedure that offered itself was an arterial bypass. Again it would demonstrate to the President that they were trying everything to avoid amputation. He agreed to the procedure and first results were encouraging, but it was clear twenty-four hours later that this had not been successful and gangrene was now a distinct possibility. Amputation was the only option but nobody wanted to engage with the President and deliver the prognosis.

Djuric refused to be involved so the hospital decided to call the President's sons, Zarko and Miso. After resisting for days, the President finally agreed to the surgery whereupon his health began to improve and he moved back to his residence at Brdo Castle. But he was never the same man and in March, kidney, heart and lungs all began to fail.

Back at home, his wife took over his care although he was hardly a compliant patient. He knew the prognosis. "Mother of God," he muttered, then stopped himself. "Where did that come from? Bloody Catholicism! You just can't get away from it. How is that stuff still in my head?"

After a stroke at the end of April, it was an ambulance with its strobing lights and emergency sirens rather than a dignified motorcade that arrived back at Ljubljana's hospital. His adjutant rode in the back of the ambulance ready to play his part.

After a succession of daily calls to Belgrade, his final call was on 4th May 1980 at 3pm.

"I trust you have good news." The statement was delivered in a flat monotone.

"I have," said the adjutant.

Chapter 4 — Belgrade

IT WAS 2.50PM on a chilly Belgrade afternoon. Not the middle of winter, but May 1980 found the people still waiting for spring to really arrive. It was almost if the gods who ruled the weather wanted to make a point – after all a President was dying, maybe had already died. Who knew? Not many dared to be out and about unless they had to, but these men did. Senior apparatchiks of the ruling Yugoslavian Communist Party were making their way to the Party HQ in their official Mercedes. There had been no hard news about the President for days even to these men, although rumours abounded in the city.

They gathered solemnly as befitting the occasion, no-one wanting to be accused of disrespecting the President alive or dead. In addition to these middle-aged and elderly men was one, Borislav Kovac, a senior intelligence officer, there ostensibly to note decisions made and make sure his master's bidding was done. He was in his early forties and usually remained quiet, on the edge of debate taking notes and observing his elders. Blondish hair, rimless glasses, clean shaven, in a rather anonymous looking grey suit and ignored by the senior men, just as an intelligence officer should be. He didn't have any friends nor did he spend time in bars or clubs, as far as anyone knew. What acquaintances he did have directly related to his work. No-one knew exactly where he lived or with whom he lived, if anyone.

The room looked like an ordinary corporate boardroom, a large glass and steel table surrounded by rather ordinary chairs except for the one at the head of the table, which was larger and demonstrably more comfortable than the others. It also seemed to be a little higher. All imported from Germany – nothing but the best. Immediately behind the chair was a private door leading to a very large and imposing suite of living accommodation with private office, living room, kitchen and a master bedroom together with more moderate accommodation for lesser mortals. Few were invited to enter and when they did, it was with rather mixed feelings.

Today all were now assembled and a quiet buzz of conversation had broken out. No-one appeared through *that* door so it was left to another to call the meeting to order at one minute to three. At precisely 3pm the single telephone on the table rang and it was Kovac who had the responsibility of answering it. His, "I trust you have good news" was designed to signal to the assembled group that he was hoping that the news was that his President was still alive. The adjutant's terse reply, "I do" meant something entirely different to him and it forced a grimace, or was it a grin, on the intelligence officer's face. His face changed to a more sombre expression as he turned slowly to the assembled figures.

"I'm sorry to have to report," he began, "but our illustrious leader passed away not more than a few minutes ago."

There was now complete silence in the room. It was not unexpected of course, for he had been lying on his deathbed for nearly four months. But no-one wanted to say anything out of place in front of fellow comrades and put themselves in any firing line. It was left to the Deputy Chairman of the Party, a rather large man, to respond. He pushed his chair back and pulled himself to his feet signalling a mass shuffling around the table as they all stood to attention in silence. Heads were down but brains running at full pelt. When eventually they all sat down again, he looked around the table.

"Fellow comrades. I am scheduling a Party meeting here tomorrow at ten," he announced. "There will be two items on the agenda. The first will be to agree final arrangements for the funeral and the second will be to discuss the implementation of the President's wishes as to the governance of this united country."

Tito had already made arrangements for how Yugoslavia should be governed after his death, his one preoccupation being to retain the disparate country as a whole. His legacy. The Constitution had been amended in 1974 for just that purpose. His plan was that the Presidency should rotate on a yearly basis, trying to ensure that each republic and province would have their turn to assume overall control of the 'parliament' of representatives, thus keeping the various power points relatively satisfied.

"Thank you. You are dismissed."

As the attendees gradually moved out of the room, the previous quiet buzz of conversation erupted into a louder discourse as men began to discuss together, trying to secure bilateral meetings with whoever they believed would come out of the situation secure, and with power. Re-positioning had started. Each briefly queued before getting into their personal Party limousine and being whisked away by their respective Party chauffeur.

Ever the professional, Kovac trailed them as they made their way out of the building, watching and listening as they went. And as the final one disappeared into the Belgrade streets, he ducked back into the building to use the phone.

At precisely 12 noon the next day after the official Party hierarchy had met and concluded their business, the Yugoslavian intelligence officer was in another meeting with an entirely different agenda to the one he had just left. Also present were Serbian General Petar of the Yugoslav Peoples Army (JNA), two rather rich Serbian businessmen, a top ranking Party civil servant called Bojan, and a well known intellectual called Goran, all under the chairmanship of someone they all just referred to as M.

Kovac lit a cigarette, comfortable in the company of like-minded friends. Now it was M sitting upright in his chair and ready to command. With blackish hair greying at the sides and combed straight back leaving a high forehead, he gave off an air of intellectual superiority, as one who rarely smiled. He was dressed in the double-breasted dark blue suit of a bureaucrat, for that is what he had been up to now.

"Comrade Kovac will update you on the situation today," began M, casting his eyes around the room. Kovac quickly reported that Tito was dead. There was not much interest in the funeral arrangements that had been made or how the Party would implement Tito's plans for the government of the country. This was the past, and it was over as far as these gentlemen were concerned.

"Thank you," said M. "I have had informal discussions with each of you over the past year," continued M, "but now the time has come to pull it all together and begin to create a Greater Serbia."

He paused and looked round the table. There were no histrionics, no clapping, no tub-thumping. Each man looked serious and dedicated to the agreed objective.

"We will begin to execute our plans for disruption and division in the various Yugoslavian provinces, particularly where our fellow Serbs have been discriminated against. Comrade Kovac will steer these efforts and I will call upon each of you as and when required to secure each province." M finished and looked to Kovac to carry on. The intelligence officer ground out his cigarette, cleared his throat and leaned forward slightly.

"As you know, Serbia is by far the largest republic in Yugoslavia and has a third of the total population of Yugoslavia but..." His voice was rising with some emotion, "...but has been deliberately overlooked by Tito and, what's more, central investment has consistently been taken away from us and distributed amongst the other republics and provinces, who then proceeded to squander it."

Kovac looked around the table. He could see their eyes fixed on him and their mouths ready to applaud what they all knew was the case. There was no need to build Serbian nationalism, it was already there ready and waiting to be harnessed and exploited.

He continued, "There is little need to worry about any new government that seeks to impose Tito's plan. I was at the Party meeting earlier this morning. The bickering and in-fighting that was evident there will ensure it will never succeed. It's a perfect recipe for ineffective decision-making and weak leadership."

He paused, for he recognised that his voice pitch was again beginning to rise such was his passion. Rather, he wanted to be coldly rational and logical. He continued.

"As we infiltrate each province in turn and embolden the Serbian population in those provinces, chaos will result which will allow the Army to enter to restore order and protect our fellow Serbs. We will not wait for this failed state to die a natural death, we will kill it."

Heads were nodding all around the table, except for M at the head of the table who now addressed the company with no emotion whatsoever.

"We all need to have patience, for we have only the resources to do this province by province. At the moment we cannot depend wholly on the existing Yugoslavian army for it comprises members of all ethnic groups in the country."

As he said this he looked at the Army General who sat rigidly in his chair. There were many Generals in the Federal Army. It was a complex organisation designed to give each republic and province its own forces with its own hierarchy of officers. There were now just six armies allocated to the five republics, but some retaining their original numeric designation: the First Army was based in Belgrade covering the northern part of Central Serbia and the northern province of Vojvodina which was still part of Serbia; the Second Army was based at Nis covering the southern part of Central Serbia and Southern Serbia, in particular Kosovo; the Third Army was based at Skopje covering Macedonia; the Fourth Army was based at Split and comprised a coastal Naval Unit; the Fifth Army was based at Zagreb in Croatia; the Seventh Army was based at Sarajevo responsible for Bosnia and Herzegovina with the Ninth Army based at Ljubljana covering Slovenia.

General Petar was one of the generals at the HQ in Belgrade overseeing the whole edifice. He was a large man with a round head rather devoid of hair, perennially turned out in his dress uniform. Some of his staff joked among themselves that he went to bed in it and ironed it again every morning. As he addressed the group he stood to attention puffing out his chest.

"We can now begin to execute our plan for weaning out those in the service who might not share our objectives. As we do this we will make sure that such men do not form any other military force within current Yugoslav provinces, nor will they take any hardware with them. We have already begun to commandeer all the Yugoslavian Army equipment in the various republics to prevent it moving into non-Serbian hands."

He looked at Kovac. "When we have established complete control, we will be able to deploy anywhere in the country. I will let you know when that might be but it might take a few years. I trust you can all work with that timetable."

Heads nodded around the table.

"Remember," M continued, "we have to take control of Serbia itself as well, but we can do all these things simultaneously. There is no need for anyone to wait."

There was a murmur of assent around the table and Goran the Belgrade intellectual took his opportunity to speak up.

"It will be important to articulate a history of Serbia which emphasises that Serbs need to be able to live together in a Greater Serbia. This has always been, and will always be our dream, now nearing reality. We are better, cleverer and more capable than others which is why we are called a 'heavenly people'. Whilst a few of my compatriots still see a future for some sort of loose federation, many others believe it will be necessary to provide both the intelligentsia and the working people with historical reasons why this will never work for Serbs."

Again there were nods of approval around the room but Goran was not finished. He loved words, making speeches and commanding a room. It's what he did.

"It will become the rationale behind the chaos that my friend here will create. It is critical that we control the narrative in the Belgrade and Serbian media in general. So I ask fellow comrades not to contact the media or respond to anything without coming through me."

There was no disagreement in the room. The businessmen looked at each other and one spoke up. "When we secure a province we will be ready to seize key business interests which will help us to control the economy and weaken any resistance."

Bojan, the diminutive Party civil servant and accountant, added his contribution whilst taking off his glasses and polishing them. "My role will be to take over the civil service of each province once a benign government has established control. I have trustworthy Serbian civil servants who I can place in senior positions in each province and republic especially within their Treasuries. This will be critical since Yugoslavia is already highly indebted to the IMF (International Monetary Fund)"

As Bojan finished, M again took charge. "All we need now is more finance and modern weaponry for the Army which is already the strongest in Europe. We have 140,000 professionals on active duty and over a million reservists. I am currently negotiating additional armaments which, I am glad to say, should be finalised shortly."

Chapter 5 — Istanbul

IT WAS THE following month, June 1980, that a private plane flew from a little known airfield outside of Belgrade normally used by the senior apparatchiks of the regime, of which M was nearly one but not quite, yet. A not unreasonable sum of money deposited in an overseas account gave him the access he needed to travel to Turkey. M was a wealthy man compared to the majority of the inhabitants of Yugoslavia, and just wealthy enough for the time being. But he needed backers for his project and a journey to Istanbul was required now that the President was dead.

The whole of the Soviet Union was undergoing the strains and stresses of a failing colossus. Too much spent on their military build-up and not enough on the centralised agricultural and industrial economy which was displaying seismic problems. It was a broken country ravaged by the cruelty of leaders the population seemed to crave and probably deserved.

"Repairs would take more than a change of leadership," muttered M as he ruminated on the meeting to come, but it was not his problem as long as he got what he needed. Then they could do what they liked.

The Brezhnev / Andropov years of the early 80s represented the last gasp of the old guard, but they and their supporters were determined to stay in control almost at any cost. Younger men with new ideas, such as Gorbachev, were challenging but still not quite powerful enough yet and M saw a timely chance to get old-guard Soviets to back his takeover of Yugoslavia – become the new Tito, before Gorbachev and his progressive friends took over in Moscow. His visit to Istanbul aimed to meet representatives of the old who, he knew, wished to prop up the whole of Eastern Europe including Mother Russia itself.

Istanbul was a neutral city but alive with intrigue. Not only was this city the bridge between east and west but also north and south. Everyone in the diplomatic world did business here whether it was state secrets or 'machine parts'. This visit was not official and neither was the deal, so there was to be no reception at the Russian consulate, no formal recognition and nothing on paper. For the purposes of history, the meeting never happened.

M was on time having boarded a waiting car from another private airfield outside the Turkish city where his plane had landed. His driver had indicated that he was to get in by opening the door and gesturing with his hand. Not a word was spoken by him either then or on the whole journey. Just as they were entering the city the car phone sparked into life and the driver quickly switched the incoming call to his earphone. There were a few grunts followed by a low *choroso* which, even M with little knowledge of any Russian knew meant OK.

It was the first time he had travelled to Istanbul and it began to look like he was being given the tour. Clearly his meeting was going to start later than planned. They passed the Blue Mosque, the first time he had seen this UNESCO world heritage site and after that the car veered towards the Bosphorus. M was now beginning to get restless and tried to speak to the driver but in vain. This was not a world that M was used to. A man in his position in Yugoslavia was in control of most things important to him, but here he was in control of nothing. After a further phone call, the car turned and headed for the district of Beyoglu, Istiklal Caddesi, No. 219-225A, to be exact – the Russian consulate.

The car stopped outside the building waiting for the gates to open, which they did eventually. A uniformed Russian guard came out to open the door for the man from Serbia and escorted him inside where Yuri Smolov was waiting.

The Russian's welcome was rather abrupt as M was quickly led into a room off the main concourse with a "I trust your journey was easy." M said nothing but followed dutifully.

"This is a much better place to talk openly," said Smolov once they had entered the room. It was not large but had a high ceiling and an old fashioned cast iron fireplace with its wrought iron vine-leaves and curlicues which had not seen a fire for decades, if ever. The windows were small, overlooking a quadrangle where it might have been possible to see inside the offices on the other side except every single window had its blinds down. Smolov proceeded to do the same in this room and switched the ceiling lights on to provide the necessary light.

"Please," he said offering M a seat on a comfortable looking sofa. "It is from Germany – nothing but the best, eh?" He laughed at his own joke and proceeded to sit down on the opposite sofa in a relaxed fashion. "A drink, perhaps?"

M, who wanted to get straight down to business, breathed out quite loudly but said, "Turkish coffee, thank you." Smolov must have pressed some button which M could not see, for immediately a maid, also in uniform, responded and took their drink requests. Almost before the maid was out of the room, M began.

"Thank you for your hospitality. Yugoslavia appreciates your help at this difficult time."

Smolov inclined his head and faintly nodded. "How can we be of service?" Although the men had already had a telephone call where the outlines of a deal were talked about, Smolov wanted the Serb bureaucrat to make the running. M had no idea whether the conversation was being recorded or not so immediately resolved not to go into any detail in case it could be used against him at some point in the future. However, now he thought about it, maybe the phone call between both men a few weeks earlier had been taped by the Russian.

He decided to plough on. His gut told him that the Russians wanted this opportunity almost as much as he did, so he was emboldened. He leaned forward on his sofa. "As we discussed on the phone, I think it is both our interests that Yugoslavia's future inside the Soviet Union is secured. So we will need to do our best to protect the people from West-leaning liberal elements who, even now I know, are plotting to declare independence in the various republics."

Smolov continued to maintain a diplomat posture. "I understand your position and, of course, we would be delighted to help in any way we can."

M decided to jump in. He saw no need for anymore oblique diplomatic references and wanted to force Smolov into the open. "In addition to the various 'machine parts' you offered for the Army, your personal presence and strategic advice for my team would be enormously helpful."

Smolov, still relaxed on his sofa, looked at the ceiling. "Yes, I think that might be possible."

M, still leaning forward, immediately discerned that the Russian had already gained approval for this and wanted to push the point home. "Also, perhaps you might be able to afford some experienced 'feet on the ground' as this is such an important issue for Moscow?"

Smolov frowned as if this had now gone beyond his remit and what he had agreed with his bosses.

M noticed the hesitancy, "Of course, all this will secure your investment in our country." He wanted a flow of arms, weaponry and experience for the Army, envisaging the high probability of using such resources on Slovenia and Croatia to bring them into line. To have Smolov himself in Belgrade would be a guarantee of that. At least, he hoped it would.

"Indeed," responded Smolov in a non committal way.

M wanted to tie down some details. "My next team meeting will be in three weeks time. Perhaps it would be possible for you to fly to Belgrade a few days earlier and I can fully brief you on our situation."

Smolov retaining his diplomatic stance replied, "Please send me the dates and times and I shall respond as quickly as I can." With that he rose from the couch and advanced to M with an outstretched hand. M quickly rose, their hands shook and M was ushered to the door accompanied by a stream of platitudes about working together for the good of the people of Yugoslavia.

The same car and driver were waiting to whisk him back to the same plane which had brought him. He looked at his watch. He had been on Russian soil for not more than twenty minutes. He hoped it had been worth it, but he wouldn't know until Smolov, or whoever he sent on his behalf, was in Belgrade and the product ordered started to flow.

On his way back M was both troubled and satisfied; troubled because he knew Russians never did anything for a single reason, neither did they ever reveal their true intent; satisfied because Russians and Serbs were so much alike that he felt he could manage them.

For his part, Smolov went straight upstairs to meet his boss who had been listening to the conversation. "The trouble is," said the senior Russian, "we don't yet know if this man is the right one to back. When you go, put together a paper on any other contenders who might be better positioned to achieve our objectives."

Chapter 6 — Kosovo

July was a hot summer month usually and this July was no exception. Kovac was now on his way south to the province of Kosovo with the windows open to try and cool the interior of the car. It rarely worked and it wasn't working now. His shirt was wet with sweat particularly under his armpits. He hadn't noticed, not that he could do much more about it. He was thinking.

"It's not a question of purist Communist doctrine," reflected Kovac to himself, "simply a question of blood loyalty." He admitted to himself that he had nothing against Tito personally; in fact he rather admired him, coming from nowhere to become head of state. But could personal admiration ever trump blood? He didn't think so. His loyalty was centred on his Serb blood. Tito, after all, was a Croat.

And Kosovo? Full of Albanians as far as he knew. Not a great Serb population, but an important place since it claimed to be the original Serb homeland and would serve as a useful test for their strategy and organisation. Croatia and Slovenia? Now they would be completely different. A much harder test.

"In fact," he was thinking, "we might have to do a deal with one of them, probably Croatia. Yes, we will have to be at our best if we were to take on either of those countries."

Montenegro would be relatively simple as would Bosnia, provided they could keep the European Community out. Not really a problem. The EC bureaucracy was more concerned with their internal rules and the individual countries with making money. They had no stomach for more wars. They were fat and content to think they were the answer to all Europe's problems, and anyway Christian Europe would never come to the rescue of a broadly Muslim province like Bosnia Herzegovina.

He smiled to himself as he thought of the shock the EC had coming and all the angst that would spread around before the wringing of hands and the inevitable decision that they couldn't do anything.

"Ummm, but would the US feel it had to come in?" His thought was probably not but you couldn't rule it out, especially as an election year was not far away. Perhaps we'd better have someone in Washington to slant the discourse in Serbia's direction. He made a mental note to talk to M about that.

As he drove, it was becoming cooler. The car had been trudging uphill for a while now and the engine sounded like it was needing a rest. But he ignored it and kept his foot on the accelerator. His mind was ranging around the whole mass that was Yugoslavia. How on earth had Tito managed to keep this together? It was a marvel. Well, all that was about to change, he would make sure of that. Might take a year or two, but there would be a Greater Serbia one day soon.

He was so taken up with his thoughts that he had completely missed what his passenger was saying. Andrej Djuric, the late President's adjutant, was sitting next to him in the car and was talking.

"Where are we going?"

"What?" Kovac dragged his mind back to the present.

"Where are we going and what do you want me to do?"

Kovac smiled. Djuric was not going to like this, but he would go anyway. He wanted to be part of a Greater Serbia.

"We are going to Kosovo, Pristina to be exact."

Djuric turned up his nose, "*Shiptari,*" he sneered.

"Exactly," said Kovac.

Djuric was a military man and Tito's adjutant for over ten years. Military service for him had been just basic training before he was moved into administration, responsible for organising shows, pageants, marches etc. He did this so well that Tito grabbed him to be his adjutant. Djuric had no say in the matter. As with all military personnel, even in administration, he was groomed to hold himself erect at all times showing off his six feet plus height and broad shoulders. His handsome looks and military bearing made him quite striking in his off duty hours around the bars and clubs of Belgrade, but the women knew who he was and that he was therefore untouchable. Now in his forties, he was a much more sociable person than his new boss.

They were still making their way through the mountains near the Sutjeska National Park, some say the site of one of the most important and bloody battles in WW2 as Tito's partisans defeated Italian forces leading to Italy's capitulation. It was becoming a slow journey, but a better one than Kovac had expected for Djuric was turning out to be rather quick witted with a good grasp of what they were about.

But Kovac noticed that the needle indicating engine temperature was entering the red zone. The Yugo 1.1 was not really built for cross country journeys. It was no Mercedes and now was in danger of overheating and they had to stop. Not a bad place though to have a break with such amazing views over the mountains. Unfortunately there was no coffee shop, or indeed shops of any kind anywhere near them and Kovac was not the sort to have prepared food or drink. They sat together waiting to the car to cool down.

"We're going to defend the Serb population against Albanian aggression," started Kovac, looking across to Djuric who nodded. Kovac said nothing but let the implications begin to sink in.

After a few minutes, Djuric spoke up. "I have some ideas," he offered. Kovac looked across at him and waited for more. His underling seemed to be studying the road ahead.

"I think we might need to approach this from two angles," he was saying quietly as if thinking aloud.

"Go on," encouraged Kovac.

"Well," continued Djuric, "on the one hand we need to stir up the local Serb population so as to alert them to what might shortly be happening, and on the other, somehow, we need to fuel the fire by getting the Albanians to realise they're vulnerable."

"Good. I like it." Kovac was nodding. "So how will you do it?"

The car descended into silence for a while, with Djuric thinking and Kovac waiting to see if he came up with the same ideas he had already agreed with M.

Djuric began speaking. "What if we established some kind of Serb organisation, a committee maybe, something to coordinate the publicity around any crimes committed by Albanians against Serbians?"

"You mean 'exaggerate' the publicity?" asked Kovac.

"Exactly," replied Djuric. "So we create a pincer movement."

Kovac looked across at Djuric, quietly impressed with his protégé. "So how are you going to do that?"

Djuric thought. "Well, heightening Serbian fears will be the easy bit. But for that to be successful, we will...."

Kovac interrupted, "*You* will...."

Djuric looked across at Kovac. "This is my show?"

"If you want it?"

"Sure. Almost certainly I will have to engage with the Albanian Mafia, and that will cost money." Djuric looked across at Kovac. "How much can I have?"

Kovac smiled at Djuric, "You're going to have to be creative. The odd rape here and a bit of harassment there won't cost a lot, but will get the job done. Don't forget Kosovo is Serb land."

While Djuric was contemplating the task ahead, Kovac started the engine and shortly the downhill part of the journey began to the driver's relief. Within a few hours, Pristina began to come into view and, as Kovac confidently drove the car into the city, Djuric had the distinct impression that his boss had been here before.

"Where are we going?" Djuric asked

"Wrong question."

"OK. Who are we going to see?"

Kovac didn't reply. He just pulled into the Hotel Begolli and parked.

"There's someone I want you to meet," he said.

Djuric got out of the car and looked around. He had not been to Kosovo before let alone Pristina, its capital. It all looked a little run down, including the external façade of the hotel they had stopped at. However, he quickly changed his mind once he entered. The décor, the furniture, everything looked classy and expensive. Kovac moved quickly through the check-in area to the lobby, and seated on one of the white leather upholstered chairs sat a blond-haired lady with two substantial males lurking near by. She looked up and smiled as Kovac approached tentatively.

"Hello Luljeta. I see you brought company."

Chapter 7 — Kosovo

"THERE WERE TWO of them," she stuttered. It was cold and late. Too late. It had been a fun evening and, as a confident single girl, she had shunned the many offers to walk her home. She was not in the mood and after all, home wasn't far away, a walk she had done many times before. Although she knew these were not normal times, she had thought, "I have many Albanian friends; it won't happen to me."

She should have stayed at home. Her parents had not know she was going out, but she was a headstrong girl and liked to flout the conservative conventions of her country. It wasn't far from home and not as if she was going to a pub, where just the men go. It hadn't even been her birthday party but one of her friends, and it had been a good bash. She had a thoroughly enjoyable time: good food, good music and good friends. Yes, she should have refused the last few drinks, but hey. She knew the local roads like the back of her hand and, although the summer had truly finished, it was not winter by any means. And it was a full moon giving lots of light in the early hours. She was fine.

Not the first to leave by any means but having glanced at her watch, it was now time to go. Hugs and kisses to her friends, she stepped outside of the warm womb of her friends house into the chilly air of Peja. The fourth largest city in Kosovo was in the west of the country near the border with Montenegro and boasted great mountains and the Rugova Canyon. Although the peace of multi-ethnic co-existence in the city was being severely threatened by random acts of racism, many citizens on both sides continued to resist this slide, as did Tanja. They were all determined that life should carry on as normal across ethnic divides, although truthfully, it was getting more and more difficult.

The police were interviewing Tanja on her own in the street where she had been found. The officers already knew that it was a waste of time taking her to a police station but they needed to go through the motions as quickly as possible to cover themselves, then get back to the bosom of a warm station. A passer-by had heard faint calls for help and had gone to investigate but, having called the police, had now disappeared not wanting to get involved or become a target himself. It was becoming a familiar scene in the Serb part of the city. The police who had responded to the emergency call were ethnic Albanians and half suspected that this Serb girl had been 'asking for it' in her party clothes. And anyway, the Serbs had been doing similar things to Albanian girls for some time now. There was no doubt such crime had been increasing between the two communities since about 1982 but, according to the police, this year had been the worst.

"They came from nowhere. They had balaclavas." Tanja was crying now, wanting just to get home.

"Tell us what happened again?"

She paused, wiping her face with a tissue and hitching up her skirt above her knees.

The two officers looked at each other. If it had been in another, less crowded, part of the town they might have taken a different course, but there were still people spilling out of the clubs and making their way home. As they saw the police, most gave the situation a wide berth.

"One held me down and the other..." She started sobbing.

"Yes, go on."

"The other got on top of me."

"Why didn't you shout for help?"

"...there was a knife."

"That's the first we've heard of a knife," said what looked like the senior officer. "Are you sure?"

"...and then they took turns."

Tanja was now sniffing and regaining some of her composure. It was with a little defiance now that she added,

"....and they took photos."

The police officers again looked at each other.

"Photos?" They both echoed her words with some incredulity.

"What exactly did they take photos of?" asked the younger officer. He seemed more eager than his senior to get more of the gory details.

Tanja looked at him. "I just saw some light flashes as I was on the ground," she replied.

"So you didn't actually see a camera?"

"No," she admitted.

The senior officer looked at his watch and cut to the chase asking that familiar question which, already knowing the answer, was preparatory to saying that they could do, would do nothing.

"Would you recognise them again?" There it was.

Tanja raised her voice a notch. "I told you they came from behind and covered their faces."

"We'll see what we can do," said the senior man, and with that both officers hurried back to their car and drove away. Tanja leaned back against the wall to steady herself. She hadn't expected anything from them and wouldn't have called them herself.

Unknown to her, there was a witness to the whole incident standing in the dark shadows of the street opposite. Having seen his two compatriots do their job, Luka had been about to make his exit when the police arrived but had held his ground not wanting to be seen and drawn into any questioning. Not that he feared the police. He worked out every day in the local gym and reckoned he could take both of them if it came to it, but his orders were to stay out of sight. Now he also disappeared.

The next morning he travelled from Peja back to Pristina and reported to his boss just after midday. Luljeta sat on her couch in a room at the back of the restaurant that bore her name with the two 'heavies' still in attendance. Clearly, one could not be too careful. She scowled as he came in.

"You're late," she declared, eye-balling him. He anxiously looked around for any movement from her to the 'security', but her attention was elsewhere.

"Well, what happened?" She demanded now not even bothering to look at him. As he told his story, she idly pushed back her blond hair behind her ears at the same time as continuing to look at some photos on the coffee table that had been delivered earlier that day.

She put them back into an envelope and said, "Take these across to Djuric.

He'll know what to do with them." Luka was just about to go back through the door into the restaurant when she called out, "Wait."

He turned around at her command. "I think we might be able to do better," she said thoughtfully. "You know the girl?"

"No, but I can find her."

"Do it and ask her if she wants her friends, any future boyfriend, husband or children to see these photos."

"And the price?"

"One thousand American dollars."

Luka smiled as he turned to exit the restaurant. He would ask for just a touch more as his commission. Before he hit the road, he called in to see Djuric.

"So how did the operation go in Peja?"

"Yea. We did a girl like you said and here's a photo we took." He proffered a single photo as proof. Djuric took it and examined it. "This is it?"

"Yep. Just the one as evidence." Djuric said nothing. He sensed there were probably more but didn't want to alienate either Luka or Luljeta. He let it pass.

"I've got something I'd like you to do in Peja." Djuric looked at Luka. "Take the video camera and interview your two friends, hiding their faces of course, and get them to tell how they have been falsely accused of this girl's rape and how local Albanians were behind it. And the police did nothing."

He smiled at Luka.

Djuric had not only promised Kovac a gradual build up of tensions between the Serb and Albanian communities, but that he would start some sort of organisation to pull the Serbian voice together and engage their nascent nationalistic feelings so that Metohija, the Serb name for Kosovo, would become a cleansed Serb homeland again. This element of his task had proved more difficult than he had imagined and the best he could do was a hotchpotch group called the Committee of Serbs and Montenegrins. But it had to do. Goran, the Belgrade intellectual and one of the authors of the Memorandum of the Serbian Academy of Sciences and Arts, had produced a series of pamphlets which catalogued Serbian grievances in rather plainer language than the Memorandum itself.

In short, it outlined how the Serbs were victims of both economic and political discrimination, although they had made the most significant military contribution for Yugoslavia. Specifically in Kosovo, the literature claimed Serbs faced genocide and the greatest liberation struggle including the 'Battle of Kosovo', against the Turks which they lost but claimed as a big victory. The tracts more generally accused Slovenia and Croatia of conspiring against Serbia.

It was just what Djuric needed in Kosovo and indeed they were circulated to the Serbian population throughout the country. Such rhetoric was music to Serbian ears everywhere and successfully harnessed the latent nationalistic tendency that was always just under the surface. Djuric was desperate to succeed for he knew his future depended on it. It had been three years of hard work which was now beginning to pay off. But he was becoming impatient and wanted more progress quickly.

While Luljeta was Djuric's passport into the underworld of Pristina, not only had he to rely on her for contacts in other parts of the country, but in the absence of any hard cash given to him, he had to turn a blind eye to her extra curricular activities as his way of paying for her services. He couldn't do without her. She had provided Luka in Peja and he was having some success, but Mirko in the northern city of Mitrovica was a different matter. He took orders from no-one and did what he wanted, when he wanted.

It was said that Mirko controlled the whole of the north of the country from here. It was not where he was born, or brought up. Not that many people knew, but Mitrovica had been a place he had fled to after some unpleasant business in Romania. Djuric didn't care. Something bigger was needed that could give him and Luljeta a suitable pay-off otherwise he might lose her just as his strategy was beginning to bear fruit.

"Mirko?" asked Djuric, having dialled the number previously given to him by Luljeta. A gravelly voice answered.

"What's it to you?"

"It's Djuric from Pristina. Luljeta advised me to call you.

"So."

"I have an idea which might suit us both."

"I'm listening."

Djuric proceeded to outline what he had in mind. There was a grunt at the other end of the line and the call was disconnected. What Djuric didn't know, nor Luljeta for that matter, was that Mirko was not Serbian, Albanian, Croatian, Bosnian, Slovenian or Montenegrin, but Roma. Originally Roma were an ethnic group of itinerant people originating in northern India but now were settled in countries all over the world, but especially in south eastern Europe. The culture and traditions of the Roma meant that it was a close knit population often living on the edge of traditional societies. Those in Kosovo were no different and Mirco was a leader on his patch and had many men he could call upon.

Once a flourishing economy, Mitrovica had fallen on hard times since Tito had died and federal money had ceased, making way for a very black economy. It had been the Trepca Mines and its satellite industries and services that had been the centre of the economy. Once Europe's largest lead-zinc and silver ore mine, it had all collapsed. Sheer neglect, no investment, absence of any control over the business, not to mention continual robbery of equipment from the workshops. Of course Mirco had made sure he had his share.

It was a couple of weeks later that an old Yugo car disappeared from outside a house on the outskirts of the city in the early hours of Sunday morning. One of Mirko's men had a gift. It wasn't that difficult, he would say. Instructions were to drive it to a garage to the other side of the city which he did without mishap. There it stayed for another three weeks until any police interest had faded, the owner had given up and the car was readied for its new occupant.

A prominent Albanian businessman in the city had crossed swords with Mirco on a number of occasions with the latter having already planning retaliation when Djuric's call came. Another call. The Roma lifted the receiver, gave his usual grunt and then asked,

"Is the car ready?"

"Plates changed and a full tank," came the answer. A fat finger disconnected the call and lifted the receiver for the next.

"You know what to do," he said quietly down the line.

"Yes, boss."

Within a few hours, at about 8pm in the evening, a teenage girl was violently snatched from her bedroom in a well-to-do house with the mother tied up, gagged and a message stuck to her forehead. At about midnight, the father drove his BMW up the drive, opened the front door and called to his wife, "I'm home," as he always did. This evening, however, there would be no answer until he found his wife upstairs in their bedroom, calmed her down and read the message concerning his seventeen year old daughter.

It was in a disused warehouse near the river that had previously stored mining equipment that a girl was being photographed, making sure that the vestiges of the bloody struggle she had put up were still evident on her face and hands. It would add to the urgency of the situation for the parents. There were many such buildings in that part of the city so that even if they suspected where she might be held, there was little chance they would find her. And if by any chance they did try and came anywhere near, she could easily be moved from one building to another. Nothing was left to chance otherwise, the men knew, Mirco would wreak havoc.

Predictably the place was damp and cold on the top floor where rainwater had been allowed to seep in since the building had been abandoned, but that didn't bother her captors. They had made the room secure with the obligatory bucket in the corner and an old mattress on which she sat. Her captors didn't want anyone to think they were savages. With a gag tightly across her mouth, she wasn't able to eat, drink, cry or shout but it didn't stop the tears streaming down her face. That wouldn't matter for she would not be there that long,

So far, all was going to plan. There would be a telephone call soon enough .... and there it was. Mirco picked up the receiver.

"Good evening," he said in an unusually bright and cheerful voice. The caller on the other end was evidently angry and began swearing vengeance and bloodshed. Mirco interrupted.

"Call back when you've calmed down." He said cheerfully again, disconnected the call and waited. He didn't have long to wait.

"I want to see my daughter."

"Ah, that sounds a lot more tranquil." Mirco was cheerful and happy, baiting his nemesis.

"Now," Mirco's tone changed to be anything but bright and cheerful. "All in good time," he sneered. "You Albanians always think you can call the shots. Well, not this time. Listen to these instructions."

Mirco didn't care if the police were involved. He had contacts and was confident he could deal with any enthusiastic detectives but he did want to collect the money and he had worked out a simple if violent way to do it. The publicity would satisfy Djuric who he wanted to keep on side because he could already see how the wind was blowing. Suspicions were that it wouldn't take much more for the Yugoslavian, now Serbian, army to intervene in Kosovo and he wanted to be protected.

So he pocketed the money allowing the girl to be gang raped by his men as their reward. She was then killed; after all, she could identify them and that could not be allowed to happen. Her body was dumped unceremoniously on some waste ground with her ripped clothes. It was a job well done and he waited for the backlash.

Chapter 8 — Belgrade

IVANA WAS LATE. He remembered that she often was but he suspected that tonight she was making a point. But he didn't mind, after all he had been away off and on for a few years. If standing him up for a while helped her to even up the score then he could handle it. It was the least he could do; in fact, he readily admitted to himself, it didn't come anywhere near making up for the asshole he had been. The problem was that he couldn't promise any change, at least not in the short term.

Djuric settled down at his table with a few beers and tried not very successfully to relax. His foot was tapping continuously on the table leg, showing his nerves to everyone on adjacent tables. He had booked her favourite restaurant, at least it used to be. He had no idea whether it was now; in fact he had no real idea of how Ivana might have changed in the past years. Would he even recognise her? He desperately wanted to demonstrate to her that he was really trying, but he had nothing to promise her. He was feeling guilty but trying not to show it. This place was going to make a dent in the money he was getting from M via Kovac, but the Restaurant Dva Jelena was one of the oldest Belgrade taverns opening back in 1832. It had a real Bohemian feel to it and suited Ivana's character. He was hopeful.

This was to be a quick trip to see his girlfriend. No, he couldn't even take that for granted anymore, but hopefully still a friend. Being in Pristina on his own for some time, he had been missing her company; actually any female company if the truth be known. He didn't want to get tied up with anyone in Kosovo just in case the people he was working with got to know about it and tried to blackmail him. As far as Kovac knew he was still in Pristina, still causing inter-ethnic strife, still following orders.

He looked at his watch again. Perhaps she really was going to stand him up. He knew he deserved it, but ever the optimist, he started to rehearse what he was going to say when she arrived since he was not coming back to Belgrade permanently as he had promised. She would surely understand his reasons since she worked, or at least did the last time he saw her, for the Party machine. Obviously an apology first, since it must have been a year since he had been back in Belgrade but even then he recalled, he hadn't really spent any time with her. Why, he briefly wondered. Work had come first, middle and last. That had to change.

He began to speculate which Ivana he would see tonight: the one who was something of a romantic and held a torch for him back in Tito's days or the sarcastic, rational Ivana who could see right through most men. He would have to watch his step. He had arrived back in Belgrade the previous day so he could clean up his apartment and make sure it was warm and inviting. On arriving, he had opened the door of the apartment block's entrance hall and headed straight for the stairs not even bothering to check the old cage lift. Even if it was working, which was not very often, it would probably get stuck. Not worth the risk. He paused at the bottom of the stairs and looked around. Not a great place to bring a lady; the whole entrance and staircase was musty as if no air had entered for years despite a supposed weekly clean by the old lady who lived on the ground floor, for which she received not a lot. Still the same threadbare blue carpet, he noticed, or was it grey? Perhaps he could find some kind of spray that would cover the mustiness.

He was anticipating a lovely meal and her coming back to his place. As he hadn't been back there for a while, he knew it would take a bit of time to cajole it into a female-welcoming place. Did he have some candles? He would go out and buy some. They could make all the difference and flowers which she could take back with her. Yes.

Ah. Here she was. He noticed heads turning as she walked in slowly, slightly swaying, with her head held high and looking stunning; tight jeans, white blouse open at the neck and showing a bit of cleavage and three inch heels. What have I been doing, he was asking himself. I could have been enjoying life here instead of slumming it down in Kosovo. Perhaps she would come down to Pristina with me. Then another thought occurred. Just because she's accepted my invitation to dinner, didn't mean there wasn't another man in her life. He couldn't blame her, but he had to find out. She saw him and wandered over.

"Look what finally rolled in." Her smoky voice and tendency for sarcasm reminded him to be on his guard.

"You look gorgeous," he began, offering an olive branch. "And thank you for coming."

She settled herself at the table and looked at him. He suddenly felt very ashamed of himself. When Tito had died he had promised her that life would be different, that he was done with the military and politics. But he had done the complete opposite.

"Perhaps the lady would like a drink?" she said looking at him.

"Of course. Sorry." He signalled a waiter over, ordered drinks.

"So, how have you been?" he asked, tentatively.

"How do you think?"

"I had to go. The Party ordered me. I couldn't say no."

"Did they now? And which Party would that be?"

Djuric looked at her wondering just how much she knew about what political undercurrents were going on. Turned out, quite a lot.

Their drinks arrived and they took a moment to order food. The game halted until the waiter had retreated, then play could resume. This is how it had always been from the beginning in Tito's employ. Of course she didn't dare do it with the great man. Or did she? Perhaps he enjoyed the cut and thrust of her humour. Maybe it was her way of flirting with him. Maybe it turned him on. Maybe she was still doing it to someone else. He'd better find out.

"Where are you working now?" he asked hesitantly.

She smiled. "I'm still with the Party."

"Oh?" said Djuric, his voice rising in a question.

"I'm currently personal assistant to the President."

He stared at her open-mouthed.

"Of Yugoslavia, that is." Djuric didn't miss the insinuation since it was common knowledge that M wanted to be President of Serbia. Either she was well informed on what he was doing or it was a lucky hit. He tried to avoid rising to it.

"Er... that's great. And er... how is the President?"

Thoughts were flashing through his mind at some speed. Was she 'comforting' the man as she did with Tito or maybe having a more open affair with him, or maybe it was even more? Did she know what M was up to? Did she know what he had been doing? Was she about to denounce him? Was he going to be arrested and jailed?

"He's a very nice man, a patriot. He has the country's future at the top of his agenda."

"Er... that's good. I hear there's quite a bit of discontent about though?" Djuric thought he needed to do a bit more fishing to see what she knew and where her loyalties lay.

The food arrived which stopped the conversation flow for a few minutes. Ivana toyed with her *Sopska* salad, (tomatoes, cucumbers, onions, peppers and white cheese), while Djuric tucked into his *Cevapi*, (sausage-style fingers of mixed meat, served with *lepinja* -bread, onions and *kajmak* – a type of cream cheese). Both were silent, wondering where the conversation would go next, but neither wanting to initiate it.

Finally Ivana spoke, "Is there?"

"Pardon?"

"Is there discontent about?" She was regarding him out of the corner of her eye.

Djuric took a second or two to think about his answer.

"Well, if you believe the press, Serb nationalism is growing stronger each day and could threaten the situation." He kept his head down, aware now that they were both sounding each other out. How much did she really know and whose side was she really on? He was sure that M was going to take control of Serbia very soon and that fact was causing him some concern that Ivana might end up on the wrong side and be purged.

He thought about what Kovac would say about this meeting if he knew and what Ivana would say if she knew what he had been doing in Kosovo. No, he couldn't reveal anything, so decided to play a neutral hand and see if she gave any hints as to where she stood. If nothing emerged, he would keep an eye out for her when M made his final move.

She then changed the subject and the rest of the meal was just pleasant, though not what he thought it might have been. At the end of the meal,

Djuric asked if she would like to come back to his place to which she replied that, yes she would but not tonight which confused Djuric somewhat. So nothing was what it might have been.

They said goodbyes outside with a brief hug and each made their own way home.

Chapter 9 — Kosovo

In Peja after Tanja's rape, there were nightly demonstrations by the Serb community against the Albanian Kosovos for the rape of a number of their women and for hiding the perpetrators. There were also reciprocal demonstrations against the Serbs by ethnic Albanians for falsely accusing their community and harassing their women. Djuric arrived back in Pristina still knowing it was just the beginning and was still waiting for something to happen in Mitrovica.

"It's still not enough," he muttered to himself. He needed more fuel for the fire. That same day he got a call from Luljeta who suggested he put his TV on. He did. The breaking news item was about a daughter of a well known Albanian businessman in Mitrovica who had been found dumped on a refuse site. This may have been news to Luljeta but not to Djuric.

He drummed his fingers on his armchair and said aloud, "Well, Albanians, what are you going to do about it?"

He didn't have to wait long. Fifteen minutes later the news agenda was interrupted by a report of riots against the Serb community in a number of different towns and cities. It was said that even peace-loving people were now saying that enough was enough. As Djuric looked on, sure enough the whole of the Albanian dominated country seemed to be up in arms and frenziedly attacking Serb communities and businesses everywhere. It was starting to get ugly. The police were watching in the main, going through the motions, their sympathies clearly with the Albanian mobs. The pump priming had worked. He was just about to call his boss when suddenly there was banging on his door. He opened it to find an excited Luka.

"They're burning and looting Serbian shops," he said with glee.

"Where?"

"Here, in Pristina. They're all those coffee and pastry shops they love."

"What!" exclaimed Djuric. "Go out and get pictures and interviews. We'll publicise them tonight and soon Albanian stores will be alight." Time to ring

Kovac. Time for the army to rescue us.

Kovac answered immediately. "We've got a situation down here and if the army is ready, we need help." Djuric was trying to sound calm, but inside he was anything but. "The Albanians are going nuts," he added.

Kovac grinned to himself. He wasn't bothered about the girl or that a few of his countrymen might die. The plan was working and he was a happy man.

"The army has been doing manoeuvres near the Kosovo border for a few weeks now, but M is planning to come down and talk with Kosovo Albanian leaders in a few days."

The phone went down in Belgrade while Djuric hunkered down in Pristina amid the sound of shattering glass and whoops of delight from the mob outside his window. Serb shopkeepers and workers were being dragged out on the street and hit with anything the Albanians could lay their hands on.

"A few days!" he muttered. "I hope I'm still alive by then."

Djuric made sure the word had got out among the Serb population that a Communist Party leader from Belgrade was coming to Kosovo to support them. He wanted to stir up the Serb population and provoke the Albanians even more.

"Get hold of a truck," Djuric was instructing Luka, "fill it with stones, and park it near to the House of Culture in Kosovo Polje."

"Why?" asked Luka. Djuric ignored him. "Stay with the truck and when you get a signal, shout out to the crowd, 'Here are your weapons.' Have you got that?"

"What's the signal?"

"Someone will appear on the balcony of the House of Culture and give a speech. When he says 'change it', that will be your signal. And, by the way, do what you can to whip up the crowd."

M arrived at Fushe Kosove railway station some five miles south west of Pristina and went straight to the House of Culture for a meeting with the Kosovo Albanian leaders. Kovac was at his side. Luka had done his job well and crowds of local Serbs had already begun to gather at the building to press their grievances and complain about Albanian aggression, so much so that all the political leaders struggled even to get into the building.

Fearing violence, the police began to use their batons to keep control and disperse the crowd where they could. But almost as if someone was orchestrating the proceedings, the crowd began chanting, "Murderers" at the police and an ominous scene was beginning to develop. Inside the Kosovo leaders pressed their issues with M who quietly listened.

"Look at the crowds," one of them said. "There's going to be bloodshed unless you do something to calm the Serb community down. We need to be able to discuss in peace and without the threat of disorder." Other Kosovo leaders nodded and pressed M to do something.

"Yes, I will address the Serbs," M said and marched off to the balcony with the other leaders following.

The crowd suddenly hushed as key figures appeared on the balcony. Kosovo leaders thought M was going to do as they asked him and put a stop to the demonstration, but M had other plans.

"Fellow Serbs," he began. The crowd roared.

"Fellow Serbs, no-one should dare to beat you," he bellowed. The crowd went wild. "This is your land. These are your houses, your memories, the graves of your ancestors. This is your place. Never give up when facing obstacles when it's time to fight. Don't tolerate this situation." M went on in the same vein for quite a while and ended with, "Change it."

"Here are your weapons," someone shouted. The crowd lost no time picking up the stones provided and pelting the police together with any other Albanians who happened to be around. It was reported that not a single police officer escaped without a severe beating.

Having wound up the nationalistic fervour of his fellow Serbs in Kosovo, M was optimistic that he could use a spreading nationalism to take full control of Serbia itself. On the return journey he and Kovac sat in a private carriage.

"Now I have to part with a long term friend," said M. Kovac looked at him uneasily.

"You're not having second thoughts are you?"

M returned his look and smiled, the first smile Kovac had seen from him.

"Not one single bit but I have to execute him, metaphorically of course."

Neither man said anything for a few moments. Each thinking this could be a pivotal moment for their strategy. If M lost here, the game would be up. If that were to happen they would be charged with treason and summarily executed. The risks were huge. They knew a win in Kosovo meant nothing if Serbia itself was not secured. Eventually M spoke.

"This is what I want you to do. You've heard about the four army recruits who were murdered a few days ago?"

"Of course."

On September 3rd at the Paracin barracks, a nineteen year old Albanian recruit shot four fellow recruits in their beds. Whether he had been bullied in some way, no-one knew but he then seemingly killed himself shortly afterwards. Although the four dead only included one Serb, the others being two Bosnians and a Croat, the Belgrade media called it 'an act of Albanian separatism against Serbia'.

"We have control of the media, but now we have to deliver the coup de gras. I want you to organise thousands of Serb nationalists to attend the funeral and make it a political demonstration for change."

Kovac thought for a moment. "The parents won't like it," he observed.

M looked at him as if to say, "So what?"

Both men lapsed into silence again. Kovac decided to recall Djuric from Kosovo to do the job. He had done well down there and was sure that the Kosovo pot would continue to boil without his direct intervention. He needed someone for this job who he could trust completely; the next few weeks would be make or break.

When they arrived back at the Belgrade Waterfront Station, M disembarked and strode off without a word. Kovac watched him go for a moment, then turned and walked in the other direction.

There was a phone booth next to the station. Kovac pulled at the door to be met with the stale smell of urine and cigarettes. He gagged – but trying to breathe through his mouth rather than his nose, he put his call through to Djuric urgently.

"I have a job for you back in Belgrade. I presume you have people who can keep Kosovo bubbling?"

Djuric was surprised but pleased to be going back to Belgrade officially.

"Of course. I'll catch the train first thing tomorrow."

"Tonight please. Meet me at the usual place at eight o'clock tomorrow morning."

The phone was disconnected. Djuric wondered what on earth the urgency was, but his was not to reason why, his was to do and hopefully, not die. He immediately called Luljeta and explained he would be going away for a while and would Luka keep Kosovo in its present unhappy state.

"That's not my job," rejoined Luljeta. "Luka is a very expensive asset and you have had his services for free."

"Not exactly for free," contradicted Djuric. "Our arrangement has been quite beneficial for you financially. And of course, there will be long term advantages if you continue to partner with us."

Luljeta said nothing.

Djuric took control of the conversation. "Much appreciated," he said and cut the line. He then called Luka and briefed him, assuring him that his boss had agreed and warning him not to get on the wrong side of history.

One hour later he was at the railway station and fifteen minutes after that he had settled into a first class carriage and closed his eyes in a dreamless sleep, which was rather miraculous because he hadn't had one of those since he had started living in Kosovo. He woke just as the train was pulling into Belgrade station. He quickly got his backpack of personal items from the rack and set off to his small apartment. He entered the roadside door into the entrance hall and was pleasantly surprised to find his spray scent was still lingering.

He continued up to his floor, the fourth, where he opened the door to be met by a freezing temperature again. He couldn't afford to have the heating on when he wasn't there and because he hadn't anticipated being back again so soon, he had switched everything off. It had only been a few days but it seemed the cold had got right into the walls again. He switched on an electric fire but even after an hour or so it made not a jot of difference. He couldn't afford to do this very often so he decided to slum it, taking to the couch and loading extra blankets on top of him, but even they seemed to have imbibed the cold. Sleep proved impossible. After a few hours he gave up, cobbled together some breakfast items that he had planned for Ivana from his cupboard, ate quickly and went out.

It was another cold grey morning with rain drifting across his path at an angle of forty-five degrees. He wanted to be at the meeting place early to show his commitment to the cause so it was 7.30am when he arrived to find Kovac already there with a map spread out on the table. Without any chat, he explained to Djuric what he had to do in the next 48 hours and said he would be back that evening to be briefed on what plans Djuric had made.

Once Kovac had gone, the first thing he did was to go out himself to get a decent breakfast and some strong coffee which would hopefully keep him awake for a few hours. He sat by himself in a corner café thinking about what he needed to do and making some notes before thrusting himself into a busy day on the phone asking, persuading and cajoling where necessary, all fuelled by caffeine. He took a break at lunchtime, had more coffee then slept for about two hours before going over his plan again and making a few more calls. By 6pm he felt he had it covered. Kovac was happy and added,

"Oh. By the way, within twenty four hours, M will be Serbian President. Everything we do now will be legit."

The turnout at the funeral was everything Kovac had hoped for. Djuric was certainly showing himself to be a superb organiser. Needless to say the parents of the dead Serb army recruit were appalled and appealed, as best they could, for people to go home. As far as one could see, not one person moved away. It was a powerful statement and M knew it. The Belgrade Party chief, Pavlovic, also knew it and tried to counter it.

He contacted his office and instructed them to get media editors on the phone. He appealed to them.

"This is creating a dangerous atmosphere. Explosive words bring nothing but fire. The smallest mistake now, even made in good faith, could be tragic for the Serbian nation."

However, he had lost the media's attention long ago. They listened and ignored him. A fiery article in the following week in one of the main dailies attacked Pavlovic, virtually destroyed his credibility and put the Serbian President, Stambolic, in the firing line for he had been defending Pavlovic. A hurried meeting of the Serbian Central Committee was called by M ostensibly to resolve the dispute. In reality, it was execution time.

It was a meeting that lasted days. During that fateful time, it was reported that,

"The atmosphere was terrible. People were standing and biting their nails in the café. Everyone turned greyer and greyer. Some people carried two different speeches in their pockets depending on how things turned out."

Members of the Central Committee were clearly realising that their careers and futures, and maybe their lives, depended on the final outcome. At the end of this momentous session in December 1987 Pavlovic, the Belgrade Chief, was expelled from the Party, the ultimate punishment, and at that moment everyone knew that Stambolic's time was over as well. At one time he had been the most feared politician in Yugoslavia, so the leaders of the republics and provinces thought that getting rid of him would play to their advantage, after all M was just a bureaucrat. Surely they could better control him now he was going to be Serbian President.

Alas all too late they realised that Kosovo had just been the launch pad – the goal for M was first Serbia, then the whole of Yugoslavia. He was to be the new Tito.

Chapter 10 — Vojvodina

THEY WERE ALL commanded to gather back in their meeting room with M in the chair. Kovac was first to arrive and, while greeting Mira, noticed that M was in deep conversation with a visitor with M doing most of the listening, which was unusual. The intelligence man caught the words 'artillery' and 'siege' which didn't take much imagination to understand what they were talking about. It was old fashioned warfare probably with new fashioned weapons. He glanced across at M's wife who steadfastly avoided his gaze.

As the rest of the team came in, M and his visitor abruptly ceased their conversation. General Petar, dressed as usual in his army regalia, gave a long sideways stare at the visitor recognising at once his military bearing. He turned to look at Kovac who took a long drag on his cigarette and shrugged, as if to say, "I don't know either," and making a mental note to let Petar know about what he had overheard. M didn't bother to introduce the visitor who sat upright a little away from the rest of the group, almost as an observer. He was built like a chunk of granite with a broad, rugged look and closely cropped black hair. A twitch in one eye implied he had seen action and been injured at some point. To Bojan he looked rather ominous, as though he might have been some powerful man's 'fixer' in his younger days, now perhaps risen to the level of one who orders others to fix situations of one sort or another. Even though he had not spoken a word, the businessmen had immediately tagged him as a Russian and even Goran, the intellectual was looking puzzled.

The invited Serbs present looked at him and then at each other wondering what this was about. It was well known that Tito followed his own path and the Soviet leadership were happy as long as he stayed loyal to the Communist bloc. However to have a Russian, presumably representing Moscow, at a meeting of Serbs intent on planning a different future for Yugoslavia was interesting to say the least. As newly elected Serbian President, M was noticeably more assured and more spirited now that Serbia itself was under his control. And he was in decision-making mode maybe to impress his guest.

"I want to congratulate Kovac," M began, looking at the intelligence officer. "Yes, and his team for what they have accomplished in Kosovo with Goran's help, of course." He nodded towards the Belgrade intellectual. "Without these contributions, we may not have had such success."

He looked at the others around the table. "Soon we will be able to complete the takeover and allow others in to do their job." He nodded to the businessmen, Bojan, the Party civil servant and General Petar. "But for now, we will keep Kosovo boiling through political means. We may need the army in other areas."

He turned to Bojan. "You have been doing some background work in Slovenia. Tell us what you've found."

Bojan cleared his throat and looked down at his papers through his tortoise shell glasses. "Comrades," he started with a glance at the visitor, "you will all know that Slovenia, although a mostly conservative country, has been flirting with liberal ideas, even gay rights." At this point, Bojan looked up expressing his disgust and expecting his audience to agree. They probably did, but were more interested in what would come next.

The civil servant hurried on. "It is the most developed and, arguably, the most industrious of our republics. But Kucan, the head of the Slovenian Communist Party, believes reform is definitely the way to go. I would agree," stated Bojan pausing for effect, "but perhaps not the particular reforms he has in mind."

Adjusting his glasses, he went on. "There was an article in an influential journal called *Nova Revija* which, among other things, called for the replacement of the Yugoslavian, that is the Serbian, Army with their own."

Kovac joined in. "We have been spreading rumours of a planned military coup through the fake leak of some military documents," he said. "Of course, we had to act as if was genuine and pursued the person who took them. My esteemed General here was able to leak further information which led the army to arrest a number of people. It all adds to heighten tension and confusion."

At this point, General Petar interrupted with a side glance at the Russian as if he was about to divulge state secrets. "This just affects the Army based in

Slovenia. They are determined to hold those whom they consider traitors to account but I fear they are making some serious mistakes and, if not careful, will only promote calls for Slovenian independence."

"This can still work to our advantage," said M quietly. Pausing and turning to his guest, he explained, "We have been secretly encouraging an anti-Slovene movement across the board, which is now seriously pressurising the Slovenian Party Committee. Shortly I will have finished purging the Yugoslavian Central Committee. Then they will realise that we mean business."

He paused, laid back in his chair, his eyes raised to the ceiling. "However, there's one province in our back yard that we need to take care of before we tackle Slovenia."

Vojvodina was a province in the north of Serbia itself, and its leadership had been living quite a comfortable life with little regard to Belgrade. M wanted to bring them to heel and unite Serbia under his leadership. Before issuing his orders, M surprised everyone by choosing this moment to introduce his visitor as Yuri Smolov, explaining his role was to supply whatever weaponry was needed for the Army. So no longer anonymous but little further explanation and no-one was going to object.

Everyone around the table waited for their orders.

Later that day, Kovac called Djuric again. "M wants you to get a large demonstration going outside the Vojvodina Party HQ in Novi Sad."

Djuric, however, was reluctant to leave Belgrade. He was trying to get hold of Ivana at the old President's office, but was getting nowhere. She wasn't there and his subtle enquiries were also drawing a blank.

"Kovac, I really need at least another two or three days in Belgrade."

"Why?"

Djuric really didn't want to tell all to his boss, so rather lamely replied, "There's someone I'm trying to find."

"Who?"

Djuric was silent. He didn't know what to say and he definitely didn't want to talk about Ivana who wasn't Serbian, but Montenegrin and almost certainly not on their side, yet. Djuric thought he could persuade her of a better course, if only he could find her.

"Just a family member."

"Umm." Kovac didn't want to upset Djuric, as his right hand man, so he said, "OK. You have forty-eight hours, then I want you in Novi Sad."

The call was disconnected. Djuric breathed again, but forty-eight hours later he was no nearer finding her.

So Djuric did what he does best and there was a huge demonstration outside the said Party HQ which became known as the 'Yoghurt Revolution' as the crowd laid siege to the building and came armed with cartons of yoghurt and milk to throw at the local apparatchiks who were trapped in their Party HQ and, by all accounts, were quite terrified and seriously afraid for their lives. They had done everything they could to stop the protest including ordering the turning off of power and water supplies, but there was no stopping the crowd who began shouting *"Dole foteljasi"* – down with the armchair governors. In desperation, they called for units of the Army based in Vojvodina to intervene and save them. General Nikola, the general in charge of the Ninth Army in Ljubljana, readily agreed since the police seemed to be unable to do anything; after all, the army was the last resort for keeping the peace. This immediately angered M once he heard of it.

" You are to block any intervention of the army. Is that clear?" M's instructions to General Petar were crystal clear.

"Perfectly," responded Petar and, since he outranked Nikola, the army stayed right where it was with the besieged leaders forced to appeal to M to call off the hordes and save them. He almost smiled for he had them just where he wanted them.

"It won't hurt them to stew in their own juices for a couple more days," said M now relishing their discomfort, allowing the mob to continue to taunt them and threaten to invade the building. It was not a large edifice as these things go and built in traditional Communist public town hall style, emphasising the status of its occupants rather than their protection. Its large rooms and high ceilings elevated a past importance now crumbling in front of its present dilemma.

Inside, relations between the men were beginning to get rather strained, each blaming others for the mess and, it was reported, fights were even breaking out between them. When the solitary working phone in the building rang, someone snatched it up. They were ready to capitulate. M was statesmanlike.

"Of course I will....." he said gently, "on one condition." His voice hardened. "I want your immediate resignations." Their resistance had already crumbled and they were ready to agree to anything. An easy victory. The Belgrade media, under M's control, made the most of it. M was a hero and his supporters made sure that his picture was everywhere in the city; on posters, banners and photos hanging out of every window in offices, homes and government buildings. In their eyes, e was the new Tito.

It was still 1988 and M's strategy of harnessing Serb nationalism mostly by political / constitutional means was succeeding beyond his wildest dreams. But he still had Slovenia, Montenegro, Bosnia, Croatia and Macedonia to go. A few would be easy, the first not too difficult but the fourth might be a problem. But there was time. No need to rush.

Unlike many of his ilk, M was not a man who liked crowds or even making speeches to them, although the few he did make were momentous. Outside the public gaze he was quiet and a devoted husband to Mirjana, or Mira as she liked to be called. They had met at school and perhaps the tragedies they had both endured pulled them together. At different times both M's parents had committed suicide; Mira had never known her father and lived apart from her mother, who was shot as a traitor in 1942.

They remained together through it all, not only as husband and wife but as co-conspirators and co-strategists. At key moments in their quest, it was he who was uncertain and nervous and it was Mira who had steeled him to go on. He would come out of a meeting, phone her and recount how the meeting was going.

She would respond "There's no going back now. You're too exposed." He would return to the meeting buoyed up and determined to get his way.

He knew the constitution, the procedures, the loopholes better than anyone – after all, he had been the supreme bureaucrat. Once each meeting had been successfully negotiated, it would be back at their modest flat in Belgrade that they would re-group with their team. This was the hub where all the planning was done and the orders given.

Chapter 11 — Montenegro

MOST OF THE team were pleased with the progress and, as they gathered, were smiling at each other shaking each others hands celebrating their success to date. Others were not so happy. The businessmen had nothing to show so far for their support and nothing in the pipeline seemed to have any prospect of an increase in their market positioning or bottom line profit, not that they would have ever used such capitalistic concepts. They saw themselves as key players in the Greater Serbia movement but, as far as they were concerned, they didn't seem to be in the game yet. A pre-meeting had been arranged to determine which of them would speak up at the team meeting.

"We were wondering," he began cautiously, "when we might be of some service to the project."

There was quiet in the room. Mira was playing the host in their Belgrade apartment and seemingly innocuously passing around *turksa kafa* but she was carefully assessing each person. M reckoned she was an excellent judge of character and looked to her for an evaluation of their team each time they met. He wanted to know immediately if anyone looked anxious or shifty. They couldn't afford to have a traitor in their midst. Kovac was casually smoking, Bojan alternatively taking off his glasses, polishing them and putting them back on again and Petar sitting ramrod in his chair as only a general could.

The words of the businessman had been softly spoken but what they meant and who they were directed at was crystal clear. All were aware that these two considered themselves big fish in their respective pools and it was now apparent that they also had big egos. They liked the finer things in life, had the money to pay for them and wanted more. They had been the main contributors to M's 'fighting fund' calculating that supporting M would be a good investment. The other members of the team stopped talking and the room went quiet. Would the future President of Yugoslavia, as they saw it, see the question as a challenge to his authority? M glanced across at Mira for her judgement. She laughed, allowing M to respond more cordially than others thought he might have.

"Well gentlemen. We're certainly glad to have you aboard and I might remind you that we have not finished in Kosovo yet. I know you will appreciate that we have to move step by step. The first wrong move we make and any number of presidents or ex-presidents will be lining up to execute us, perhaps literally."

Before there was the chance of a riposte, General Petar spoke up and confidently confirmed that he was satisfied with progress to date. "The move we made to keep the Army from intervening to support the Vojvodina Party leaders was, I believe, crucial in our gaining that Serbian province."

M, Mira and Kovac all nodded their agreement. M looked like he was going to say something but the General went on,

"I know you all think that generals just like to fight, but they also like to win, and win with the minimum of casualties. I believe," he continued, "that we may come into our own when we get to Bosnia Herzegovina."

The General's play for operational control of any Bosnia operation did not go unnoticed by anyone and Kovac, for one, nodded his agreement. Mr Smolov, who was present again, sat quietly in an armchair again slightly away from the rest, his hard features making even the hardest Serbian look like a Boy Scout. It looked as if he was going to be a permanent team member. Bojan glanced at him wondering what was going on behind those lidded eyes and what his real role would turn out to be. At that moment, the Russian had made a decision – to get more acquainted with the General.

Kovac had been the busiest of the team with the exception of M himself, being used in his intelligence capacity all over Yugoslavia. He was quite happy with how the strategy was developing but still with reservations about taking on Croatia. A personal concern over Djuric was growing in his mind but currently on the back burner to be brought to the front if any further issues arose. It wasn't a subject for this or any other team meeting though.

Bojan had been used just to get a view on what was going on in Slovenia, but was itching to get his hands on some real action somewhere. He was thinking that Montenegro might be that place. Once he could prove himself to M, he thought he might get a bigger slice of the cake elsewhere.

M cleared his throat, signalling an end to that discussion. "The next target is Montenegro," he announced.

Bojan looked up expectantly. "I believe I might have something to contribute here, especially," he took his glasses off again, "as the place is all but bankrupt."

M and Mira were both from Montenegro so they understood that republic well. Montenegrins were closely connected with Serbia in history, religion and identity and, with only just over six hundred thousand souls in the country at this point, no-one really saw a problem. But the population was not homogeneous. In the distant past, they had been a warrior people of some thirty-five tribes emanating from the Dinaric mountains and, although most were still able to trace their ancestry to one of those tribes, their warrior days were long gone. Now the country was full of social unrest with workers demanding higher wages which no factory or mine could afford.

M looked at him, "Yes, I believe you may be right. They will need some specialist help." Having taken off his glasses for cleaning, Bojan now replaced them carefully with a satisfied smile.

"You probably all know the history," M continued, "but today, politically, they divided into two factions: the Greens who want independence and the Whites who are with Serbia. We will do the same thing we did in Kosovo." He ended by looking at Kovac again.

"It will be easier than Kosovo," M was addressing Kovac, "so get your team to organise a series of 'Truth' rallies to mobilise the Whites. My guess is the police will move in with rough methods and then we can use that to cause unrest and threaten them with the army if the Serbian population is discriminated against."

"Should be no problem," responded Kovac, "I'll get right on it." He sounded positive for the benefit of his boss and the others, but was feeling far from it. He knew he had to handle Djuric carefully at the moment. He didn't want to lose him, but neither was he about to go soft. After drinks were finished, M wished everyone a good night, asking Kovac and Bojan to stay behind for a minute.

"Our businessmen friends and the General already have mobile phones, as do I, and I want you to have one so we can be in touch all the time. My number is already on both phones and I have yours on mine." With that he gave each a box.

Djuric was already in Montenegro. Not many knew that he was half Montenegrin on his mother's side but his father was a Serb and a Party chief of some sort in Belgrade – he never knew exactly what. His parents were always vague when it came to explaining what he did. Whatever it was, legal or illegal, it was enough to live quite comfortably in Belgrade. Djuric was only twelve his father had died, in odd circumstances apparently, but he vividly remembered secret police arriving at the house after his death and roughly questioning his mother. He heard most of the questioning as he hid at the top of the stairs and decided that his father must have done something wrong. He began to wonder whether that was linked to his death but, listening to his mother crying, it was evident she knew nothing about it.

She drank quite a lot after that, and the failing relationship with her son finally fell apart in his late teenage years. By this time the military was looking a good option for the young man so he joined up, never bothering to keep in touch with his mother since they hadn't had much to say to each other for years. She died shortly afterwards of an alcohol-related illness and the state quickly took possession of the family home since, as a Party official, his father had been allocated the house as a lifetime privilege.

Before leaving home he decided to try to find out what his father had done. So while his mother was comatosed one afternoon, he had searched his father's study for anything that would tell him what his father had been up to, but found nothing. He assumed the secret police had removed everything of interest. He then went up into the attic remembering how often his father went up there. After a thorough search with a torch he was about to give up when he noticed a brick in the back of the chimney stack where the mortar had been scoured out. Taking out the brick, he had found a small box with a key together with an address at the back. He replaced the brick but kept the box and its contents.

The address related to a place called Igalo. He had no idea where that was but found that it was on the coast at the southern tip of Montenegro in the Herceg Novi municipality. He had known that his father had gone away occasionally without his mother, 'on Party business.'

"So this is where he went," muttered Djuric. Clearly the secret police hadn't discovered the existence of the Igalo residence for which he was grateful, but it almost certainly meant that his father had some illegal source of finance in addition to his Party income, hence their interest. It was not unknown for Party officials to have other interests but he had never thought of his father in that way. But then, he had never really known his father. His curiosity was now piqued.

As there was a lull in M's activities, he had decided to drive down to have a look. As he came into Igalo, the streets were narrow and hilly with not many street names so it took a little while to find the apartment block which he did with the help of a local green-grocer. What he found wasn't a typical Soviet block which was rather refreshing, rather an older block with a lot more character. He was directed by a sign to drive into a car lift which would take him down to a lower ground floor car park. He hesitated, knowing the country's record on maintenance wasn't great but there was nowhere else to park his car, so he decided to risk it.

He made his way up to the third floor with his bag, opened the door to a rather stale and musty smell and headed straight for the window to let in fresh air. As he settled in he began to notice odd things, apart from the dusty evidence signifying that no-one had been in there for years. For example, there were no family photos, no decorations, no sign of a woman's touch except in the wardrobe where there were both male and female clothes, old but quite expensive-looking. Looking at the female ones, they seemed a lot slimmer and a lot dressier than he remembered his mother wearing. Well, it wasn't unknown for Party chiefs to have a bit on the side. He wondered who it was, whether she was local or not. But after all these years, he didn't care and anyway, he wasn't planning to stay long, just long enough to think how he could locate Ivana.

He had not left any telephone number with Kovac, but had said he needed a week or two to sort a family issue and would call regularly.

"Just calling to find out what's happening," Djuric was checking in.

"Where are you?"

"In Montenegro."

"Good. Get yourself to Titograd, if you're not already there," he paused to let Djuric confirm that's where he was. Djuric said nothing and waited.

"Find a place that sells mobile phones and get one. I'll pay and put this number on it immediately. That way I'll be able to get you when I need to."

He gave Djuric the number and closed the call. Not much thought was given to signal accessibility but it was a start. Titograd, the capital, was only seventy miles or so away. By ten o'clock the following morning he was there, had found a shop, was shocked at the price but intrigued by the device and felt he had moved up in the world.

He sent a message to Kovac so he would have the number on his mobile and received a long message back instructing him to organise more 'Truth' rallies. He cursed and began to realise what a short leash he was now on. Well, he would make some phone calls, then spend the rest of the day looking at the national records for Ivana Popovic. It was a common family name so he had no high hopes of immediate success.

It was true that Djuric didn't make a great deal of effort over the first demonstration. Titograd was the only city worth working on and he didn't think it was going to take much to cause an upset. But the Montenegrin regime got wind of what was about to happen and were well prepared. It didn't go well.

"What the **** is going on?" Kovac was yelling down the phone to Djuric who profusely apologised and blamed it on the short notice. He promised to do better. The hunt for Ivana had to be put on the back burner while he gave his full attention to the job. He decided to call up Luka and his compatriots whom he had used with great success in Kosovo and directed them towards the steel workers, workers from the aluminium plant and any other industrial workers they could find. It was Djuric's finest hour. A superbly organised event which shook the regime to the core.

"I think one more demonstration will do it," Djuric was on the phone to Kovac confidently predicting the outcome.

"We'll see." Kovac wasn't given to awarding accolades for anything and Djuric wasn't expecting one. He gathered together his team and told them exactly what he wanted. A third demonstration was going to be even better. As it turned out, it wasn't. It was more the actions of the police who used truncheons and tear gas on the workers before a baton charge injuring at least seven people. That was sufficient for Belgrade to accuse the regime of suppressing the will of the people. The regime lasted another few months before it capitulated and M's men took over. Bojan finally got his wish and the Central Bank of Montenegro got a new governor. The two businessmen were not so happy – loss-making steel and aluminium works were not top of their list of takeover options. They had their eyes on the riches of Croatia.

Djuric didn't stay around to see the riots, neither did he care who or how many got injured. Not his concern. He was busy burying himself in records of Montenegrin births, marriages and deaths. Day after day he searched, not able to lay the task on anyone else. It was his private burden. Finally, he identified three possible Ivanas who were about the right age and seemed to fit with his limited knowledge of her background. One was on the outskirts of Titograd itself, one in the north of the country in Pljevlja and the other near the Albanian border in a place called Gusinje.

He retreated to Igalo to review the three possibles and get some rest for a day or so. He was feeling quite exhausted and wanted to work out exactly what to say if he ever found her, especially as her loyalties had never been clear. He felt sure he could persuade her to come on to his side if it came to that, at least he hoped so. As he settled down for the first night, his mind began to work through all the different scenarios he might meet. It was by no means certain that she was at any of the places he had identified and even if her family were there, she might not be. He would have to visit each locality in turn which might take a while if Kovac called again. It was a relatively sleepless night.

He woke in the morning not refreshed but with a plan to walk around the bay to clear his head accompanied by his new mobile phone. It was a beautiful area almost fjord-like; steep cliffs descending into clear sparkling waters. There was a footpath right next to the water which seemed to go on for miles with floating restaurants moored to the side. Djuric took some long deep breaths as he strolled along the path. He hadn't done anything like this for years, certainly not in such a beautiful setting. So carried away with the scenery that Kovac and the mission he was on seemed irrelevant. Perhaps he could find Ivana and persuade her to stay here? It would be idyllic. He sat on a bench opposite an island on which stood an ancient church. He consulted a plaque giving details of the history of *Gospa od Skrpjela* to find that it had been artificially created on 22 July 1452 around a rock where an image of the Madonna had been found and every year on the same day, the locals row over with more stones to continue the task of building the island. Part of him hankered after the simple lifestyle of these folk. They were totally oblivious to what was unfolding in other parts of the country and in some ways he envied them. Yes, when it was all over, he wanted to come back here.

Turning around, he made his way back to Igalo feeling refreshed and a determination to bring Ivana here. He ate out that evening hoping to have a better night's sleep, but no. Because he wanted to wake early to make a start back to Titograd he woke every hour or so to look at his watch, not yet having understood that his new mobile was much more than a phone. Finally he got fed up with laying in bed not sleeping so after a very early simple breakfast he was on his way.

He was tentatively making his way through an unfamiliar city with just an address indicating that this Ivana's birthplace was located in the west of the city. With a few rough directions from people he stopped, he began to get close enough for people to recognise the street name. It wasn't long before he was driving down her road with increasing excitement building up within him. He tried to keep calm as he drove, telling himself that as this was the first place he was checking out, it was unlikely to be the one. This part of the city was filled with six storey concrete apartments built in zigzag fashion, Soviet style. A few cars were parked along the road with waste ground opposite and a concrete football pitch with torn down wire netting around it. The grass, if you could call it grass, was yellow and sparse. The few trees looked as if they were dying, if not already dead. He drove along it once to get a feel for the place, turned around at the end and came back slowly. There weren't many people about, children still at school and just a few women trudging to and from the local shop.

He stopped the car, got out and moved nearer to the block to look at the numbers. Yes, this was the right block and there it was, number 108 on the top floor. He climbed the concrete steps and found himself outside the door. Water was dripping from the flat roof and the paint was almost gone from the walls and the door. No-one had done anything to this since it was built, he surmised, but that was how it was with all these buildings. He knocked. No answer. Knocking a few more times didn't elicit any different response from the apartment. His excitement had drained now and he was becoming frustrated.

He decided to knock at number 107, a floor down. An old lady opened the door ajar and looked suspiciously at him.

"I've knocked several times on the door of number 108 with no response. Do you know where they might be?"

"Agh, agh." the woman coughed. "And who might you be looking for?" The old lady was giving nothing away.

"Ivana."

"She's gone."

"Where did she go?"

"She went to Belgrade years back." Perhaps this was the right house. How many Ivanas went from here to Belgrade?

"Yes, I know that," said Djuric. "But didn't she come back recently?" He asked the question desperately hoping for a positive reply. The old lady looked him up and down, with some interest now. "How do you know?"

"Err.... we're friends."

The old lady's eyes twinkled and she smiled at him. "Are you Djuric?"

Djuric frowned, wondering how much he should admit to. "Yes," he said cautiously.

"She said you might turn up one day."

"Did she? So why is there no-one in the apartment?"

"Well, I suppose there's no harm in you knowing, seeing that you're 'related'." She grinned knowingly showing her lack of teeth and pinkish gums. "Her mother died a few weeks ago which is why she must have come back."

She paused to engage in another fit of coughing. "Nice girl to come and look after her mother, unlike some." She sniffed. Obviously her own daughter had no intention of coming back to look after her.

"Where is she now?" Djuric wanted to end this encounter.

"Agh. Agh." The lady began yet another long bout of coughing forcing Djuric to take a few steps backwards. Once recovered, she said, "Out. I saw her going down the steps at nine o'clock this morning, all prim and proper like. She must have a nice job." She sniffed again.

"Where does she work?"

The old lady brought her hand up to her mouth. "You know, I really don't know."

Djuric had had enough of this and started to move away when the old lady called out,

"She'll be back at four o'clock this afternoon. She's always back at that time."

Djuric turned back as the old lady cackled and burst into another coughing bout. She shut the door and Djuric made his way back to the car. He was buzzing to have found the right place first time and now just had to wait. Sleep seemed the obvious course since he had had precious little the previous night. He settled down in the car having put the seat back as far as it would go, which wasn't far, and it wasn't long before he was happily unconscious.

Chapter 12 — Belgrade

GENERAL PETAR WAS a complicated man. On the one hand he was one of the highest generals in the Yugoslav Army used to having his every word obeyed instantly, yet on the other he was happy to submit to M's orders and strategy. The reason: he saw the total disaster facing Yugoslavia without a strong man at the political helm. M was the leader he had decided to back. A group of about two hundred Serbian officers of all ranks were members of a secret cabal in the Army under his authority. Each of them sworn to secrecy on pain of death until the time came for them to reveal themselves and execute their orders.

The General was head-quartered at the Stone Palace at 33 Kneza Milosa St. from where he saw to it that M's instructions were carried out. Today, however, he had an appointment with a Mr Smolov whom he had seen twice at M's flat but had never been properly introduced, and to whom he had taken an instant dislike. It was never good to incur the dislike of a senior general in the Yugoslav Army but then Smolov was not under his command. He could tell the man had a military background, perhaps in Special Forces but it was his self confidence, no, call it arrogance that presented a challenge Petar had not faced in years.

At 10am promptly, Yuri Smolov presented himself at the reception desk and asked for the General. The corporal on duty checked the visitor's diary for the day to ensure he was expected and seeing that he was, asked Mr Smolov to be seated and the General's adjutant would be along shortly. In fact, the adjutant had already been instructed to be positioned on the ground floor out of sight and to greet Mr Smolov immediately he sat down. The adjutant came to attention in front of the Russian, clicked his heels and saluted.

"Would you follow me, sir?" The two of them walked to the lift and headed for the top floor. Once shown into the outer room of Petar's office, Smolov was invited to sit, duly informed that the General was running a little late and offered coffee, which he accepted.

The Russian smiled. He recognised the game. The immediate appearance of the adjutant downstairs was to demonstrate efficiency and the wait in the outer office to demonstrate who was senior. But the General wasn't very long; he didn't want Smolov to give a bad report to M. He burst in through the door from the corridor as if he always walked around in a hurry.

"Apologies. Sorry to have kept you waiting. Ah. I see you have been offered coffee. Bring one in for me, will you? Let's go into my office shall we?"

The two of them entered Petar's nicely furnished office and indicated that they should sit on two facing chairs near a window with a table in between for drinks.

Immediately he said, "To what do I owe the pleasure?" Petar was trying to be cordial and at the same time indicating that he was a busy man. The Russian was in no hurry, though.

"I felt I needed to get to know you a little better. These meetings in M's flat are fine for those who know each other but I'm a late arrival." He chuckled as if he had made a little joke. He sat forward a little. "Tell me, what additional weapons do you require?"

Petar was taken aback a little at this sudden change of direction. He decided to take it head on. "Am I to suppose that you are able to supply us with everything we need?"

The Russian responded calmly as if nothing Petar could say was going to rile him. "Well, I suppose that depends on what you need. By the way, have your troops seen any real action. I suppose I should ask whether any of your generals have ever operated in a war environment?"

Petar was now staring at the Russian, who noted Petar's surprise but carried on. "It makes a difference, you know. I liked what you said about winning and minimising casualties. In Russia we don't have a problem with manpower, as we demonstrated against the Nazis. But you are a smaller country and I'm guessing many of your existing force who are not Serbs, might not want to support your specific objectives. So with a much smaller Army, minimising casualties will be critical to success."

Smolov looked at the General who was now visibly uncomfortable in his own office. The conversation was definitely not going as anticipated. But

Smolov hadn't finished yet.

"I recommend that you adopt a strategy of bombardment and siege. On no account allow your men to face the enemy hand to hand, even gun to gun. Use large artillery units to surround and blitz the infrastructure of the city you are trying to break. They can be tanks or just large field guns."

Petar just looked at the Russian who could see the man's discomfort, so he smiled and continued, "It takes time but works ever time. So what have you got?"

The General got up from his chair and went over to his desk. He was not going to share the status of his force with this man, but he had been working on a wish list of arms and armaments ever since M introduced him to the team. But before he could speak, the Russian again took control of the meeting.

"Oh. Incidentally, I have offered an experienced strategist to be embedded with each force you have in the battlefield. They will be invaluable and will, of course, be under your orders completely. M thought that might be a good idea." He didn't mention the probability of Russian feet on the ground which was not necessary at the moment since he was entirely sure Petar would not be long in his job.

The General was still rummaging around on his desk trying to retrieve a document from his desk and looked up when M's name was mentioned. He nodded, not really knowing what to say. He returned from his desk and proffered the document to the Russian who quickly looked at it, page by page, saying nothing. Petar sat in his chair facing Smolov also saying nothing. Eventually, the Russian, having glanced all the way through the document, pronounced that he understood it.

"Thank you, General. I would like to take this back to Moscow if I may, and see what we can do for you."

He got up indicating that as far as he was concerned, the meeting was over. "I would like to meet again when we are further down the track and your strategy is better developed. If that's agreeable to you?" He lifted his eyebrows.

"Of course, of course," responded Petar. He got up and showed his guest to the door and ordered the adjutant to escort Mr Smolov through reception.

General Petar retreated back to his office and sat down, wondering about the Russian and his relationship with M. He was not entirely happy with how things had gone and started to think about what report Smolov would make to M. For his part, Smolov went back to the Russian embassy in Belgrade and checked in with his boss in Moscow.

Chapter 13 — Slovenia

M's strategy of using constitutional manoeuvring backed up by large public demonstrations had given Serbia far more political power than any other republic. He refused, however, to acknowledge that those public events had partly been brought about by criminal activity fostered by his own team.

There were eight votes within the group called the Federal Presidency, which represented all the republics and provinces of Yugoslavia for this is how Tito had designed it. Serbia by now controlled three votes out of the eight which had incurred Slovenia's indignation. They felt they should have had a special position in Yugoslavia and certainly more votes than Serbia in the Federal Presidency. After all, they were the richest republic, by far the most progressive and Tito himself had come to the central hospital in Ljubljana because it had the best reputation in the whole of Yugoslavia. This complaint was continually encouraged by their Party machine among their own people, namely: that they were being exploited and their prosperity sucked away to other parts of Yugoslavia who were living off their wealth.

It was a thorn in the side for M who wanted to take control of Slovenia, not just because of its riches, but to clear out what he saw as arrogant leaders who were focussed on opposing everything he wanted to achieve. He was in deep conversation with Mira, his wife and co-strategist about the Slovenian leadership.

"It's getting out of hand. Now they want to propose amendments to their own constitution which will effectively relegate Federal law to internal Slovenian law. Next they will want to declare independence." He was pacing up and down physically manifesting his outrage.

"They're learning" Mira observed wryly watching her husband with some amusement. "That's almost exactly what you did in Serbia. It's going to be difficult to argue against." These considerations weren't unknown to M. He was looking for a way that not only protected his gains but, having become President of Serbia, to take control over Slovenia.

"This is essential if our plans are to be fully realised," he declared.

"But if such changes are merely a build up to an effective UDI," said Mira thinking aloud, "and it could be argued that they are, it would mean the certain breakup of Yugoslavia with Slovenia able to do whatever they like."

M pondered for a moment, "And it also means," he said, responding to his wife's comment, "that they could annex the Yugoslav army that is stationed in Slovenia and make it their own whenever they wanted, provided they had good relations with the military hierarchy there."

"Quite possible," agreed Mira. "You have control over much of the Federal Army but not all of it. You need to get complete control quickly before they act."

"Treacherous bastards," M snorted. Mira sat quietly waiting for her husband to calm down. She was possibly the only person who could challenge M directly, but even she knew there was a time to speak and a time to be quiet. He knew that the process of 'Serbianising' the army had to be speeded up somehow. He would get on to Petar, but in the meantime he had an uncontrolled Slovenia on his hands. Not a situation he liked. On impulse he called Kovac to organise 'something' that would rid him of these people. Kovac was not happy but recognised M's anger, so began by sympathising with M about the Slovene leadership and then quietly began talking him down as best he could steering him away from what he thought was the wrong path. He was taking a big gamble for M could be quite unpredictable if anyone contradicted him.

The advice was to play it softly, at least to begin with. "That way," explained the intelligence man, "you don't alienate the other republics and you demonstrate how reasonable you are and that you have Yugoslavian Federal interests at heart. We still need Croatia on our side, at least for the time being."

M grunted and disconnected the call. "He's right," he finally admitted to Mira, deciding to take Kovac's advice, "but just for now. If all our meetings, negotiations, talks, whatever they are, do not succeed and they go ahead on their own," he added grimly, "it will be over to the Army."

Next he called General Petar. "What progress are you making with the Army?"

"We're working on it but it takes time. There are Federal Army barracks all over Yugoslavia. Each has its own commander and not all are Serbs."

"We may not have time to wait any longer. If Slovenia declares independence we will lose Croatia for certain."

The Yugoslavian Presidency group were trying to head off the Slovenian actions but without much success. M was not encouraged. Continuous discussions back and forth were not producing any results. The Slovene leadership were not in a compromise mood. They had decided that things were going their way and if they held out, they would get everything they wanted, which was independence. M decided he needed to take his own action. He was frustrated to be on the sidelines because he could see the whole situation deteriorating rapidly and all he had achieved so far undermined at a stroke. Since the meetings had concluded without any agreement and everyone had gone back to their own republics, M embarked on a series of calls to pressure the group to invite the Slovene leadership back to Belgrade one final time. But would they come?

M's mobile rang. The intelligence man had information from someone high up in the Slovene leadership.

"The Slovenes have decided to come to the meeting."

M breathed a sigh of relief. Maybe he had one last chance and, he thought, if they didn't compromise he might take matters into his own hands.

Kovac continued. "But they have secretly arranged various escape routes via a series of rental cars just in case things don't go their way."

"Why?"

"They suspect if there is no agreement, there may be assassination attempts on them."

"If I had my way...." muttered M. "How are they going to do it? We could easily block the road back to Ljubljana."

"They're going to drive over towards the Bulgarian border, then back to the capital."

"Are they indeed?" M was thinking hard.

Kovac could almost hear the wheels grinding in M's head. He cautioned. "I still think we should just wait and see. We still have Plan B."

It turned out to be the worst possible outcome for M. Although at the end of another 'exchange of views' there was a vote by the Yugoslavian Presidency group which Slovenia lost, one of the most powerful republics, Croatia, voted with them. The Slovenes saw they had an ally and immediately ignored the majority decision against them and went ahead to declare themselves to be a sovereign state. Their leaders were welcomed back in Ljubljana as heroes – rental cars not required. The Slovenian Parliament was also jubilant and started singing patriotic songs whilst unanimously passing a motion to refuse to contribute any further monies to the Federal state.

M was incandescent at the Yugoslavian Presidency Group. Even Mira kept out of his way for a day or so as did Kovac.

"Those ******* incompetent fools. They couldn't organise a pissup in a brewery. I'm not having it. If they can't do it, I will. And I will use whatever force I need to."

Plan B was the Kosovo strategy. If political and constitutional means didn't work, mass demonstrations might with a bit of criminality thrown in. Kovac was on the phone to Djuric who was still in Montenegro.

"This is urgent. We have to rein in Slovenia. So we want a mega 'Meeting of Truth' rally in Ljubljana."

Djuric put the phone down and called Luka.

"Luka, I'm stuck in Montenegro for the moment, but Kovac wants another demo in Ljubljana. Get up there as soon as you can. I'll call the others and we'll do the usual. I'll see you there."

With those words, Luka disappeared towards the Pristina railway station to catch the train. Whilst he was moving north, Djuric used his new mobile phone to pull together the rest of the cabal for another 'Meeting of Truth'. They were getting good at these events, enjoyed creating chaos and getting well paid for it.

However, the government in Slovenia had got wind of what was happening. Some tried to dismiss it at first calling it 'M's travelling circus', but wiser heads were regarding it as a serious threat. They eventually banned the rally and posted guards on both rail and road access from Serbia with orders to search incoming Serbs for weapons, confiscating any and turning them all back.

Back in Belgrade, Mira was counselling her husband. "I think you should call off the rally," He looked at her questioningly so she explained her thinking. "It could result in our people being killed, and we're not ready for that sort of conflict yet."

Reluctantly, M agreed and decided to call it off. "Perhaps," he said thinking aloud, "we might make better progress with economic sanctions instead."

"It will cut both ways," she warned. "It will harm Serbia as well, so don't let it go on too long."

"I won't," he said getting up to kiss her on the cheek. "What would I do without you?"

Serbian businesses lost no time in responding to M's call and in a matter of weeks over one hundred of them cut ties with either suppliers and/or customers in Slovenia. The Belgrade press lambasted Slovenian companies who dared to import their goods into Serbian shops, and major institutions abandoned relationships with their counterparts over the border.

The timing was perfect. M's inaugural speech as President of Serbia was due and he was not going to pull any punches. This, he knew, was another key moment. Somehow he had to begin to prise Croatia away from Slovenia because if the northern republic established their independence, the western state would follow. Yugoslavia, and therefore Serbia, would be left with the economic runt of the brood.

The bitter divisions which Tito had successfully but thinly cemented over were about to erupt big time. The Fourteenth Congress of the Yugoslav Communist Party was about to begin with M's speech.

"You," M said pointing his finger accusingly at the Slovenian representatives, "have acted aggressively towards Yugoslavia. It is clear, comrades, that this republic is intent on dividing our country and they MUST be stopped."

The Slovenian delegates had their say. "These are unfounded and absurd assertions which have NO basis in fact. On the contrary, it is Serbia who wants Yugoslavia to disintegrate so they can claim a Greater Serbia for themselves."

It was clear that the passion and emotion of it all was getting the better of all the delegates. It was becoming a total free for all. Motion after motion put forward by the Slovenes at the Congress were defeated which eventually led them to walk out, closely followed by Croatia. Some thought it was a victory for Serbia. Mistake.

One of the Serb representatives turned to Croatia's leader, Racan, after they started to vacate the hall and shouted insults at him. He stood up and advanced towards him pointing his finger threateningly at him.

"I have had enough of you," he shouted, red in the face. "You are a disgrace to Yugoslavia." Other Serb delegates tried to pull him back but the damage had been done. It had the immediate effect of pushing Croatia against Serbia and firmly into the Slovenian camp. M was furious. He grabbed the lapels of the delegate.

"You idiot. I have deliberately steered clear of criticising Croatia because I don't want them supporting Slovenia. You, my friend, are finished. Go." Despite some back-room apologies, a personal insult thrown publicly at Racan by a Serbian delegate was never going to be successfully pulled back. Even the Bosnian leader, Durakovic, did his level best to engage with the two dissenting republics knowing all too well what this might mean for Bosnia, but to no avail.

Communism all over Eastern Europe was disintegrating and so it was in Yugoslavia. Croatia and Slovenia made the decision to hold free elections for their populations and everyone knew what that meant. Kovac had been listening to the exchanges and had his head in his hands.

"It's over," he moaned to himself. "After all our efforts, that imbecile torpedoes our total strategy. If M wants to continue, it's going to have to be with the Army and I'm not sure I'm going to like it."

M did, and Plan C was about to be dusted off.

Chapter 14 — Montenegro

IT WAS BEYOND four o'clock. Evening had come and Djuric, who had immediately nodded off in the car, was now wide awake and had been for some time. He was beginning to think the old lady in107 had been having fun with him and maybe she wasn't here after all. Then Djuric saw someone coming in his rear view mirror that looked like her and walked like her. He sat up immediately thinking she would stop, but it was clear she had serious things on her mind. She was walking head down, taking little notice of anything in the road.

Oblivious of the strange car parked outside her apartment block, she passed it and began to ascend the concrete steps, when suddenly she stopped and looked back as if a sixth sense had told her something was unusual. She glanced back towards the car ready to either run up the steps and lock the door or aggressively approach and confront any stranger. She had no middle way. When she turned and looked at the driver, recognition finally dawned on her and she smiled to herself. He'd come.

She impishly thought of ignoring him and going up to the apartment and watching from her window to make him follow but she suspected the old lady from 107 would also be watching through her ancient net curtains. So she made eye contact indicating with her head that he should follow her and, without waiting, she carried on up the concrete steps.

Djuric watched her. As soon as she disappeared he got out of his car, smoothed himself down, locked the car and followed. He found the door of the apartment left open and cautiously went in. The hallway was quite dark as he made his way through until he got to the living area at the front where there were large windows with a view across the city. There she was, sitting in a chair waiting for him.

"So you found me." She was toying with him. He was still standing, getting used to his surroundings and waiting for an invitation to stay. He knew if he sat down before such, he would be asked to get up again. She liked playing games.

"Did the Party send you?" she asked sarcastically.

"Which Party would that be?" he replied, quoting her question at the restaurant back at her. He could play the game to. She smiled indicating he should sit down and make himself comfortable. He dropped his bag and slumped in his seat, but still regarding her with some apprehension.

"They don't know where I am, but..." he pulled out his mobile phone, "they will want to know soon."

"Ah. In high demand, I see."

"Sometimes. Look," Djuric sat up. "Can we cut to the chase here? I know that after you left Tito's ....er employment, you became the Private Secretary to the Yugoslav President.

"Personal assistant."

"OK, Personal Assistant. And I'm guessing in the light of recent events, you thought it would be diplomatic to move away and keep a low profile?"

"Always the man in a hurry, never any foreplay, that's your trouble."

He looked unsure of himself, not certain how to approach this situation. She got up, took him by the hand and led him into the bedroom. When he eventually reached over her to look at the alarm clock it was past midnight, but as he stretched in the bed so she awakened.

"You awake?" she mumbled.

"Yes. Can we talk now?" he asked.

"What now? You do choose your moments." She yawned and swung her legs off the bed and padded to the only bathroom in the apartment. It was about ten minutes before she reappeared, head in a towel and body in a dressing gown.

"So what is so important that you want a midnight discussion? Is this now business after pleasure?"

Djuric didn't say anything for a few seconds, as if thinking about how to approach a delicate subject.

"Things are changing," he eventually said.

"Amazing," she said, "If you hadn't told me, I'd never have known."

"It's serious Ivana."

She hugged the sheet and blankets around her. It was now quite cold in the apartment; the heating had never been very good and she couldn't afford to have it on all the time. Djuric looked at her, then looked away as he spoke.

"The thing is – Serbia has a new President and he doesn't just want Serbia. He's looking for the whole country and he's probably going to get it."

She looked straight at him compelling him to turn around and look at her. "Please don't take me for a fool. I'm Montenegrin. Why do you think I fled back home?"

Neither spoke for a few moments. She then added, "Is this what you've been doing these past few years instead of keeping your promise to me?"

Djuric was now shuffling uncomfortably in bed, her bed. "I apologised back in the restaurant and I meant it."

He turned to her. "It was for the future of the country."

She laughed at him, "Oh that's all right then, if it's for the future of the country."

"Look," he said, "It's going to happen. If I can help do it politically that will be a whole lot better than doing it militarily. And, believe me, if it comes to deploying the Army, they will not hesitate. In fact, he's under pressure to do just that."

Ivana wasn't going to let that stand. "It doesn't take a genius to see it. And that doesn't make it right whether politically or militarily. He just wants power and he's happy to use any means to get it. He doesn't care about ordinary people, just himself and his legacy. He wants his place in history."

She was sounding rather bitter now. "Tito held the country together and all the men who subsequently became President on the rotating basis Tito set up, also tried to keep the country together. It was only Serbia and …. him, who wanted to grab it all." She spat it out.

He had come hoping she would see his point of view but it didn't look like that was going to happen. They both sat in silence. He didn't know what to do. After a few minutes he got up and went to the bathroom, had a shower and returned to dress.

"So, you're leaving?" she asked. "You don't have to. It's still dark."

"I think I do." he said.

She suddenly skipped out of bed and into the kitchen. "Let me make you some breakfast and then you can go.... if you want to." She eyed him as she went and saw total confusion on his face.

Ten minutes later they were sitting at the plastic table in the kitchen, he eating a *burek,* a minced meat pita and she some healthy granola, both washed down with Turkish coffee.

"I need to switch on my mobile and it's likely there will be a message or two. I'll have to go," explained Djuric avoiding a response to her offer.

"Go ahead."

He switched it on and there were missed calls galore from one person. Djuric sighed. He moved into the other room to take them. There were no messages so he didn't know what he was needed for. He returned Kovac's calls to be met with a blast of curses. He held the phone away from his ears and waited for the frustration to subside. He wasn't concerned that he might lose his job for he knew he was good at it and Kovac depended on him, at least for now.

"Where do you need me?" Djuric thought he might as well try and dispense with the 'where the hell have you been etc.?' and move on.

He heard Kovac take a large breath. "Things are happening in Croatia. M wants you in Zagreb and he wants lots of other people there too."

"On my way," answered Djuric.

"And by the way, keep your bloody phone on." With that the line was cut.

Ivana had come in from the kitchen and could hear both ends of the conversation. "So are you going or staying?"

"Well, I need to make some phone calls first but I could stay for a few hours longer, but then I really have to go."

"Pity," murmured Ivana. Djuric made three calls so his crew could get to work and sat down in the living area trying to work out where he stood with this woman, while she got dressed. After twenty minutes she reappeared and began to clean the room around him. So he got up and began to leave.

"Give me your number," she asked. "I haven't got a mobile yet but I think I'll get one." He did so and she said, "Now there's no excuse not to call me."

Chapter 15 — Croatia

SEEMINGLY OBLIVIOUS TO the inexorable move towards the splitting up of Yugoslavia, its current Prime Minister, Markovic, set about implementing free market reforms thinking that perhaps better economic conditions would head off the various nationalist movements. True, the populace were becoming much better off and the blue eyed Prime Minister was becoming quite a favourite with the people, but the governments of the various republics and provinces had no intention of submitting to any Federal Prime Minister.

"Is he living in a dream world, or just stupid?" asked Kovac. They were at M's apartment discussing next steps. Not all of them though. "Where are the others?"

"The General is meeting with our Russian friend. I dare say he is listing a very expensive range of military hardware which he wants for the Army." M was nonchalant. Kovac wanted to ask for more details about the Russian dimension, but decided to wait for M himself to offer more insight. Rather, he asked about the funding of this new relationship.

" I'm thinking that such hardware doesn't come cheap. Where is the money coming from to pay for it all?"

"Ah. That's where Bojan comes in." The accountant looked up importantly. M continued, "Every republic and province will help to fund their own demise. Clever, eh! The task will be to get people into the Treasury of each one that we control. Not a difficult job."

Bojan nodded, glad at last to have a role he knew he could excel at. Kovac shrugged. "But without Slovenia that won't amount to much."

M agreed. "Much will have to be done by 'encouraging' the civilian population to ditch their current leaders. I think the military might have a role to play in that 'encouragement'." He smiled. But the mention of the military again caused Kovac to frown. Bojan saw it and seem to recognise this as area of growing discomfort for Kovac. So before M began to expand his military views the accountant switched the conversation.

"What are we going to do about Croatia?" He was asking the question they were all thinking about but no-one had mentioned. Addressing Kovac, M asked, "From what you've said, your demonstrations in Zagreb didn't go so well."

Kovac, grateful for the change of topic, confessed. "It did the opposite, so I've pulled them out."

They all knew that Croatia had finally woken up. The walkout at the Congress had emboldened their leaders and everyone suspected more actions would follow. They did. The Party hierarchy began to invoke some past history to reinforce latent Croatian nationalism. Discontent had been building since the 1960s initially concerned economic nationalism. The reformists wished to reduce transfers of hard currency earned in Croatia to the federal government in Belgrade. This gradually morphed into political demands for increased autonomy and, in particular, opposition to real or perceived over representation of ethnic Serbs in the security services, politics, and in other strategic fields within Croatia. And there was still bitterness over the 1971 Maspok movement which had been harshly crushed by Tito. A long time ago, but in this part of the world it was as yesterday.

Even though ostensibly a communist country, religion was still alive and was always a sure way of expressing identity. The Roman Catholic Church in Croatia had continued to operate albeit with some Communist Party persecu-tion but now it started to see a revival as people used their growing attendance at its churches to signify the end of Communist Party influence and to place themselves squarely against the Serbs' Orthodox Church. New elections were announced which, their leaders hoped, would give them a mandate to break away from the Federal government of Yugoslavia. Racan was the man who had spearheaded this new movement, but in the run up to the elec-tions ex-General Franjo Tudjman had formed his HDZ political party to rival Racan's party and, surprisingly, had won.

It all indicated that Croatia was going to be a major stumbling block to M's vision of a Greater Serbia, since thousands of Serbs lived in Croatian villages and towns. Bojan's question was the overriding issue of the moment, and no-one knew quite how to handle it.

There was a long pause until Mira spoke up. "You know, if Markovic gets his way, Croatia will lose all their foreign currency earnings from tourism to the central Yugoslav Treasury." She left the comment hanging in the air.

Kovac replied glumly, "That might ensure that Tudjman declares his UDI sooner rather than later." M was quiet, thinking of any way to get a hold on the situation in Croatia.

"I've been listening to what Tudjman has been saying. He's slagging off everyone, Serbs, Bosnians, even the Army. We need to respond just to show we're here and not going away, and I think I know how."

Red Star Belgrade, the premier football team in Serbia, were due shortly to play Zagreb Dinamo in the Croatian capital. M turned to Kovac and said, "Get a group to Zagreb at the football match and have some fun. We're not taking Tudjman's threats lying down, but I need Djuric for another job, if you can spare him?"

"Of course," responded Kovac. "Not quite sure where he is but I'll call him."

Djuric's team, minus Djuric himself, went off to the football match determined to enjoy themselves.... and they did. After the Serbian supporters had been wound up, they charged the Croatian supporters leaving seventy five police and fifty-nine spectators injured. The police were totally outnumbered and completely unable to cope with seats ripped up and thrown like missiles at them. Old style English supporters would have been proud. This news spread around Croatia like wildfire. The reaction of some was anger, wanting revenge and soon. For others, it was fear.

For the Tomic family, it was the latter. They were Croats and lived in a place called Kijevo; a Croatian village surrounded by Serbian settlements in the Krajina region near the border with Bosnia. Before the present troubles life had been good but hard, managing the seasons as they came and went in their mainly agricultural village. It was basically a subsistence economy, but the opportunity was there to sell some produce to nearby Serbian villages. Relations between the two ethnicities were relatively friendly although there was little inter-marriage.

The family consisted of father Jakov, mother Vesna, older sister Zora and baby Ivan. Jakov managed a small holding inherited from his father and had married his school sweetheart Vesna when they were just twenty years old. As Croatian Roman Catholics, they attended Mass regularly all squeezing into an old pick up truck, inherited from his father-in-law and driving through neighbouring Serbian villages to the church. Their Serbian neighbours also travelled on a Sunday but in the opposite direction, to the local Orthodox church.

There weren't just farmers in the village though; there was a blacksmith, a catholic primary school, a few shops, two inns and a small police station, with other amenities in neighbouring Serbian villages. Jakov was in his fields where he was everyday, but now the sun was beginning to go down over the Dinara mountain and he was straightening his back thinking it was time to call it a day. Just twenty five, he was a caring man anxious to do everything he could to feed and clothe his little family. He trudged back home, his back hurting a little but nothing he couldn't cope with. He took his boots off as he went in through the back door and greeted his wife.

"Are you all right?" As he kissed Vesna, he sensed there was something wrong. "Yes," she responded, "but I think Ivan has a temperature and he's definitely not himself today."

"I'll go and tuck him in." He was back in a few minutes. "Yes, he's very hot. Have you given him anything?"

"Just what was available at the shop. They said this was all they had and if he didn't respond we should take him to a doctor."

Jakov thought. There was a Serbian doctor not far away, but he would have preferred to go to a Croatian medic. If it turned into an emergency, then the nearest doctor would have to do. The alternative was to wait for the morning and see what the situation was. He might even be better then.

"Maybe we should give him another dose before we go to bed and see what the morning brings?" Although Vesna was hesitant, she absorbed her anxiety by getting Zora ready for bed. She was an easy child and could already detect her mother's emotions. "Don't be afraid mummy."

When both parents were free of the children, they sat down to their simple meal. They sat in silence for quite a few minutes before Vesna brought up some rumours she had heard at the school gates.

"This football game in Zagreb. Some are saying that it was deliberate Serbian aggression sanctioned by Belgrade and just a preliminary to much greater incursions."

Jakov stopped eating and looked up at his wife. "Just Serbian hooligans my dear, playing at soldiers." He carried on eating. Vesna was not convinced but held her peace. Jakov decided that his wife was projecting her anxiety about Ivan on to this hooliganism. "Natural enough," he thought, "the lad will probably be fine in the morning, and so will she."

Nevertheless, Jakov did have some misgivings about the changing attitude of his Serbian neighbours. The garage where he got fuel was in a nearby Serbian village and he had noticed a reluctance to fill him up on the last two occasions. He had initially put it down to the garage owner being out of sorts – he did have a reputation of frequenting the local inn a bit too often – but now he began to wonder.

On June 28 Djuric was in Kosovo at M's request. He had been asked to spread the news among the Serb community that St Vitus's Day was going to be really celebrated this year. He had commandeered Luka again and, as this was a massive family day for Serbs, Djuric had invited Luljeta as his guest who had arrived together with her two minders. This day was always a celebration day for Serbs. It marked the defeat of Serbs by Turkey some six hundred years earlier in Kosovo's Field of Blackbirds. Serb commanders had been offered an opportunity to surrender but refused and fought to the death. Virtually the whole of the Serb aristocracy, including their leader Tsar Lazar, had died gloriously that day. The whole episode had so integrated itself into the life blood of Serb culture and identity, that each year lines of pilgrims would queue at the Gracanica monastery to view Lazar's bones. M saw some parallels and was determined to use the occasion to reinforce his version of Serb national identity.

"Look at them all," Luka whispered to his boss, Luljeta who had joined him to look at the celebrations. "Serbs are coming from all Yugoslav republics."

"I understand," said Luljeta aiming her barb at Djuric, "that Serbian culture is obsessed with the graves of their ancestors and with dying gloriously, maybe even with death itself," Luljeta was shaking her head as Djuric tried to disregard her gibe.

"What's that famous joke about three Serbians going to Mars?" asked Luljeta of Luka. She knew of course, but she felt like riling Djuric's Serbian roots a little more.

"Ah yes," responded Luka. "The one where as soon as they land one turns and kills his compatriot. The third says, 'why did you do that?' and the instigator responds, 'where you see Serbian graves, you know you are on Serbian land."

They both laughed at Djuric's expense.

"Look at all the different countries' flags, Luljeta." Djuric was trying to recover some dignity for his nation. "They're coming from all over the world." Luljeta paused to look at the crowds. "This is nuts."

"They all want to commemorate this day and see the modern-day Lazar."

"My God, he's coming in by helicopter."

"Listen to the crowd. I've never seen anything like it."

"It's like a messiah descending from heaven."

"And they love it."

"Look at the other Yugoslav leaders on the stage. They're wetting themselves."

"Listen. M is coming to the microphone."

'Serbs in their history have never conquered or exploited others..... the Kosovo heroism does not allow us to forget that we were one of the few who went into the battlefield undefeated. Six centuries later, again we are in battles.... they are not armed battles, though such things should not be excluded yet.'

"Did you hear that?" Luka asked. "That's the first time I've heard him mention using the Army in public."

"I think your struggle has now reached another level," murmured Luljeta. "I hope you know what you're doing."

Djuric said nothing.

Buoyed up by such adoration, M wanted to move against Croatia in a more structured way and got that opportunity when the new Croatian leader produced his draft constitution. It made no mention of the Serbs who made up the majority of Krajina and Knin, a region which was both strategically and economically important to Croatia. M decided that this was the moment to mobilise the Croatian Serb population in his favour. But he had one problem; the leadership of the SDS party of Croatian Serbs were split, one section favouring an 'uprising without weapons', the other under M's influence, willing to do anything.

"We need to take full control of the SDS party and settle for nothing less than taking this area out of Croatia into Serbia." M was in ebullient mood.

"It's already moving in our favour," added Kovac. "I've just got hold of the details of a private conversation Tudjman is supposed to have had with the SDS appeasers." M looked up. "Apparently," continued Kovac, "he accused Serbs of being a 'crazy people'. That hasn't gone down well at all."

"Right," said M in decisive mood, "get down to Knin and talk to Martic. He's currently leader of the Serb party there in Croatia – the SDS – and on our side. Assure him of our support and I'll get Petar to get a supply of arms into a local Serb warehouse so that our people can be armed and stand against whatever the Croats throw at them. The Army will also stand by just in case. This time there's going to be war, and we're going to win."

Before Kovac got to the area, the Serbian Krajina police had already refused to wear the uniforms of the Croatian police. A civil disobedience campaign from the Croatian Serbs was getting underway which directly challenged the central Croatian leadership. Tudjman immediately ordered a delegation from Zagreb to bring the Serb dissidents to heel and stamp central authority on them. However, after an angry and volatile meeting the Croatian delegation left with their tails between their legs and high-tailed it back to Zagreb. The local Croats were devastated. They had wanted the Serbs to be brought into line but now it was clear that in any contest they could no longer trust that their government had the capability of defending them.

Kovac laughed as Martic told the tale. "M's going to love that," he said.

"Seriously though, why don't you organise a referendum among the Serbs to build a Serbian state within Croatia?"

Martic thought about this. "Yes, maybe we can do this. We're not actually breaking away, so I think those within Krajina who want to stay within Croatia, will still vote for it. Yes, we can do this." And he set the wheels in motion.

Just two days before the referendum was due, news reached Martic that Zagreb had declared it illegal and that seven armoured Croatian police vehicles and three helicopters with more police reservists were on their way to ensure the vote did not take place. Martic contacted Kovac who alerted M who, in turn, warned General Petar. Army jets were scrambled to intercept the helicopters and turn them back. On the ground Martic had announced a full alert and the warehouse full of arms stored for exactly such a purpose, was opened up. Once the armoured vehicles from Zagreb heard that the helicopters had been grounded, they turned back before reaching their intended destination.

A great victory for the Croatian Serbs without a shot being fired but with many of the population now armed and on a war footing. M was ecstatic but Kovac not so much.

Chapter 16 — Slovenia and Croatia

A NEW SLOVENIAN nationalist government was about to be sworn in. M had already been on the phone to General Petar who was now reasonably confident that he could trust the Federal Army stationed in that republic to obey his orders.

"I want to kill this government before it starts." M was now going to the next level. "How do we do it?"

The General had been expecting such a move and had already worked out a strategy. "We first need to capture the arms dumps of the local forces." These TO's (Territorial Defence) forces represented a potentially huge civil army in waiting. Each republic had such a force owing its allegiance not to the Federal government in Belgrade, but to their own republic. It was Tito's idea to ensure that any enemy of Yugoslavia would find it extremely difficult to conquer the country. An extremely unlikely and illogical scenario but then dictators can be extremely irrational when their position is threatened.

"Do it," said M. Two days after the swearing in, before ministers knew what was happening, the Army had managed to confiscate over 70% of the stored weaponry in the TO warehouses before a stand-off began.

Petar reported the results as satisfactory, "but," he outlined to M, "they will try to recover the situation by smuggling in the arms they need."

"What do we do about that?"

"Well, first we can try to monitor the borders – not easy though – maybe the best route is to find out who will be supplying them."

"I'll talk to Kovac – he's the intelligence man who's supposed to have contacts and informers everywhere."

The showdown with the Federal Army had the effect of uniting the new Slovenian regime which previously had been divided on the question of smuggling arms. At M's command, the Army declared that all TO's outside the Federal military were banned and shortly afterwards the Slovenian TO HQ in Ljubljana was completely taken over by the Federal Army. However, it didn't stop the continued accumulation of arms by the Slovenian government. Anti-tank weapons, shoulder to air Ambrust missiles and a mass of small weaponry had been secured and hidden by Slovene Special Forces ready for use should the Federal Army decide to invade.

Kovac, as ordered, had been out and about himself in Slovenia. Intelligence was hard to come by but he did learn one thing. He called M. "They are going to broadcast a firing of some anti-tank missiles they have on television tonight. Might be worth watching."

M and Mira watched and noted the commentary as well as the demonstration. It was full of patriotic fervour almost challenging the Federal Army to try to take them on. They looked at each other. "Perhaps we'd better change tack," said Mira.

"For the time being," said her husband. So M agreed with Slovenia not to prevent their secession from the Federal state, after all, there were no Serbs living in Slovenia. But it was at a great economic cost to the project for M had been counting on the Slovene Treasury contributing to the purchase of the Russian arms. It made securing Croatia even more important.

Kovac returned from his intelligence trip into Slovenia. "I've done a little investigation into where these arms have come from and whilst it seems a little opaque, I suspect that our Russian friend was somehow involved."

M and Mira looked at each other. "I'm going to have to have a word with him," said M. "This is not at all what was agreed."

Kovac was listening intently for this was the first time he had any insight into the deal M had made with Moscow, if it was Moscow. When the co-strategists stopped talking, he moved hurriedly on to hide the fact that he had heard secrets he probably should not have heard.

"I think we should get General Petar to ensure the Army disarms the TOs in Croatia quickly, before they have time to copy Slovenia. If not, we might lose them as well as Slovenia."

M confirmed that General Petar's troops were already on the ground. It was done exceedingly efficiently as if they wanted to make up for their failure in Slovenia, and the incoming government of Tudjman found they had no force capable of defending the country except the police. They were left with fifteen thousand rifles of varying capabilities, one armoured personnel carrier and no heavy weaponry at all. They had no option but to try to turn their civilian authorities into a military force. There were many obstacles to achieving this objective and one major issue was that Serbs represented a significant portion of the police force. The government decided they couldn't trust their loyalty so thousands of police were sacked or sidelined because they were ethnic Serbs and thousands of young Croats recruited as part of a nationalist drive, promoting them to positions way beyond their capability. Such was the fervour and hatred towards Belgrade that Croatian Serbs from all walks of life were fired 'en masse' or forced to sign loyalty pledges.

Kovac's counter-intelligence colleagues were monitoring Croatia carefully. Arms smuggling through their Adriatic ports was becoming very evident and on a much larger scale than in Slovenia. Their messages to Kovac were becoming increasingly urgent.

"They've now installed a retired General of the Federal Army, General Spegelj." Kovac was reporting their news to M over the phone. "He will oversee all of their military preparations and my information is that it's beginning to look very impressive."

M put the call on hold and turned to Petar who was visiting the Serbian President in his official office for the first time.

"What do you know of Spegelj?" M asked Petar who was walking round the office admiring the impressive furnishings which was always important to Petar.

He answered without turning, looking at some of the paintings on the wall. "Spegelj? Yes, I know General Spegelj." He suddenly looked round as if conscious of being rude, "Yes, he'll be a consummate adversary." Then added, "These pictures look like originals."

M ignored the comment and waited for the Army man's full attention with hands folded behind his back. Petar realised M's impatience was rising to full blown anger.

"My apologies. Spegelj. My guess is that he will be forming a completely new command structure which will need mass training since many will be given posts they are ill equipped to fulfil. It would be what I would do. When that happens they'll be preparing for war."

M's only question for Petar was, "Can they beat us?"

Petar responded, "Absolutely not, but we might lose a lot of men."

M sat back down behind his desk and pressed a button on his mobile to connect with Kovac again. "Will they invade the Serbian regions of Croatia?"

" As far as I can tell, there's a stand-off in government circles," answered Kovac. "General Spegelj wants to launch a pre-emptive strike at Federal Army bases in Croatia but others think that they would be immediately classed by the outside world as the aggressors."

"Who's going to win the argument?"

" Difficult to tell."

"We need to know. Recruit some Croatian agents and get inside their network."

"Not going to be easy."

"There has got to be some who are in favour of keeping Yugoslavia together and against the secessionist polices of Tudjman."

"Got it." Kovac didn't like arguing with M. He knew the man well enough to know how far he could go and when to give in. He knew that Croatia now was brimming with rumour, intrigue and espionage. Trust was in short supply and sides were being taken which split families, friends and neighbours. His task wasn't going to be easy.

But then he had a piece of good luck. A Croatian colonel, Jagar, who had been approached to side with the new Croatian army, decided his future interests would be better served on the other side. After being thoroughly checked out by Kovac's counter-intelligence people, Jagar was approved. He turned out to be a most exceptional spy and was given strict communication protocols for contacting Kovac directly.

"In a matter of days there's going to be a consignment of kalashnikovs coming through Austria across the Hungarian border," reported Jagar

"Right. We'll get the borders under surveillance," responded Kovac.

He was right. They soon found out which border, for the relevant one was crawling with Croatian police, somewhere between two and three hundred.

Kovac's men could do nothing except watch as two large trucks with outlying Croatian police vehicles came across the Austrian/Yugoslav border with no checks at all.

Kovac was stunned to receive their briefing confirming totally inadequate planning. He was incandescent at his agents but also at himself for not getting Djuric to do the planning. As he began to calm down he knew that M would be more than stunned. This needed careful handling otherwise his job, maybe his life, was on the line. He decided he needed positive information to go with the negative. Jagar's activities were not known to the Croatian authorities as far as they were aware, so Kovac decided both to test that and hopefully get some decisive intelligence at the same time.

He spoke to Jagar and ordered him to contact Spegelj, engage him in conversation and elicit plans, strategies, anything of note, equipping him with a wire for the purpose.

"Your rank and loyalty will speak for you. So go straight to his house in Zagreb." This caused him a little anxiety for if his treachery had been known, he would have been shot immediately. In fact, Spegelj answered the door himself with a pistol in his hand causing Jagar to take a step backwards for a moment thinking this was the end, but the General motioned with his hand that he should enter putting his finger to his mouth indicating that he clearly thought his house, and maybe his garden was bugged.

Jagar breathed a big sigh of relief feigning a concern for the General's safety and whispered, "Are you all right?"

"Yes," whispered Spegelj. "But I'm not taking any chances. Let's talk in the car."

Jagar wondered who could be bugging Spegelj's house. He didn't think it was Belgrade, so it must be his own side. Interesting.

Once in the car, the General was quite talkative, almost as if he hadn't spoken to anyone for days. Spegelj seemingly had few people he could relax with so felt he could talk easily to Jagar who was a good listener, offering occasional thoughts of his own which he knew would be acceptable to the General but not give anything away that might impact his new friends.

Over the following weeks, Jagar accrued almost a hundred hours of taped conversations about arms smuggling and secret liquidation squads who were apparently ready to kidnap and murder senior Serb officers and their families. At one point, such was Spegelj's faith in Jagar that he accepted an invitation to Jagar's house where the spy had set up a camera to secretly film the General trying to persuade a friend of Jagar's to join his network revealing much of the planning for the newly formed Croatian army. The more Jagar's friend hesitated, the more information was revealed.

Kovac now had more than enough information for M and tried to re-position the border *faux pas* as deliberate strategy to see what was happening without the Croatian authorities knowing they knew. Whether M saw through the ruse or not, he was immensely pleased with the overall package that Kovac presented. The intelligence man breathed a sigh of relief. But it was to be short lived.

On the basis of all this information, a dossier was prepared by the Serbs and presented to the Federal Presidency group with a motion that called for all paramilitaries to be disarmed. The whole of Croatia knew what this was about – neutering their dreams of an independent republic with its own defence force. By now the whole country was simmering with anger and teeming with weapons. The motion only passed when Croatia agreed to limit the seizure of weapons to the 'illegal' ones. Croatia then claimed that none of the weapons were illegal. Stalemate.

"Although we now own half the votes on the Federal Presidency, we haven't got enough to defeat Croatia," M was grumbling to Mira.

"But you have Jagar's film of Spegelj's treachery, why not use it?" Mira had a good point and M called the television executives ordering them to put it out immediately. They decided to trail it without any names the day before. At this point Bojan's ears pricked up knowing Kovac had been in Croatia and called him to see if he knew anything about it.

"What!" shouted Kovac down the line. "When is it going out?"

"Tomorrow," said Bojan a bit taken aback. "Didn't you know?"

"No, I did not," Kovac said firmly. He tried to toned down his next response. "And thank you Bojan. You have hopefully saved a good man's life."

Bojan put the phone down wondering what it was all about. No doubt he would hear about it one day.

M either didn't care if Jagar's cover was blown or it didn't even cross his mind. Kovac was on the phone immediately trying to contact Jagar without success. So he left some terse code words instructing Jagar to disappear quickly. He had no idea if he ever received these messages or indeed acted on them but he never heard from him again.

The film was released on television and while it created a stir, it didn't change the Federal Presidency votes and the Federal Army continued to refuse to invade Croatia without a veneer of constitutional authority. General Petar was living on borrowed time as far as M was concerned and Kovac was furious that all the effort expended on getting Spegelj's information was wasted and his informer was now blown, maybe permanently.

M had played his last card and reluctantly came to the conclusion that if he could keep the rest of Yugoslavia together under his rule, he would have to let Slovenia and Croatia go but not before taking control of the Croatian Serb territory of Knin and Krajina.

The seemingly inevitable slide towards war had, perhaps for the moment, been halted. But few issues had been settled in M's mind and they were surely destined to resurrect themselves.

Chapter 17 — Sarajevo

ISMET WAS A teenage lad who lived in Sarajevo with his parents and sister and today, on 7 July 1980, he celebrated his eighteenth birthday. He was now a man. Unknown to him, at the same time as his family was celebrating his birthday the Safra massacre, or the Day of the Long Knives, was happening in the coastal town of Safra, north of Beirut, which claimed the lives of eighty three Palestinians. If his mother had known maybe she might have seen it as a premonition.

His father, Nurija Terzic however, would have dismissed such a notion out of hand. He didn't believe in such nonsense; taxi drivers had their minds focussed both on the sports pages and where to go to get the best fares the following day. Priorities varied depending on how each day was going. Business wasn't good. It never had been great but he had managed to keep in the black, just. But his passion was football and, of course, FK Sarajevo. Their current manager was Fuad Muzurović who, in his playing days, had been a centre back with a good grasp of the strategic nature of the game, but international success was now hard to come by.

"We just need money to get some better players," moaned Terzic, echoing the lament of supporters the world over. "If Red Star Belgrade can do it, why can't we?" He was back in his comfy chair after another day swapping stories with other taxi drivers waiting for fares which rarely came.

"We also need more money by the end of the month for the rent," his wife stated in a tone which suggested she had said this mid-month for years.

"And I'm doing my best," was the well worn but half hearted reply of her husband as he continued to read the sports page at the back of the local paper.

"Our ground, Asim Ferhatović Hase, is not good enough." He continued to rehearse the conversation he had had with his fellow taxi drivers. "A multi-purpose ground with a full size athletic track between us and the pitch?" His groans were reaching their climax.

"It's ridiculous. It does nothing to create any atmosphere. No atmosphere, no supporters, no investment." He finished his sermon with a triumphal flourish and put down the paper, expecting his meal to be on the table.

Ismet had overheard some of the conversation and it confirmed to him yet again that he didn't want to drive a taxi all day and most of the evening just to scrape a living. He had bigger ambitions which his mother encouraged and, being the only child, he felt a burden to help the family's income at least until he got married. Although he had a steady girlfriend, a lovely Serbian girl called Ana which had the approval of both sets of parents, any marriage would be a few years away.

Ismet was aiming higher. He had already been accepted by the School of Economics and Business at Sarajevo University and was due to start in a few months time. It was the largest and oldest university in the country tracing its origins back to 1537 as an Islamic madrasa. This history didn't figure in Ismet's thinking for he was not an overly religious person and neither was his family. Anyway, he didn't see his future in Bosnia but wanted to travel westward while vowing he would never forget his home country. He would make sure that any children he had would be able to speak the language and know its history.

After a tea-time celebration with his family, he had arranged to go out with Ana for the evening. A warm July evening was ideal for going down to the river. Maybe they would go to the Latin bridge; perhaps then on to the brewery up the hill. It was founded back in 1864 and some said it was the only brewery to have operated in two great empires: the Ottoman and Austria-Hungarian. Obviously, he thought, the Communist empire didn't count.

He walked up the hill to Ana's house. Sarajevo was full of hills which surrounded the valley where the city lay. He knocked and Ana's mother, Mrs Lukic opened the door and smiled a knowing smile at him.

"Happy birthday Ismet. I think Ana may have a present for you. Come in."

He went in. Ana and her parents lived in a large house in a posh area of town in contrast to the fifth floor apartment where his family lived. Her father, Mr Marko Lukic, managed a small factory which produced office furniture and it seemed business was good as he had just bought himself a new car, a red BMW. It was sitting on the drive as Ismet walked up to the front door. It all confirmed his own ambitions to get the best education he could and move away, hopefully with Ana, not that he had broached the subject with her yet. That would be pushing things too far at the moment.

"Hi Ismet." Ana was coming down the stairs with her hair still a little damp but she had her 'going-out' clothes on and he could see a little make-up on her cheeks. They went into the lounge where her brother, Stefan was relaxing with a drink. As he saw them come in, he glared at them both and made his exit. Stefan was two years older than his seventeen year old sister and worked at his father's factory as a foreman but it was clear to everyone that he was doing the rounds in order to take over management of the business at some point.

"Don't take any notice of him," Ana assured Ismet. "He'll get over it. Besides, my mother said to give you some space as it's your birthday."

Ismet and Stefan hadn't got on from day one and, although Ana explained that he was just being overly protective of his younger sister, Ismet saw the gulf between the two families and assumed the animosity was because Stefan didn't think he was good enough for her. And perhaps he wasn't.

Ana and Ismet had known each other from school days, but the relationship had only grown since they, and some others, were both assigned to produce a play about the history of Sarajevo at their high school. As well as getting to know each other, they also began to appreciate the special place that the city was. Of course, they already knew of the infamous happenings in 1914, when the Archduke Franz Ferdinand was assassinated triggering the start of the First World War. On the plus side, it was one of only a few major European cities to have a Mosque, Catholic church, Orthodox church and Synagogue within the same neighbourhood with no significant tensions between the different religions. And the second city in the world to have a full-time electric tram network running through the city, the first being San Francisco. Not bad.

"I have a little present for your birthday," Ana said hesitantly. "I hope you like it." She withdrew a package from behind the sofa and presented it to Ismet. He tore off the wrapping paper and found a small box containing a men's personalised silver neck pendant.

"It's...... it's beautiful," he stuttered. He immediately put it on and said, "Thank you so much. I'll never take it off."

Ana laughed, "Glad you like it. So where shall we go tonight?" she asked expectantly.

"I thought we might go down to the Latin Bridge.

She smiled, "That's so romantic."

"And maybe walk along the river and perhaps up to the Yellow Bastion if we have the energy. We can view the whole of Sarajevo from there."

"OK. Let's go." They left the house with Stefan watching them from an upstairs window. Hand in hand, they began making their way to the Wilson Promenade. It was a long walk but they didn't care; they were together. Neither did it matter if they never got to the river, they were just enjoying each other's company. After about twenty-five minutes they passed the Sacred Heart Cathedral and zig-zagged past the City Hall and on to the Miljacka river bank. There were lots of people out on a balmy July evening, many of them walking along the river.

To a visitor it probably seemed rather small and not very long, only about 20km from its source before it flowed into the larger Bosna river, although when flood waters arrived as the winter snow melted, it could fill up quite fast. It was known for its brown colour and distinctive smell probably caused by sewage leakage upriver, but somehow it attracted people to it and the many bridges that crossed it especially the Latin Bridge.

Love was in the air. Life was good. The future was bright.

Chapter 18 — Washington DC

"MR PRESIDENT."

George H W Bush lifted his head from his desk in the Oval Office. He looked alert and had been reading the latest intelligence on Desert Storm and the Gulf. Although Kuwait was now freed, the whole military operation seemed to have disturbed something in the ether, almost as if tampering with one bit of a complex jigsaw in the Middle East somehow put the rest of the pieces out of kilter. He couldn't understand it.

His Chief of Staff put his head round the door. "Secretary Baker is on his way over, as you requested. His flight departs in two hours."

"Send him in when he gets here and you come in as well."

"Thank you Mr President."

"Also," the President paused, "ask Brent to come over too."

"Yes, Mr President."

It was twenty minutes later when Baker arrived and the meeting began. President Bush came around from his desk and sat on the sofa next to Chief of Staff John Sununu, with James Baker and National Security Advisor Brent Scowcroft on the opposite sofa.

The discussion was all about Iraq, Kuwait and what was going on in the Middle East generally. The President allowed everyone to say their piece and after thirty minutes of detailed discussion Baker was given the task of 'peace in the Middle East'. The atmosphere in the Oval Office was confident, even strident. The Soviet Union was no more and China was still an emerging economy. The US had no competition.

The President was ebullient. "We are the respected and undisputed leader of the free world," he stated implying that the US could do almost anything it wanted, as long as it sat well with certain lobby groups and the pollsters. As the meeting was winding up, the President asked,

"James, by the way, what on earth is going on in Yugoslavia?"

Baker winced. He didn't want to get tied up in that. "Mr President, it's just a local scrap between the various parts of Tito's old empire. Nothing to worry about, and anyway, we don't have a dog in that fight."

The other men quickly shuffled out of the room. They didn't want to get involved in Yugoslavia. That was down to the Europeans. The Secretary of State also moved quickly down the corridors of power and into his car taking him straight to Dulles where he boarded a flight to Kuwait. However, the subject of Yugoslavia was not going away, much as he hoped it would. Waiting for him when he landed was a message from the President who apparently had just spoken with John Major, the British Prime Minister. The upshot was that he, Major, would be grateful if he, Baker, would drop in on Belgrade on his way back to talk to the various parties.

Baker swore. "Since when has Belgrade been on any route from here back to the US? And what the hell has it got to do with us? Bloody Brits." He turned to one of his Under Secretaries, "You'd better get me some briefing papers..... and a map so I know where on God's earth it is."

When it was announced that James Baker, the US Secretary of State was travelling to Belgrade, the leaders of all provinces and republics of the federal government wanted to see him. They all set great store by his visit, hoping that they could convince the US of their version of the future. But his scheduled time in the city was short, deliberately so.

"I've had to schedule in eleven meetings tomorrow," confessed his Under Secretary. "They all want to see you."

"Eleven! Are they trying to kill me?"

Baker yawned. It was late and he hadn't slept on the bare bones military flight which had taken him to Belgrade airport. There was no other way of getting to Belgrade in time. He was focussed on the Middle East, an area which had global implications, as well as for the next Presidential election. Most folks in the US had no idea Yugoslavia existed, let alone where it was or what was going on. This responsibility was not at all what he wanted.

"We'd better start early. Get Ambassador Zimmerman in for a breakfast meeting. He can give me the low down before we start."

"I'm sorry Mr Secretary, but you have a breakfast meeting already booked with the Yugoslav Federal government."

"Shit. Well get him in for pre-breakfast coffee, or something."

"Yes Mr Secretary."

Warren Zimmerman was the US ambassador to Yugoslavia and had been putting the US position to whoever would listen in Yugoslavia for months. It was his staff who had arranged all these meetings once he had been told of the Secretary's short stopover.

Zimmerman arrived at the hotel at 7am and immediately apologised to his boss for the frantic nature of the day he was about to have. Baker didn't reply but issued his instructions for the meetings.

"Let's not give anyone any hope that we're going to put men on the ground in this God-forsaken country. These meetings will give us an opportunity to outline a clear and unambiguous position that we want to see a united Yugoslavia."

Zimmerman broke in. "Mr Secretary, we have been stating that clearly for months now, but no-one seems to be listening."

"Ummm. Warren, I want you in these meetings so you can take over when I'm gone." This is a European problem, as far as I'm concerned. We're just going to go through the motions, making an effort. If we don't, some son of a bitch will blame us. So let's get it over with, and I'll need a strong drink when this is over."

As far as the Secretary was concerned the day dragged on endlessly. But when Croatia's Tudjman said, "Thank God my wife is not a Jew or a Serb," Baker sat up and stared at him. Tudjman then launched into a tirade over Bosnia calling it "a national state of the Croatian nation." He claimed the Bosnians were "dangerous fundamentalists" wanting to use Bosnia as a springboard for spreading Islam into Europe.

Serbia's position was no less hard line, accusing the US of being completely influenced by Germany which wanted to see the breakup of Yugoslavia so it could gain a Croatian warm water port in the Mediterranean. When it came to Montenegro, Baker had all but given up. He had only two notes on his briefing paper, one of which said, 'the smallest republic in Yugoslavia,' the other similarly inconsequential. Afterwards, the Montenegrin leader let it be known that Baker was clearly confused as to who he was talking to, and most of the conversation was quite incongruous.

Within a few hours of finishing his marathon of meetings, Baker was breathing several sighs of relief and on his way back to Washington, leaving behind some confused and other very determined leaders in Yugoslavia.

Chapter 19 — International

IN LONDON, THE weekly cabinet meeting at 10 Downing St was ending when Prime Minister Major whispered to the Cabinet Secretary that he would like to see the Foreign and Defence Secretaries in his office immediately afterwards. A senior intelligence official was already waiting when first the Prime Minister arrived and a few minutes later the other two invited Ministers and the Cabinet Secretary.

"Gentlemen, thank you. Foreign Secretary, can you give us an update on Yugoslavia?"

Douglas Hurd looked a little puzzled as to why this had not been discussed at Cabinet. However, he cleared his throat and began. "Our Ambassador, Peter Hall, has confirmed that Secretary of State Baker landed in Belgrade yesterday evening for a whistle stop visit at the request of President Bush following, I understand, a conversation with you Prime Minister, a day or two ago?"

John Major ignored the attempted challenge. He had acted alone which he had every right to do as Prime Minister to President. But, according to protocol, he should have got No.10 staffers to at least inform the Foreign & Commonwealth Office (FCO), but as he knew himself, having been a previous Secretary of State for that particular ministry, the latter would have preferred the PM do nothing. They preferred to 'monitor' situations rather than do anything pro-actively. The PM had no regrets.

The Defence Secretary, Tom King interrupted with his usual combative style with an eye on the intelligence officer in the corner, "We're not changing our mind about any troop deployment are we?"

"No," said the Prime Minister quietly. "Douglas, do we have any feedback yet?"

"Not yet, Prime Minister."

"As soon as you can. I'm in Brussels tomorrow and I want to brief our EU colleagues."

"Of course, Prime Minister."

The intelligence officer looked at the Prime Minister with an eyebrow raised and Major nodded.

He joined the table and the conversation. "Feedback from the cousins and our own intelligence colleagues over the pond indicates that the White House is not at all interested in Yugoslavia and this visit is purely going though the motions, and not likely to lead anywhere. As far they're concerned, it is a European matter and to be dealt with by Europe."

Hurd cleared his throat again preparatory to making another contribution. "It is the Foreign Office's position that this is a UN issue. I propose we brief our Ambassador at the UN and prepare a resolution which encourages all sides to reach an agreement which prevents war and maintains the integrity of the country."

It was a typical FCO move to procrastinate and put the onus for action on another party, in this instance, the UN. Prime Minister Major didn't question the strategy because he didn't have another one and this suited him. Everyone knew Europe would do nothing substantial other than make some media pronouncements. The UK could not and would not act alone. It was either with the Americans – that seemingly not possible at the moment – or with the Europeans – even more unlikely since they didn't want to spend money on Yugoslavia.

"Agreed?" Major looked round at his colleagues. They nodded.

In Brussels a scheduled meeting of EC leaders was getting underway and Prime Minister Major had asked for a slot on the programme to brief continental colleagues on the Yugoslav situation. He had been allocated ten minutes in a packed session mostly crammed with EC internal matters. After all, the European Community was about to become the European Union and there was excited talk about a common foreign and security policy. Jacques Poos, the Luxembourg Foreign Minister had declared, "The hour of Europe has dawned."

"Two days ago," began Major in their plenary session, "I spoke to President Bush about our concerns over Yugoslavia. Although his attention is very much on the Middle East, especially the Gulf, he promised to direct his Secretary of State, James Baker, to return to the US via Belgrade to meet with various Yugoslavian leaders." He paused, momentarily reflecting how on earth had the FCO not got some feedback from Belgrade in time for this meeting as he had asked. "That was yesterday and as yet I have not received any report from those meetings although the UK Ambassador in Belgrade has another meeting with Warren Zimmerman the US Ambassador tomorrow."

The UK Prime Minister paused again, "We have agreed our policy not to recognise separate declarations of independence. The first priority is to hold Yugoslavia together."

The current president of the Community was Hans van den Broek who responded. "I'm sure we're all grateful to Prime Minister Major for his efforts in this regard." Then seemingly placing much more emphasis on what the EC had in mind, he added, "Our troika of ministers will go to Belgrade shortly and I trust that banging a few heads together will prevent war breaking out. I think I speak for everyone when I say that no-one is in favour of putting troops on the ground in another European country at this stage."

There was a murmur of agreement around the table and the agenda moved on.

In Moscow, Mikhail Gorbachev hadn't been in the Kremlin for very long and already he was proving to be a different kind of Soviet leader, one with whom the West could do business with. But there were many within the highest ranks of the Russian Communist Party who were not happy. One who was in agreement with *perestroika* and *glasnost* was his Foreign Minister, Eduard Shevardnadze.

"Eduard," Gorbachev was talking to his friend in his Presidential suite in the Kremlin. He had a worried look on his face, "I'm not sure who I can trust anymore, but I don't think we have any option but to press ahead with economic reform."

Shevardnadze nodded, "I see reports every day of mounting scarcities of food and medicines, long queues to buy essentials and only 50% of the fuel we need for the coming winter."

"What are the chances we could get emergency supplies from the West?" Shevardnadze looked startled.

Gorbachev continued, "What options do we have? Millions could starve or die over this winter."

"We would need to do this quietly somehow, otherwise we will be gifting our enemies a big stick to beat us with." Shevardnadze was hesistant.

"See what you can do." With that Shevardnadze retreated and Gorbachev was left alone until his wife, Raisa, came in.

"I hear rumours that a number of our hard-line comrades are unhappy," she said.

"Yes, well it was those very people who caused this mess in the first place. Inflation at 300%, factories with not enough cash to pay workers, Baltic states in rebellion, Yugoslavia close to fracturing. I fear that unless we get some economic help, the Soviet Union will be no more."

She stared at him, "You mustn't say such a thing."

He smiled, "I know."

At the United Nations (UN) in New York, Perez de Cuellar had been Secretary General for two full terms and was due to stand down. Although the Cold War had warmed somewhat, appointing a successor wasn't proving any easier and the New York HQ was alive with the manoeuvrings of potential candidates and their backers. Not a lot of time for solving any problems, therefore.

The staff rumour mill was in full swing and enjoying every minute of it, for normally if the Secretary General was any good, he (and it was always a he) would serve two terms and this unique enjoyment was only available for the staff every ten years.

"I hear the next Secretary General could be from Africa."

"Did you know that the US and UK tried to block the regional rotation?"

"Yes but China is backing Africa."

"Well, we all know what that's about!"

"Nevertheless, the OAU have said they will block any non African candidate."

"How many African candidates are there now?"

"Six and I understand they're going to use straw polls to select the candidate."

Apart from such tittle-tattle, the various ambassadors did manage to get some useful work done that year. A cease-fire in the 16-year civil war in Angola was negotiated, then administered by the UN Angola Verification Mission, and Resolution 713 on Yugoslavia was passed which attempted to impose '*a general and complete embargo on all deliveries of weapons and military equipment to Yugoslavia.*'

When Smolov got to hear of it, the Russian just laughed.

Chapter 20 — Serbia

M WAS QUIETLY confident that neither the US nor the EC would intervene in Yugoslavia giving him confidence to push on with his amended grand plan. Kovac, who was still looking at immediate issues, decided to raise the issue of Belgrade and Serbia again.

"We have all been concentrating on other republics, Kosovo, Slovenia, Montenegro, but we must not neglect Serbia itself."

Mira jumped in shielding her husband from what she saw as criticism. "What do you mean?" she questioned. "M is Serbia's President and we now have four votes on the Federal Presidency."

Kovac cast his eyes round the table looking for support in particular from Bojan, but he stayed quiet. So rather haltingly he went on. "I'm picking up the beginnings of a student movement in favour of liberalism, a free press and other reforms that might damage us. They're calling it the Serbian Renewal Movement."

No-one was sure whether M had been listening. His eyes were shut. Everyone was quiet, waiting for his verdict. Suddenly, in a commanding voice unusual in this company, said, "I think we have everything under control."

Kovac didn't know whether he could risk one further comment with no other support in the room. What he wanted to say was "Let's not let this Movement become a rallying point for the liberals." But he buttoned his lip. He saw a change in M's demeanour which he hadn't noticed before. He glanced over to Mira who, in the briefest of moments, glanced quickly back then turned away and ignored him for the rest of the meeting. He decided he had been wise. There was no more to be said.

There had always been small demonstrations in Belgrade about some issue or other, but the police had usually been able to deal with them without much fuss. Road blocks, dogs, horses, the usual – were used to successfully corral the protesters and they had never threatened to disrupt the city or the politicians. There was little doubt that such demos were growing both in number and frequency but on this particular Saturday some forty thousand people descended on Belgrade's central square intent on causing damage, so much so that the unprepared and outnumbered police found they needed to retreat. Something was indeed changing.

Kovac continued to be disturbed both by M's dismissal of his warnings and by the growing demonstrations. He sought out Bojan, the only other member of M's team he knew was in Belgrade at that moment. The intelligence man was feeling distinctly uncertain. His gut was telling him that there was a different feel in Belgrade, something he could not put his finger on but was real all the same. He was concerned – no, more than concerned. He was troubled. Bojan was not his natural company, not that he had anything against the diminutive civil servant, but he needed to check his own inner anxiety with somebody. Djuric was somewhere else, probably Montenegro with a woman he suspected, but what did a military man know that he didn't? After all, he was supposed to be the intelligence man. Mira, he knew, would never say anything against M to anyone else, although she might in private. He wondered what she was saying to him now. She had good instincts, but were they the same as his? That brief glance had told him that even if they were, she would give way to M.

His mind was wandering, a clear sign to him that all was not well. His instincts had served him very well up to now and he trusted them. Nevertheless probably for the first time in his life he required some third party corroboration and he certainly couldn't share what was on his mind with M's wife.

"What's going on?" Bojan looked up from his desk surprised to see the intelligence man in his office. He had handed over the Treasury of Montenegro to one of his lackeys and was back in Belgrade, legitimately employed by the Serbian state. Kovac had never been to Bojan's office before but knew roughly where to find him when he wasn't in one of the other republics creaming off funds for M's cause. Wherever he worked, the man was a consummate civil servant with routines that rarely changed unless M had otherwise instructed him.

"I'm not sure," responded Kovac, lighting up a cigarette. That caused Bojan to look up quickly with a look of concern. Predictably he took off his glasses and began to rub them with a cloth. This was the first time he had heard any word of doubt pass Kovac's lips. Usually the man was super confident and always had the answer.

Bojan looked around. "Shall we take a walk?" he said already getting up and putting his coat on. "These offices are no place to have the kind of chat that you seem to need." They descended by the stairs – Bojan didn't trust lifts – and left the building, moving down Decanska towards Pionirski Park.

For a moment they walked together silently, Kovac having second thoughts about trusting Bojan but then he thought, "Who else?"

"The thing is," he began, "I'm now not sure we're on the right track. Look around you. Look at the debris, the destruction. Did you see what happened the other day?"

Bojan replied neutrally, "I saw it on television, although I must say it didn't look as bad as this."

Kovac grimaced. "At least M's control of the media and the TV station in particular has served him well." He paused, "But this isn't Kosovo or Vojvodina. This is Belgrade, the capital of Serbia." His voice was raised in dismay.

"Yes," replied Bojan. "I understand the police took quite a drubbing in spite of their riot gear," Bojan was cautious and answering in neutral statements until he was sure of Kovac's agenda. But Kovac hadn't finished, although talking more to himself than to Bojan as if trying to make sense of it all.

"They were singing 'Give peace a chance.' And it's not just students. I saw ordinary people coming out to give them blankets and food as they stayed out in the freezing temperatures. And there were messages of support from other cities in Serbia."

"I must admit that is quite concerning," Bojan still responding cautiously.

"But there were tanks on the street.... in Belgrade." Kovac was shaking his head and going to add, "ordered by our leader," but quickly thought better of it.

Bojan began to realise that his colleague wasn't out to test his loyalty, but was genuinely upset. He replied, "It did surprise me, I have to say. I hope it's the first and last time we see that."

"But I warned him," continued Kovac, "and he took no notice." He paused and looked at Bojan, "You know, it's almost as if he wanted to put tanks on the street as a symbol of his control." There, he had said it.

Bojan picked this up and responded rather more positively, "Yes. Once you deploy such force, it does become easier to do it the next time and even easier the time after that."

Kovac had somehow emptied his pent up angst and said, "Perhaps that's how it's going to be from now on. Perhaps we have reached the end of constitutional and political manoeuvring." He stopped in his tracks and turned to Bojan.

"I bet that Russian had something to do with it," he declared. Then a thought crossed his mind. "I wonder if M did it at Smolov's suggestion as a test of what they might do later?"

Bojan didn't answer straight away. He had his own view of Russians which had never been shared with anyone.

"My mother was half Russian," he confessed. Kovac looked intently at him, wondering where this was going and whether he had made a monumental mistake in confiding in Bojan without doing some digging. That, as an intelligence officer, would be inexcusable.

"Her father was some high-up in the Party. I met some and didn't like what I saw." Kovac breathed a sigh of relief. "Those I did meet, and I was still quite young, were greedy even exploitative. Never any kindness. Of course, the ordinary peasants in Russia only have themselves to blame. They have, over centuries, willingly allowed themselves to be governed by autocrats who, whether the Tsars or Communists, systematically exploited them and amassed huge wealth for themselves. Tito, for all his imperfections was not like that."

Kovac could have disagreed with Bojan on a number of points but merely responded, "I know what you mean. There's a brutality about them, an animal-like rawness, at least in the ruling classes and certainly in the military."

Bojan was quiet and Kovac, thinking that perhaps he had said too much, said, "Let's head back. I'm sure you've got things to get on with."

Bojan hesitated before confessing. "I do have my own sources within the Yugoslav Presidency," he admitted shyly.

"Have you indeed?" Kovac looked at Bojan with a new interest. "And what are these sources telling you?"

"That M has been ensconced in his Presidential office with General Petar and Mr Smolov for days now trying to find a way to get the Army properly mobilised."

"What?" exclaimed Kovac aghast. "He wants to put the Army permanently on the streets against his own people?"

"If he loses Serbia, what has he got? Kosovo and Montenegro? He would be finished."

They were both walking back silently, thinking. Neither wanted to end up on the wrong side and neither had been involved in discussions about deploying the army, let alone on the streets of Belgrade.

"Who's preventing army deployment?" asked Kovac.

"The senior Generals. The same as in Croatia. They want the fig leaf of constitutional approval, but the Federal Presidency is divided."

"That's nothing new. It's a hopeless mess."

"But I also understand," said Bojan, pausing as if to deliver his coup de gras, "M is going to address the nation tonight."

Kovac looked at Bojan with new admiration. "I didn't know. Where did you hear that, not from M surely?" he asked.

"I haven't seen or spoken to him for some time."

Kovac went back to his bachelor's apartment, turned on the TV and, while waiting for the address M was going to give to the nation at 7pm prime time, he made himself some *gibanica* (a cheese pie). He decided he needed to pay more attention to the Belgrade media, even if he didn't believe everything they said. He ate as he listened to the speech.

To Kovac, it was all normal PR stuff, until.....

"I have ordered the mobilisation of special reservists and the urgent formation of additional Serbian militia units. Yugoslavia has entered into its final phase of agony..... The Republic of Serbia will no longer recognise a single decision reached by the Presidency under existing circumstances because it would be illegal."

Kovac watched with his mouth open as M effectively declared UDI for Serbia. "I hope that General Petar can do this for you," he thought, "because if not, you are going to lose."

He immediately phoned Bojan. "Did you know this?" he asked.

"Not all of it. But apparently, all the mayors of the republic have been invited to a meeting at the Parliament."

"What's that going to accomplish?"

"I suppose if M doesn't involve them, they're not going to back him. He needs their support."

"He hasn't bothered with them so far and now he hasn't even bothered with us." Kovac stopped thinking he had gone too far again in front of Bojan. He continued, "Unless he's got something new to say they are definitely going to be pissed off. This could seriously backfire. Who's giving him this advice?"

Bojan didn't answer, so the conversation ended. Kovac, the prophet, was proved right. M didn't even come to meet the Mayors. They were indeed pissed off. But he did agree to meet with some two hundred students but with not too dissimilar results.

It seemed M didn't really care what any of these people thought. He would ram through whatever he wanted and, as he commanded a significant majority in the Serbian parliament, he calculated that he was safe. What he did want to do was to ensure that the Serbian parts of Croatia were 'returned' to Serbia so he secretly met with Tudjman, the Croatian leader, and promised him part of Bosnia and Vojvodina in return for the Serb enclave in Croatia.

Later M denied ever making such promises and within a few months a real war would break out beginning with Serb rebels taking control of the police station in Croatia's Plitvice National Park.

Chapter 21 — Sarajevo

THE WHOLE OF Bosnia Herzegovina was watching the unfolding events in Serbia and Croatia with some concern. Bosnia itself was an amazing example of a multi-ethnic community where all lived side by side in relative peace but, perhaps because religion and ethnicity went hand in hand for the most part, it did have the potential to become a powder keg if nationalism reared its ugly head. Once the rumour had circulated that Serbia and Croatia were discussing the partition of Bosnia, the population became very concerned. Rumour or not, everyone was thinking about the consequences even if only a few people were talking openly about it.

Ismet and Ana certainly were, at least one to the other. The wedding had been a lovely day. Ana, with her long light brown hair looked every inch the perfect bride. She had an innocently open face, high cheek bones with intelligent eyes and just a little shorter than her handsome bridegroom who had black hair cut short, a square chin and a broad smile. Everyone was happy except for Stefan, Ana's older brother. Her father, Marko Lukic had semi-retired and Stefan had taken operational control of the state-owned furniture factory his father used to manage. Stefan had never liked Ismet, whether it was because of religion or class or ethnicity, who knew? But it was his sister's wedding and family pressure had obligated him to attend especially as his father was paying for it.

But that was now five years ago and Stefan had not seen his sister since the wedding. He had always managed to be out if she called in to see her parents, who didn't live that far away from where the couple had settled. In the meantime, a baby boy had been born to Ismet and Ana which had delighted both grandparents. Separately, they visited the young couple with their gifts and congratulations both commenting on how little Danilo looked like his father or was it one of his grandfathers?

"I am getting a little worried," confessed Ana. Ismet had just come home from the bank where he worked. "There are all sorts of rumours flying around about parts of Bosnia being given to Serbia and Croatia."

"Yes, I've heard them too. I don't think there's anything to worry about. It'll all blow over." Ismet was anxious to settle his little family although he was far from settled himself. He'd heard stories at the bank of what was happening in other Yugoslavian republics like Kosovo and Montenegro. Trouble seemed to be getting a lot closer.

Since Danilo had been born, life had been tough enough. Not just sleepless nights but now they were down to a single wage and making ends meet was proving difficult but the last thing he wanted was for Ana to mention this to her mother for, although her parents would have lent or given money to them, he didn't want that. It was his job to provide for his family and in particular, he didn't want to give Stefan any ammunition to criticise their marriage. Besides they were Serbs and whilst he had good relations with his in-laws, he wasn't sure what would happen if Serb nationalism came to Sarajevo.

"I've invited Mum over for lunch tomorrow. I hope that's all right." Ana wanted to keep Ismet abreast of what she was doing, not because she had to but because ….. well, she didn't quite know why.

"Of course. I'll take sandwiches as usual."

Mrs Lukic duly arrived with most of the lunch, knowing that the young couple were feeling the pinch and she brought Ana up to date with all the family news. Most importantly, her father had gone back to running the factory because Stefan had joined the army.

"It's what he really wanted to do. He's been obsessed with military matters for years and although his father persuaded him to come into the business, I knew it wouldn't last long."

"Where is he stationed?"

"Well, he has basic training first but then I think he will be assigned to the Cipran Barracks in Serbia."

"That's a long way away."

"Yes. I don't expect we'll see much of him except when he's on leave."

The women were silent both thinking the same thing, but afraid to mention it. They had finished lunch and just as Mrs Lukic was getting ready to go, Ana changed the subject.

"Danilo will be going to school soon."

"Really. Doesn't time fly past quickly. It seems only yesterday we were celebrating his birth."

"I know." Ana went quiet again. "We're not sure whether to have another baby," she confessed.

"Oh?" asked her mother.

"We think we might wait until things settle down a bit."

Her mother looked at her and nodded. "Perhaps that's wise." And with that they kissed each other and Mrs Lukic left. Ana, who had been hoping for some solid reassurance, was left without it.

Ismet returned home that evening and over dinner casually asked Ana how her mother was. She told him about Stefan and the final conversation before her mother left. He pulled a face at the mention of her brother, then said,

"I'm hearing stories at the bank that there are demonstrations in Serbia and there have been riots in Belgrade. The authorities actually put tanks on the streets to maintain order."

"Ismet, what does it all mean?"

"I don't know, but there's also talk of the Federal Presidency having meetings in all the republics to try and thrash out a deal and Sarajevo is due for one in June."

"That's only a month away." Ana was thinking as only a new mother can.

"Maybe we'll know more about what's going to happen after that." Ismet tried again to be upbeat. He had been seriously thinking of moving, but where would be safe? Nowhere in Yugoslavia except maybe Slovenia. They were virtually independent already but would they allow a Bosnian husband and a Serb wife in with their mixed race child? Unlikely in the present circumstances, and how would we get there, and how would I get a job, and where would we live? Unknown to his wife, Ismet lay awake at nights going over and over the same questions and getting no answers.

He had thought of talking to his father but while he knew everything there was to know about football teams, his political opinions were picked up from gossip and rumour at the taxi rank. He wanted facts but didn't feel he could talk to his father-in-law either. Perhaps Ana could. But would Mr Lukic feel he had to support Serbia over his Bosnian son-in-law? He didn't know and didn't want to test it just in case he got the wrong answer. No, there was nothing he could really do except keep his head down.

It turned out that taxi drivers really do know what's going on in politics. Ismet accepted an invitation from his father for a drink one evening, which was a first. The young man suspecting something serious decided not to tell his wife, giving some excuse about an after work drink at the bank. Mr Terzic was more serious than his son had ever seen him. He had no answers but he did have some disquieting news about what was happening in the rest of Yugoslavia, if Ismet decided to believe him.

"How are you both and how's my grandson Danilo?" He started with a family question, yes because he was interested, but also because it disguised the news he was about to share with his son. In fact, Ismet thought, he looked a lot older than he remembered, but then they had not seen much of each other after they had married. He had suspected that both of his parents would have preferred he had married a nice Bosnian girl, but they had never said it openly.

"He's well thanks. A few wake ups at five o'clock, you know." Ismet tried to be sociable while waiting for his father to get around to what he wanted to say.

"The word is," his father started quietly, looking around conspiratorially, "that Slovenia will declare independence on the twenty-fifth of this month and Croatia will follow a day later."

"But what does that mean for us?" asked Ismet

"Serbia will let Slovenia go because there are no Serbs there, but everywhere there are Serbs they will fight to create their Greater Serbia. That means they will fight to annex all territory that Serbs currently occupy."

"But what about us? We are a mixed community, always have been." Ismet was becoming alarmed.

"I don't know for sure, but the chances are they will try to annex Sarajevo because we are the main city in Bosnia, and if they control us they think they will be able to control the rest of the country."

The men began to sip their drinks in silence, both thinking about what had been said and what it meant. Ismet was thinking about his father-in-law and which side he would take, then about Ana and where her loyalties would lie. His father was thinking about how his fares would dry up and how would he and his wife have enough money to buy food, heat their home and live?

Chapter 22 — Slovenia

Kovac had left Bojan and was trudging back to his own apartment. He didn't want to go to his own office which was full of comrades working for the 'other side'. In fact, he hadn't resumed his place for some weeks causing some of his superiors to ask some questions. Occasionally he sent in reports containing nothing new but keeping the processes happy. As he had been Tito's official intelligence liaison, he had some cover but knew it wouldn't last for ever. As he trudged through the debris of the Belgrade riot, he wryly observing the city's municipal labour in their inadequate efforts to clean up the city.

"It's going to take the Army to clean up this mess," he thought. Thinking about the Army caused him to wonder what M was really up to. "The man does little without knowing the outcome. Yes, he has made some errors of judgement but so far, he has always come out on top."

Perhaps for the first time in his career, the intelligence man realised that he didn't have the intelligence data he needed to make any decisions, the principle one being should he continue to support M or not? He decided to recall Djuric to Belgrade to discuss the next move. Although he was Djuric's superior, he recognised the former adjutant's undoubted abilities not just to organise but to think clearly. He was smart. Djuric duly arrived the following day.

"What the hell has been going on in Belgrade," was his first question.

"The short answer is there's been a demo. The longer answer is more complicated." The men were at Kovac's apartment, the first time Djuric had been invited to this bachelor pad. The lift worked, the carpet was fairly new and there was no smell in the lobby. Djuric liked it. But, he deduced, this was going to be no ordinary meeting. Kovac made some Turkish coffee and both men sat down in easy chairs.

"I haven't seen M for some weeks," Kovac started. "When I did, I warned him that liberal elements in the country were opposing his leadership and particularly his control of the media. This demo, or riot as it turned out to be is the flexing of some serious muscle and whoever they are, their presence is being felt."

Djuric interrupted. "There have always been student types protesting over some cause or other and there have always been small demos, but from what I saw coming through the city, it looks like there was a war."

"Not quite," Kovac managed a thin smile. "Anyway, M ignored me and this was the result."

"That must have been difficult," commented Djuric, who had never been at M's team meetings, but assumed Kovac was someone in the inner circle.

"Admittedly, it was an unusual meeting. M didn't say anything to us about what his plans were and none of us were asked for our opinion, nor were we asked to do anything. Frankly it looked as if he had already made up his mind and didn't want any disagreement. Then the meeting just ended."

"What do you think it means?"

"Well, he got tanks on the streets and I think that was what finally saw off the demonstrators who, by the way, were not only students, but lots of academics and ordinary people."

"Tanks, eh," Djuric whistled.

Kovac suddenly switched as if he'd said enough to Djuric. He didn't want to disclose to Djuric the role he suspected the Russian was playing behind the scenes so he got straight to his main agenda which was getting Djuric to do some digging on his behalf.

"I think," began Kovac, "now that Serbia has been silenced, at least for the moment, the next place that is going to see some action is Slovenia. They've already set in motion constitutional measures to break away from Yugoslavia."

"But," objected Djuric, "I thought M wasn't going to intervene because there were no Serbs living in Slovenia?"

"That's what the Slovenes were supposed to think," countered Kovac. "I think he's playing a double game and if he sent tanks on to the streets of his home city, he won't hesitate to do that in Slovenia, or anywhere for that matter."

"What do you want me to do?"

"I know you have contacts in Slovenia which you used for the demos we organised. Get up there yourself and let me know what the mood is, what the rumours are and what the Slovene leadership are thinking."

Djuric let the '*we* organised' pass. He had done all the work, but he didn't want to nitpick.

By the end of the day Djuric was in Ljubljana seeking out his informants, who were not easy to find. "That's odd," he thought to himself, "usually money talks, but it seems few people want money for information anymore." From being quite confident, he began to be a little more wary. He checked into the 2 star Hotel Emonec, near the river. The hotel welcomed the custom but, it seemed to Djuric to be less than welcoming once the receptionist had looked at his papers.

The next day he managed to meet up with a few of his contacts who appeared to be quite nervous to be seen with him. He used Kavarna Zvezda as his meeting place since it was close to his hotel and had some quiet booths where he could talk in private. At the end of the first day he was able to give Kovac some good updates.

"The belief here is that Belgrade is going to send in the Federal Army imminently," reported Djuric.

Kovac nodded. "That ties in with what I've managed to get from General Petar. It's going to look like a limited police action to control the airport, the main borders and the TO barracks."

"That sounds like an invasion to me," said Djuric, "and that's exactly what they will think here. That's a declaration of war. What on earth is M up to?"

"I'm not entirely sure," Kovac admitted. "Stay up there a bit longer and let's see how it develops." Again he decided that talk of Smolov would not be helpful to Djuric at the moment, but his suspicions were growing that M had found a new advisor and his old ones were now on the back burner.

Djuric heard the order, immediately deciding he would have to work out a Plan B so he could get out quickly should the need arise. If there was to be war, a Serb in Ljubljana would be a fine target for someone looking to make their name. He booked to eat in the hotel restaurant, found he didn't have much of an appetite but rather more solace propping up the bar together with a rabble of travelling sales reps and a few hookers. He was tempted, but wanted to stay around to hear whatever other gossip was being offered.

In the morning at breakfast he joined Andro with whom he had been drinking the night before. He was a Croat from Split who broke the news to him that a helicopter had been shot down by Slovenian forces. Also, according to his breakfast companion, electricity and water supplies had been cut in certain areas and telephone lines were down. Djuric hurriedly finished his breakfast and cajoled a couple of his informants to meet him again at the Kavarna Zvezda with more specific information. For example, who had cut supplies? Was it an invasion force of Serbs, the Federal Army or perhaps the Slovenes themselves wanting to slow down any advance? Unfortunately only one man turned up and he claimed not to know anything further.

The rest of the morning was wasted waiting for others to arrive. At noon he gave up, went back to his room and turned on the television for news to be confronted with pictures of the 1968 Soviet invasion of Czechoslovakia accompanied by a breathy news anchor who proclaimed that Slovenia had declared war on the Federal Army. He had all he needed to call Kovac which he did, adding that he was getting out. He didn't wait for Kovac to comment but packed his bag and headed to the border.

Back in Belgrade, Kovac finally got a meeting with M. Although he was still undecided on whether he would continue to support M's policies, he kept his feelings under wraps for the time being. He needed to understand exactly what M was doing.

"What is our policy towards Slovenia now?" asked Kovac once coffee had been served. He thought he might as well ask the question everyone else was asking.

"I'm happy for them to be released from Yugoslavia," responded M. "But the EC troika are visiting us again in the next day or so and still want us to remain as one country. We will put up some arguments and extract some concessions from them and then we will agree."

"I'm sorry, I don't understand. You don't want to retain federal power across the country." Kovac was struggling to follow M's strategy.

"Correct," smiled M.

At this point Mira spoke up. "It's a negotiation. Slovenia is not going to come back into the fold. They're virtually independent now and the Federal Army will not be able to force Slovenia back. International pressure will inevitably be on the side of poor, western, liberal Slovenia battling against an old eastern-looking communist bloc."

"Ah," exclaimed Kovac as the light began to dawn. "So the current Federal Army leadership becomes vulnerable, giving us the opportunity to replace them and then we can ensure that Croatia doesn't follow."

"Exactly," said M.

"But what about the European Community troika?"

M scoffed, "What about them? They have no idea what they are doing. It will take some time before they realise the inevitable. In the meantime, we keep talking to them about one direction whilst pursuing another."

Mira joined in, "I hear Bob Dole, the Republican leader in the US Senate, has told Bush that he should compel the Federal Army to halt its activity in Slovenia." She laughed.

"I think in a few days we should formally recognise Slovenian independence,"M was thinking aloud.

"That won't please Zagreb," said Kovac.

"Not at all," said M.

Chapter 23 — Belgrade

M AND MIRA were on their own in their Belgrade apartment having their evening meal. They were expecting Yuri Smolov afterwards, but Mira wanted to have a serious talk with M before he came.

"Do you remember what Kovac said at the last team meeting?" Mira asked as she served the meal. M looked up for a moment, pretending not to remember.

"Remind me," he said.

Mira looked at him as if to say, "Don't play games. I'm not one of your team now. I'm your wife." Actually she said, "He warned us that a big demonstration was likely, and it happened."

"Oh that," said M. "I knew something was up. I didn't need Kovac to tell me."

"Are you telling me that you let it happen so you could put tanks on the streets of Belgrade?"

"In a manner of speaking, yes."

"Why?"

"That's what Yuri is coming over to discuss."

"Are you sure you can trust him?"

"Of course not. You're the only one I have ever trusted."

"So you believe that his advice is going to help us achieve what we want? "Yes."

There was a ring from the doorbell. Mira looked at M who indicated to let him in. She pressed the buzzer, the front door opened and the Russian entered. Mira put on her welcoming face.

"Good evening Yuri. Come in. May I offer you a drink?"

"Vodka."

"Rude," thought Mira, but said in an overly nice voice, "Of course." If he knew how crucial Mira was to M, he didn't show it. He was used to dealing with men in his world. They were the power-brokers. Many Russian men had old-fashion views of women and their place in society, and it wasn't in positions of control or influence. Mira had sensed it from the beginning when she was largely ignored by the man. But, out of respect for her husband, she played the dutiful wife role that Smolov expected.

"M is in the sitting room. Please go through." It was said sardonically since Smolov was already on his way in.

"Ah. Welcome Yuri." M was also profuse in his welcome."

The Russian dispensed with small talk as usual, and immediately took the initiative. "What did you think of our little experiment last weekend?

He took a seat opposite M and fixed his eyes on the Serbian leader in a passive aggressive pose. He was always one to try to gain control in any conversation, startling his opposite number into submission. His bosses in Moscow were still far from convinced that M was the right man to support. Indeed Smolov didn't think M had the bottle to do what needed to be done, but he had looked at all other possible leaders and concluded there was no-one else. So he had been instructed to push M hard to see what he was really made of.

"Excellent," M was up beat in his assessment. "It gave some of our forces good experience and allowed Petar and his commanders an opportunity to play with various options."

"And what about...........?"

At this point Mira had come in with drinks and the Russian immediately stopped mid flow as if Mira was the maid and they were talking official secrets. Mira immediately detected the atmosphere and took the nod from her husband to leave the room. Unknown to their visitor, this had been foreseen and a simple microphone and speaker had been setup to enable Mira to hear everything that was said from the next room.

".... the casualties?" Smolov finished his question testing M's squeamishness.

"Obviously I would have preferred that we could have done the exercise elsewhere rather than on fellow Serbs, especially in Belgrade, but the opportunity could not be wasted."

"When we get 'elsewhere' we will need to use more than a squadron of tanks."

"Of course," replied M. "By the way, did you have a satisfactory meeting with Petar?"

"To be blunt," Smolov started. M thought, "was this man ever anything but blunt?" He took a pull on his vodka as did Smolov. "To be blunt, I don't think he has the balls to do what really needs to be done. He and all his sort, are always looking for constitutional cover for their decisions, afraid to get stuck in."

"I know what you mean. But for the moment he's useful and the other generals will usually take direction from him."

"You will have to find other military leaders soon. Where will you get them?"

"I have my eye on a couple which I will test out in Croatia and Bosnia."

"I hope they prove themselves quickly because that's where the make or break is going to happen."

While M knew what the Russian was saying was true, he didn't like the way it was said. He was used to some deference, especially in his own home. He hadn't had an opportunity to get feedback from Petar over his meeting with Smolov, but if the Russian was just as abrasive as with him, the chances were that the men had not got on well. Not that the Russian cared a jot and neither did M.

"I have also arranged," continued the Russian, "as you suggested, for a platoon of our hardened soldiers to help. They will be arriving shortly in Belgrade."

"Did you advise Petar?"

"No."

"Good, but he will get to know soon enough."

M decided that the meeting was over and took what control he could. He got up thanking Smolov for coming over and promising to be in touch.

Smolov had a faint smile on his face as he got to his feet and was shown the door. As he walked up the street to his car which had been parked on the adjacent street, his smile disappeared into a frown as he realised that M and all the other leaders in Yugoslavia were not a patch on Tito. He would have just sent the tanks and artillery into an area immediately there was an hint of insurrection. These men were wimps.

Back in M's apartment, Mira appeared with eyebrows raised at what she had over heard. M lapsed into his chair in deep thought.

"He's right," he said to Mira, letting out a long sigh. "I knew it. I just hadn't put it into words."

"Did you really put tanks on the streets of Belgrade at his behest?"

"It was a joint decision when the opportunity arose. It enabled us to send a message to any republic thinking of rising up that I am prepared to quell any such disobedience with the heaviest of methods."

Mira looked at him. "It will also push Croatia, in particular, to smuggle in weapons and prepare for whatever you can throw against them. Now there's no element of surprise. They know what might come."

"That was always the risk," conceded M.

Chapter 24 — Croatia

THERE HAD BEEN many meetings and lots of hot air expended in Kijevo and other Croat villages near the city of Knin about what actions they could take to secure their homes and families. They were in a mainly ethnic Serb area and the whole village was on edge. No-one had an answer but, at the same time, nothing was happening on the political front, at least nothing that they knew about. Jakov and Vesna had put the children to bed and were again sitting down to their evening meal.

"I know this is more gossip at the school gates," Vesna began, trying to head off any instant dismissal by her husband, "but the rumours are that Serbia will use the Federal Army to take over this territory soon because it is predominantly Serb."

Jakov paused before starting his meal as if trying to avoid the 'instant' accusation. "Who is saying that?" he asked.

"Three of the women have husbands who are part of the voluntary Croat police. They have been militarised recently so they can defend us against an attack."

"If such an attack were to happen, I'm afraid sticks and stones will not defend us."

"Apparently they now have rifles and grenades." There were a few moments of silence as Jakov thought how to phrase his response.

"And what good will rifles and grenades be against the tanks of the Federal Army?"

Vesna was quiet. She knew he was right but wanted to unload all the information she had. "Apparently, it's already being called the Serbian Army." She also put her knife and fork down for suddenly she was not feeling hungry. "What shall we do?"

Jakov started eating; after all he had worked hard all day. He swallowed a couple of mouthfuls before saying, "Not a lot we can do. The only option is to up and leave." He paused and stared at his wife. "But where do we go?

How will we live? We would be homeless with two small children."

"We might still be homeless with two small children, that is if we survive at all," snapped Vesna. Suddenly Jakov realised how all this was getting to his wife. He moved over and put his arms around her to try to comfort her as she started to cry.

"I'll try to speak to my father and some of the other men and see if we can't get a meeting together to discuss what to do."

Vesna sniffed. "Whatever we do, it's probably better to do it together with everyone else, if we can."

"I agree," said Jakov.

It was an early night for both of them knowing that the children would be awake from six, if they were lucky. Neither of them got much sleep thinking about what the future might hold for their family.

True to his word, Jakov took some time to go into the centre of the village at lunchtime to talk to his father. He was not that old, but an accident in the fields had meant early retirement for him and, as in most Communist lands, he was able to get a pension each month to live on. It wasn't much but he and his wife managed. Mr Tomic senior was sitting alongside other older retired men of the village outside one of the shops, which seemed to be the general gathering place for those who weren't working. They were already talking about the war rumours.

"I heard," said one old man, "that the Serbs want to grab an Adriatic port. They say it's going to be Zadar."

"That's miles away from us," commented another who sounded optimistic.

"But what it says to me is that if the Serbs want something, they'll use the Army to get it and we won't be able to stop them."

Jakov joined them and after explaining to his father why he wasn't working, posed the question to all of them. "What are we going to do if the Serbian Army comes to take over our land?"

The older men looked at each other wondering who was going to answer Jakov. His father spoke first.

"We haven't got much in the way of weapons, so the only thing we can do is try to barricade the village with anything we can get hold of."

"That won't be much of a deterrent if they really want to obliterate us," said another.

A third spoke up, "You know we are right in the path between Knin and the main Serb area, don't you." He was directing this question to Jakov. "They'll have to come through here if they want to link up all the local Serbian areas."

Jakov sat with them until he realised that no-one had much more to say. No doubt there was not much more anyone could say. He was going to suggest they talked to friendly Serb villagers on the locality, but thought better of it. To the old men, it would seem naïve. He returned to his fields not quite sure what he was going to tell his wife when he got home.

It was just a month later that an ultimatum was sent to the Kijevo police from Martic, the leader of the local Serbs. The place was to be wiped off the map or "cleansed". What could they do? All who were able bodied were called on to begin barricading roads on all sides of the village whilst the older men and women, children and babies fled out of the Serb area joining the thousands who had already lost their homes in other skirmishes. Among them were Vesna and the two children. Mr Tomic senior was not classed as elderly so he didn't go with them. He stayed with Jakov and the other men of the village to defend their land.

They resisted the Serb militias for longer than anyone had thought possible. Kijevo's resistance, such as it was, was becoming a symbol in the country. Without seeking direct permission from M, Smolov had embedded his troops within the Serb forces. It didn't take long for heavy weaponry to join the fray and a Russian-style bombardment began. Resistance didn't last long. The remaining resisters fled as best they could but Jakov's disabled father was not able to move very fast. He should have gone earlier with the elderly but had refused saying he was as good as the next man and wanted to do his bit to protect his village and his land.

He and Jakov were moving as quickly as they could, but still too slow. There were walking down a leafy lane, Jakov helping his father as best he could, when suddenly bullets began to be sprayed about like confetti. Jakov dived to the floor but his father was too slow and caught one in his abdomen. He was lying in the middle of the road moaning and trying to hold his stomach.

"Don't move, Dad," Jakov screamed at him, "I'm coming." He crawled over to him as fast as he could with other bullets flying over his head and hitting the trees behind him.

"Dad, it's OK. I've got you."

And with that Jakov somehow dragged his father over to the verge where they both fell into a shallow ditch. There was blood everywhere.

"Don't die, Dad. Please don't die. I'm going to fix it." Ripping some cloth from his own coat, he tried a tourniquet hoping to stem the flow of blood without much success. There were no medical facilities nearby and even if there were, they couldn't move without the risk of instant death. Jakov emptied out his bag hoping to find something that would help. There was nothing. He was crying now with hopelessness. He couldn't remember when he had ever cried before but something inside was telling him it was hopeless but he was refusing to give in.

"It's OK Dad. The blood flow has stopped." It hadn't, but while his father was still breathing, he felt there was hope. But unfortunately that hope didn't last very long. His father had lost too much blood. There was nothing his son could have done. Jakov laid besides his dead father for hours hidden down in the mud and brambles until the Serbs had long gone. Only as darkness was falling did he gradually emerge and even then the sight of his dead father's body in a ditch caused him to burst into tears. He fell back down next to him, his face twisted with pain and his hands over his face almost wishing the Serbs would come back and murder him too. He wasn't worthy of life anymore and, because he hadn't saved his father, he was consumed with guilt.

He needed Vesna's arms to hug and console him at that moment, but she was long gone. As he began to think about her and his little ones, his strength and determination started returning. It was quite dark now and all seemed quiet. Trusting the Serbs had really moved on, he got out of the ditch and began the journey to his family, hoping they had got to safety unharmed.

Everyone said later he couldn't have done anything except be shot himself, but that did nothing to take the guilt and shame away. He was a broken young man. He didn't look back but if he had, he would have just seen his village in ruins. To say that the force used by the invaders was over the top was an understatement. In this campaign the Army had used old Soviet and US guns. They particularly valued towed artillery because of the mountainous terrain of the country. The Soviet pieces consisted of towed 122mm howitzers and some 130mm guns, the US guns mainly 105mm and 155mm artillery. Some might have said ancient, but they did the job against virtually unarmed opposition piling everything the equipment would give them into Kijevo which was entirely flattened. It was to be a symbol of Serb strength and determination.

Martic who was leader of the Serbs in the region was triumphant. He recorded:

We seemed superior to the Croatians. They were running away. We didn't care about the victims. We wanted to liberate our blocked villages.

Of course, there were a few burnt houses, that's the way it goes in these actions with artillery. We thought it wouldn't last long and we were right.

The Russian surveyed the impact of the bombardment and smiled grimly. "That's more like it," he murmured to himself. "Just wait until we get some better artillery, then we'll get some action." He congratulated the young lieutenant colonel in charge for following his battle plan.

"Now, you've got the right idea." His name: Ratko Mladic.

Kovac, monitoring these developments from Belgrade, found himself in two minds; on the one hand, he wanted to push for a Greater Serbia for he was a Serb but on the other, he found such destructive military action not only distasteful but completely unnecessary. Political and constitutional means yes, even using the Army as leverage, but killing people on such a scale, no. However, M had asked him to get someone into Zagreb to find out what the Croats intended to do next.

"I want you to get into Zagreb," he ordered Djuric. "We need to know if they are going to be peaceful or declare war on us."

Djuric replied, "I wouldn't blame them if they did, but I don't think they have the muscle to seriously go against the Army."

"Well, we can think what we like. M wants hard facts not our opinions."

Obediently, Djuric took a circuitous way into Croatia which would also serve as his exit route. This time there wasn't going to be any plan B. It was Plan A and it had to work. No sooner had he checked into the Hotel Puntijar on Gračansko Borje and entered the bar, than the television loudly proclaimed a national mobilisation. "Well," he thought, "Kovac didn't need me here to know that. It will be all over Yugoslavia within minutes."

Bar talk began to centre on what was happening at Vukovar, up north on the Slovenian border.

"I've got family up there," one person was saying, "and those ******* Serbs are firing mortars into the city. And what the hell are we doing about it?"

"Tudjman is a waste of time. He's done nothing but try to appease them," said a second.

"Listen," said yet another.

The news had moved on to a government announcement that all Federal Army bases in Croatia were now surrounded by Serb forces. Gas, electricity, water and telephone lines had been cut off. Tank traps had been made and all roads around the bases were now blocked. The Croatian forces were unable to get a single piece of artillery out of their own bases.

"We should have seen that coming," said the first person.

"We're always too ******* late," said the second, who seemed not to be a great supporter of the government.

"Listen," the third shouted to the other two.

The news had moved on again to talk about the bridges over the Sava river being mined and barricades erected on all major highways. As all this was being digested, suddenly there was the deafening sound of Army jets screaming low over the city.

"Bloody hell," exclaimed the first.

"I might not be able to get home," exclaimed the second.

"Listen, you just missed that, you morons." The third man shouted again, "They're saying to watch out for snipers."

They all looked at each other in horror. Snipers? It wasn't just happening in other places in the country, it was happening here in Zagreb.

"I'm off," said the first, and the others followed quickly. Soon the bar was empty and Djuric found himself a little exposed. He went up to his room, called Kovac with all the news, whether he had already heard it or not, then put Plan A into action.

Chapter 25 — Vukovar

GENERAL PETAR AND Smolov were in discussions with M about Croatia. The General was feeling pleased with himself for having taken control of the Army and getting it into Croatia in defence of the Serb population. However the Russian was critical of the Army for not totally levelling Croat villages. M agreed. He was also looking for more.

"I want as much territory as we can defend, not only the Serb enclaves, and I want Zadar and I want the destruction of Croatian areas."

Zadar was an important port on the Adriatic for landlocked Serbia but it was a long way from Serbia itself. General Petar agreed. "We'll need Zadar to bring in the armaments that our Russian friend here can provide and for which we have paid handsomely."

"What about the other Croatian areas?" demanded M.

"Well," started the General, "We now control between a quarter and a third of Croatia. But the Croatians are waging war against Serb civilians wherever they can find them. It's looking ugly."

"I know there are some Serbs there who have a misplaced loyalty to Tudjman, so I'm not worried about them," said M.

"I think about one hundred and twenty of them have been killed in Gospic," explained Petar. "Among them professors and judges."

M dismissed it all with a wave of his hand. "So what. I'm more concerned with getting our forces out of their Croatian barracks. There are a lot of troops in barracks there, not to mention the heavy artillery which we urgently need. Surely the Army can do that simple task."

The General ignored the jibe waving his hand across the map they were studying. "Here's Gospic and the commander there has been murdered trying to get his men and equipment out."

"Right. I want that place levelled. To the ground. That's an order." M was now marching up and down the room.

"Our commanders have struck many local deals which allow everyone to leave with their equipment in exchange for not damaging their town"

M stopped. "Really? Then the Croats are more stupid than I thought."

"But not in other places," continued Petar. "In Varazdin, our men were stripped of their uniforms and forced to make their way home as civilians, but in Jastrebarsko we got everything out – six hundred soldiers and all their heavy weapons, surface to air missiles, anti-tank and anti-aircraft batteries and dozens of armoured vehicles."

"Who was that Commander?"

"Tasic, Radovan Tasic."

" Make sure he gets a medal."

"Who was the commander in Varazdin who betrayed his soldiers?"

"Trifunovic."

"Make sure he's arrested for treason and put on trial. I want to make an example of him."

Trifunovic was subsequently arrested and despite his appeals, was sentenced to twelve years in prison. Many Belgrade liberals were dismayed at the way the trial was conducted. It seemed to many that M now had the judiciary in his pocket, either by voluntary agreement or serious pressure.

Djuric's Plan A didn't quite work out as he had wanted. He got as far as Vukovar, near the Serbian border, when he learnt that the Army had surrounded the town. He was stuck. Such was the anxiety to get out of Vukovar that both Serbs and Croats were constantly slipping out of the place in the hope they would go unnoticed. What was once a town of fifty thousand was now down to fifteen thousand, leaving only those who could not flee and the inexperienced Croatian National Guard. Djuric was moving around the town cautiously, trying to avoid being noticed when his luck ran out. He was spotted by a sniper who kindly sent a bullet his way. Fortunately only in the shoulder, but such was the blood loss that he decided to make his way quickly to the hospital for some urgent treatment, following other unfortunates doing the same.

Serb militias and Army forces were launching continual bombardments on the town including two bombs which directly hit the hospital. Djuric was one of ninety plus people who had come into the hospital that day and were waiting to be seen. Had he been already in surgery, he would have perished for one device completely demolished the Surgery Dept. whilst the other failed to explode. He cursed both Kovac for sending him to Zagreb and M for letting the Army loose on civilians.

Getting out was now not going to be easy. Vukovar was putting up tremendous resistance helped by the fact that the Army was filled with conscripts who had no idea what they were doing and hundreds were deserting. If it was chaos in the town, it was a different type of chaos in the Army. There were no chains of command, some didn't even know who their commanders were, and orders were seemingly disobeyed at will. Smolov was smouldering with anger and laid the blame squarely at the door of General Petar. He threatened to bring his platoon in unless he got a grip of the situation quickly.

Djuric knew the inevitable couldn't be far away but he was in the same position as everyone else or perhaps worse since he was a Serb. Having got a modicum of treatment at the hospital, where he didn't have to show any papers, he was now holed up in the basement of a building already half demolished with twelve others including a mother with two children, four old women, a young man who looked as if he had a broken leg, two old men and two corpses. He tried to get some sleep in a corner apart from the others. He didn't want to get drawn into a conversation for obvious reasons. When he awoke he had no idea of the time but light was coming through the cracks and the living were already out, presumably trying to replenish supplies of food and water.

He looked around to make sure no-one was coming back in. They weren't, so he started searching the dead men for their papers. The first had nothing but some cigarette stubs which now would never get smoked, but the inside pocket of the second proved much more profitable and he pocketed the documents quickly. Now he reckoned he could pass as a Croat or a Serb, which ever was going to be most useful. All he had to do was to keep his beard to look passably like his dead donor which wasn't going to be a problem since shaving was the last thing on his mind. He quickly moved out and made his way into the town keeping close to the side of the road and dodging the fallen concrete, masonry and twisted steel rods.

Ahead of him he could hear clashes with clouds of dust flying up and knew tanks or some other armoured vehicles were not far off. Small arms fire crackled and men were dashing from one building to another. It looked like hand to hand fighting was going on with the support of the armoured vehicles.

"I've got to get out of here," he thought. Turning away from the fighting down a dark alley he came across some Croatian National Guardsmen.

"Who are you?" they demanded. He showed them the papers he had appropriated and was allowed through.

"How do we get out of here?" Djuric asked.

They looked at one another as if to ask, " Do we trust this man?" One shrugged, another said, "Stick with us. As soon as it gets dark, we're going over the cornfields to Vinkovici."

Another added, "That means we have to go through the Serb lines. We might all get gunned down. Are you up for that?"

Djuric, knowing he might be able to use his Serb papers if there was a chance, nodded. "No problem."

The young men moved off at a pace away from the fighting which was getting ever nearer. A couple of hours later they settled into the ruins of a factory until darkness fell. They had no food, no water and did not want to light a fire for fear of being discovered. They spent the time talking to each other and ignoring him.

"Those Serbs are animals," he heard one person say. "They were shooting everything that moved. Men, women, children, no matter who."

"I saw hundreds of bodies in the main street, and animal skeletons too."

"And looting. I saw one militiaman with a rucksack filled with stuff, and it wasn't ammunition."

"Did you notice," another said, "They were beginning to separate the women and children from the men."

"What does that mean?" asked the youngest of the group. Djuric looked at him and assessed his age as fourteen or fifteen.

"It means the men are going to be shot," answered the one who seemed to be the leader. "Likely as not to be pushed into a mass grave. Just like the Nazis used to do."

A few hours later darkness was falling and there was a rustle from the younger men impatient to go. They were told in no uncertain terms to be quiet and informed that they would not be moving until well into the night when, hopefully, the Serb guards whose shift would have started at midnight would have slackened their watch. At exactly 3am, there was again a stirring amongst the men and, in single file with Djuric at the rear, they started their journey. Fortunately, there was a partially clear sky which gave them some light and a stiff breeze which could mask any noise their feet made. It wasn't a long way but they had to be absolutely quiet down the footpath and through the fields. A stumble from the youngest lad created a little stir causing them all to fall flat on the ground not moving, hardly breathing but listening hard. Nothing. His older brother grabbed him and hissed, "Walk in front of me." They got up, one by one, and continued their trek. The Serb lines were difficult to gauge so silence was kept even once they believed they had past through.

Once he was really sure they had passed the Serb positions, Djuric, still at the back of the line, quietly veered off unnoticed and began to make his own way. He wasn't much of an outdoor man but recalling his early military training, he began to navigate according to the position of the moon. He knew the Serbian border was eastwards but suspected that troops would be coming from that direction and even though he was a Serb, they might shoot first and ask questions later. So he determined to go south towards the Bosnian border and head for a town down there called Brcko.

It took him three days of hesitant off road travelling before he was certain he was in Bosnia then he knew he was safe, at least for the time being. From there he was able to call Kovac and have him come to the rescue. A day later Djuric was safely back in Belgrade, firstly visiting a hospital to have his injured shoulder checked out, then on to his apartment with Kovac there to chauffeur him about. During these travels Djuric told his story and Kovac listened. When the story had finished, Kovac was able to tell him more of the Croatian war.

"Last week, the Army stationed in Montenegro attacked Dubrovnik."

"Why?" asked Djuric. "There's no strategic reason to do that."

"Apparently, the Army commander there wanted to get in on the action and it was seen as an easy target."

"What happened?"

"Well, they bombarded it, even had a gunboat out in the Adriatic, but they never got into the city."

"Those old walls would take some battering before they gave in."

"But they did manage to hit every single yacht in the marina." Both men laughed.

Chapter 26 — Belgrade

M HAD DECIDED the call his team together to agree on some next steps, not that he needed their input just their obedience to undertake the necessary tasks. This time they were invited to the Presidential offices. Clearly M was no longer worried about revealing his secret team.

"Where is Kovac?" he asked. Everyone shook their heads.

"Didn't you ask him to go to Zagreb?" said Bojan.

"Ah yes," murmured M. "I thought he would get Djuric to go rather than go himself." No-one said anything. "Well, let's move on."

Having heard what Djuric had to say about Croatia, Kovac was having further serious thoughts about M's orders. So he had decided to stay under the radar as far as M was concerned. He calculated that everyone would probably believe he was still in battle-torn Croatia or even had perished there. The only one who knew the truth was Djuric. It was time to have a conversation.

Finally the EC had decided that since there was an undeclared war going on in Croatia with multiple casualties and rumours of mass graves, perhaps they ought to do something more. Lord Carrington, an English aristocrat and former UK Foreign Secretary under Margaret Thatcher, was given the task to 'knock heads together' and come up with a solution in two months. He was also Deputy Chairman of Christie's prestigious auction house, a post he insisted on keeping. So he was part time at best.

M was scornful. "Is that how important they think Yugoslavia is?"

Mira was more calculating. "It may offer us something. If we just hold out for what we want, we may actually get most of it without lifting a finger. The rest can come later through other means."

So M decided to play the game. His opening gambit was that he wanted all Serb-occupied areas to be part of Serbia. That meant not only keeping the territory won in Croatia, but large tracts of Bosnia where there was a majority of Serbs. Slovenia was virtually independent and had no Serbs at all, so he was not interested in that land. Montenegro and Kosovo had puppet governments under his control so they were already his for the taking.

Carrington came up with a number of plans – an *a la carte* menu some called it. All had merit but came up against Serbia's intransigence. Once he had exhausted his efforts, the UN appointed former US Secretary of State, Cyrus Vance to try his hand. He had something to offer (or threaten) that Carrington didn't have, namely blue helmeted troops.

"What did I tell you?" Mira told him. "We have virtually all we want in Croatia if we get those UN troops positioned according to the facts on the ground. That Croatian territory will be ours instantly and it won't be long before that becomes the new border."

No-one envisaged that Helmut Kohl, the ebullient Chancellor of Germany, would muscle his way single-handedly through the objections of most of the other members of the European Community and the US, to support Croatian independence. Croatia was, after all, a potentially rich state with a warm water port and quite a lot of potential oil fields. Some critical objectors claimed Europe was witnessing the rise of the Fourth Reich but, in spite of international pressure, Germany went ahead and declared Croatia an independent state to the horror of Carrington who correctly guessed what was likely to happen to Bosnia.

Bosnia was caught. If they also went for independence like Slovenia and Croatia, they risked the Bosnian Serbs provoking a civil war in their country. Yet if they stayed within what was left of Yugoslavia, they would still be dominated by Serbs, this time from Belgrade. One, Radavan Karadzic, the Bosnian Serb leader, said that if Bosnia did declare independence it would 'be stillborn and not survive a single day'. It was a no-win situation for Bosnia. But a plebiscite was held and, with the Serbs boycotting it, the Bosniaks and Croats saw the declaration passed with a huge majority. Karadzic set about keeping his promise.

M was happy with what he had achieved in talks with Vance. He had the Croatian Serb territory sorted and the input from Karadzic was that taking over the Bosnian Serb territory would be even easier. He never anticipated that the Serbs in Krajina would refuse to come into line.

"What the hell are they playing at?" M was shouting at anyone who was within earshot. Most were quickly moving out of range. He was still in his Presidential office, the other team members having disappeared. He shouted to his secretary to get Babic on the line.

"It's very simple," said the leader of the Krajina Serbs. "The Vance proposal means the UN forces replace the Army on the border we have created, but our militias will have to disband and disarm. And we are not going to do that."

"But the UN soldiers will mark the future border of Serbia and we will have got what we wanted."

"Maybe what you wanted." The two men were now shouting at each other down the wire. In a prophetic comment of what would later take place in Bosnia, Babic tried to explain once M had calmed down a little.

"Listen. If Germany rearms an independent Croatia so they can 'defend' themselves, it doesn't take much imagination to see that a thin line of blue helmeted soldiers might be unable or unwilling to stop them attacking us."

M conceded the point but needed Babic to climb down just to get the UN soldiers in. "What if we gave you a guarantee, a law passed in Parliament if you want, that if such an eventuality were to happen we would immediately bring in the Army again to defend you."

Babic, however, would only budge if M could ensure that the Serb enclaves in Bosnia near to the Krajina area were consolidated as part of Serbia. "That way," he explained, "we have a direct route into Serbia; otherwise we are isolated."

So M began thinking about Bosnia a little more deeply than he had done. Although he wouldn't admit it openly, he would have quite liked to have Kovac around to help him think it through. However, Kovac was hunkered down in Belgrade, thinking he ought to move well away from the city in case someone recognised him, but knew he had to talk to Djuric first.

"Can we meet at my place this afternoon?" He asked Djuric. Kovac wanted to get it over with and preferably before Djuric went back to Montenegro for he was sure that's where the adjutant would go.

"Sure," Djuric sounded fresh and ready for another task. He arrived at

Kovac's apartment at 2pm.

"Can I get you anything to drink?" asked Kovac. Djuric stared at the man. He had never been asked that before by a man who was usually a whirlwind, having just come from a meeting with M and ready to give his orders.

"Something has changed him," he thought. Whilst he declined the drink, Kovac poured himself a generous measure of *rakija* (a clear spirit distilled from ripe fermented quinces.) This was so out of character that Djuric was beginning to feel a little uncomfortable.

"How are you after your Croatian adventure," the intelligence man asked tentatively after he had lit a cigarette. Asking questions was not really what Kovac did. Something had definitely changed but not the cigarettes. Djuric had never smoked and hated smoke especially indoors. It got into his clothes and more especially into his lungs. Nevertheless he said nothing as he thought about how he should answer his erstwhile boss.

"I saw things, experienced things I have never done before," Djuric admitted. "For a few days I must confess I was scared. My exit plan was scuppered and there's no doubt I could have been killed by either Serbs or Croats."

His voice trailed off as he remembered hunkering down next to two dead bodies. "Anyway, you don't want to listen to me wittering on." Djuric looked at him expectantly. Surely he was going to say something, give him some tasks.

"After you told me your story I realised, perhaps for the first time," Kovac started, "that M's plans weren't just going to be political or constitutional manoeuvrings, but that he had extreme violence in mind all along."

Kovac looked at his underling, wondering what his reaction was going to be. "I know there were massacres. Women and children shot, innocent civilians just mown down, looting on a grand scale." His voice trailed off again.

Djuric looked uncomfortable as his superior spoke with such openness. "Yes there was. I saw some of it with my own eyes," he stated feeling the need to say something to acknowledge that what his boss was saying was true.

"Look can we speak in confidence? Just the two of us?" Even as he said it Kovac knew it was a stupid thing to say, so he ploughed on. "It wasn't just your story, but it's what I've been hearing from others as well. What I'm trying to explain is that I don't think I can continue to support M's policies."

There, it was out. Kovac looked at Djuric trying to discern what the adjutant's reaction was going to be. Of course, he knew that he couldn't necessarily trust what was said. If Djuric was invited by M to a meeting, Kovac might find himself betrayed. He wanted, desperately wanted, Djuric to understand and hopefully agree, but perhaps it was too early for him to appreciate what was going on.

"I had hinted to Bojan," Kovac continued, giving Djuric time to consider the bombshell he had just dropped, "that I was unhappy about tanks on the streets of Belgrade being used against our own citizens and I think he agreed, but now Croatia, Vukovar. It's becoming all too clear." Kovac was suddenly conscious that he was doing all the talking.

He looked at Djuric. "Are you surprised, disappointed, angry?"

Djuric looked a little distressed. "No. I..er..I can certainly understand how you have come to such a decision. It can't have been easy."

"Of course, I don't want to betray the cause. I want a Greater Serbia, but not at the cost of mass civilian burial sites." Kovac self-consciously stopped talking again.

For a few moments there was quiet and Kovac went over to the sideboard and poured himself another large glass of rakija. "I think I'm going to get drunk," he said. "Sure you don't want to join me?"

Djuric's mind was in a whirl, not knowing what to think so he accepted a drink, giving him a few moments to gather himself together.

"I'm not sure what I think, to be honest." Djuric tried to formulate words which didn't rubbish what Kovac was saying but also didn't express direct agreement. "I see what you mean about Croatia though. It was a terrible experience."

Kovac put his arm round Djuric as a friend. His voice was a little slurred. "If I know M, he will come looking for you because you're good. You are the one who has made everything happen. All I ask is that you pretend you don't know where I am. For all you know I went to Zagreb, not you, and was probably killed there. I'm not going to switch sides, I just need some time to sort myself out."

Djuric found he could answer that question easily, "Of course. Absolutely."

"By the way," said Kovac, "M has a Russian friend who I think is pushing for an even more ambitious military policy. I suspect he's pushing at an open door which means it's going to get a lot worse. Look out for him." Kovac's loosened tongue was now saying things he shouldn't have said to Djuric.

"Oh." replied Djuric, not quite knowing what to make of this latest revelation. Kovac suddenly turned to business.

"Now listen. I've got a new SIM card for my phone, so my old mobile number is now defunct. No-one will be able to call me, but I've kept some personal numbers. I might call you to see how you are in a month or two. Maybe you'll come to the same conclusion as me."

Djuric sensed the meeting was over and got up to go.

"Goodbye, my friend," said Kovac. Djuric shut the door and was gone. Kovac poured himself yet another drink.

Chapter 27 — Bosnia

M WAS BACK at his apartment. After some discussions with Mira, he called Djuric on his mobile hoping he had the right number. It was not a number Djuric had in his contact list, but he answered it.

"I understand Kovac is missing." No introductions, M just assumed everyone knew his voice, which they probably did. "So I would like to meet you. Can you come to my apartment this evening, say seven o'clock?" He gave the address. Djuric didn't see it as a request so respectfully agreed.

He was surprised at the apartment block as he approached it. It was certainly better than his own which he expected, but it was by no means the most prestigious block in Belgrade. Why would the Serbian President still live in his apartment? Was the 'team' so far off the grid that they couldn't be invited to his office? Or is it because of me? Anyway who was to say that M didn't have another flashy apartment or even a country mansion somewhere else? He looked round at a tree-lined avenue with plenty of space around with well looked after grass and gardens. He rang the bell for the number he had been given and a woman's voice invited him to come up.

"I'm Mira, glad you could make it." Djuric was feeling quite nervous and muttered something like, "Thanks," which upon retrospect was not exactly the correct greeting for the President's wife. However, she let it pass and indicated he should go into the lounge, where M was sitting at a table surrounded by a mass of papers and a large map.

"Ah, you must be Djuric. Good of you to come." M was pleasant, even friendly, but didn't offer his hand. Djuric was thinking maybe Kovac had got this man wrong. He was studying the map on the table, and without looking up asked casually,

"I suppose you don't know what has happened to Kovac? I understand you worked together." Djuric caught a slightly different tone in the question which made him a little uneasy.

"No. I'm afraid not sir."

"Pity. He was a good man. When did you last see him?"

Djuric was beginning to perspire a little, "Just before he went to Zagreb sir."

"Nothing since?"

Djuric knew now he had a choice. He could go on lying or he could quickly change his story. Of course, it wasn't a choice. One lie always had to be backed up with another, and probably another. He thought quickly, "What if M had someone watching Kovac's apartment?" They would both be in very serious trouble then for they were privy to secrets that M would not want to be made public. He tried to make his voice sound normal.

"No sir." Then he offered a suggestion. "I guess he got caught up in the troubles there, sir."

M looked up and stared at him. "I guess so."

At this stage he still hadn't been invited to sit down. He was actually standing to attention, which he hadn't noticed until now. It had been some years since that had happened and his back was beginning to ache a little. Then came the question he had been anticipating. "Do you think you could step into Kovac's shoes?" M wasn't looking at him as he asked the question but moving pieces around on his map.

"Well, Kovac was an experienced intelligence officer and I was only an adjutant, sir."

"You were Tito's adjutant weren't you?"

"Yes. It was me who phoned Kovac with the news of his death sir."

"Of course." M was still looking at his map.

"So can you?" The voice came from the other side of the room and Djuric turned to see it was Mrs M.

"I'll do my best. I can certainly follow orders, ma'am."

Mira again, "But we also need someone with some ingenuity, maybe even a little flair and creativity."

"I believe the operation in Kosovo showed some of both, ma'am." He replied cautiously. He actually wanted to ask, "What exactly do you have in mind?" but one didn't ask such questions at an interview with the President, for that was what it was turning out to be.

"I believe you've shown yourself to be loyal and hard-working, so I'm going to trust you with a difficult but very important job." M looked up and eyeballed him. Djuric kept his gait and gaze as he would if he was receiving orders from a senior Army officer, which he was.

"OK. Stand at ease."

Djuric relaxed a little as M invited him to survey the map. It was an enlarged map of Serbia, Croatia and Bosnia. He was stabbing his finger at Sarajevo while Djuric was looking at his hands and superbly manicured nails. "This man, has never been in the army or done any manual labour in his life," he thought, but quickly dragged his attention back to what M was saying.

"These are the Serb areas in Croatia which are now internationally recognised by the UN, and which we now control." M was a little ahead of the international community, but he didn't care and Djuric didn't know.

"And this is Serbia. Tell me what you see."

Djuric immediately saw the importance of the Bosnian Serb area particularly around Banja Luka for those Serbs in Croatia and he outlined quickly what he saw.

"Quite right. We need to get control of those areas, maybe more if we can get it."

"What do you want me to do sir?"

M paused for a few moments. "What Kovac would have done would be to get into the area in advance of any troop movement and collect intelligence which will help the Army plan their strategic thrusts into Bosnia. Can you do that?"

"Can I use any of the team I built for the demonstrations sir?"

"No. This must be between you and me only. You're on your own."

"Just like Kovac," thought Djuric, but answered firmly, "Yes, of course. I understand sir."

"You're an Army man. I don't need to outline any specifics do I? You know the type of information we need?"

"Yes sir." Djuric was back to standing to attention and looked ready to march out.

Mira again. "Let me show you out, Djuric," she said. Two minutes later he was outside the apartment block walking away as if in a trance. "Did I really just meet with the President of Serbia?" As he was walking thoughts were flooding his mind: how do I do this? do I want to do this? what did Kovac say? He didn't notice a man in a grubby raincoat walking on the other side of the road following him at a distance.

The majority Serb areas in Bosnia were mostly in the north bounded by Croatia, and in the south bounded by Serbia itself and Montenegro. There were also many cantons where Serbs would claim possession but where they had no ethnic majority. Sarajevo itself was in a mainly Muslim canton but with a majority Serb canton very close by. But as the capital, Djuric felt this was where it would all happen for if Sarajevo fell, other cities would be likely to fall quickly.

He left Belgrade almost immediately, arriving in Sarajevo a day or so later. M's tracker in the grubby raincoat reported back that the adjutant had met no-one else in Belgrade and the next morning had left the Serbian capital with a backpack bound straight for Bosnia. What he couldn't report was that Djuric desperately wished he could have contacted Kovac and got some advice from the intelligence man, but there was nothing to be done on that front. He just had to wait until Kovac phoned him.

There was certainly tension in Sarajevo. Radovan Karadzic, the Bosnian Serb leader, had instructed his men to build blockades around the city and the Bosnian Muslims reciprocated with barricades from the inside just in case the Serbs decided to invade. Neighbourhoods were cut off from each other and it was difficult to get around the city. The three communities had their own political parties and each were fastidiously looking after the interests of their own community. No-one was backing down.

Djuric sent his first report, happy that he had good data to transmit but unhappy as he realised that this was almost an exact replica of what he had experienced in Zagreb. He was stuck; no-one was getting in and no-one certainly getting out. It was clear, after a while that neither side was really ready for outright hostilities and a temporary political agreement meant that barricades could begin to come down. Karadzic was happy for he now knew the strengths and weaknesses of his militias as well as what strategic moves he might make on Sarajevo when he was ready to move. He knew he needed the Army and their heavy weaponry to take the city and had heard how Mladic had used Russian boots on the ground in Croatia which had been pivotal. He began wondering what role they might have to play in Sarajevo and under whose command they might be. But General Petar, under M's instructions, was holding back the Army for the moment. M had other plans.

Chapter 28 — Zvornik

M'S PLAN WAS to do what he had done successfully in Kosovo and Montenegro; that is, substitute the current President of Bosnia with a man more to his liking. And he had even found such a person. Called the Belgrade Initiative, the Muslim Bosnjak Party (MBO) was specifically formed to facilitate the move, but the Muslim population saw through the scheme and immediately rejected it. It wasn't difficult to see that under the control of Belgrade, Bosnia would be an apartheid country where Muslims would be second class citizens to the Serb Orthodox majority.

Djuric had already made good contacts with the Muslim population and had forecasted the rejection in his report.

"From the feedback I've received, there is no chance that the Muslim population will accept the MBO to represent them. They will see it as a trick."

But M pushed it hard and when it failed, he was enraged. "Now they will see that they have missed their only peaceful chance to cooperate with me. I will crush them." He screwed up his fists and banged them into his Presidential desk. He called Karadzic.

"Organise your militias. I've authorised the Serbian Army to support you. You are in overall command and the Army commander on the ground will be Ratko Mladic. I've watched him operate in Croatia. He's efficient and single minded."

Karadzic replied, "Thank you. While we are coordinating ourselves, I will be carrying on discussions with the locals so that when we are ready and they are unprepared, we will launch."

"Oh, and you'll also have a Yuri Smolov with you. He knows what he's talking about, so listen to him."

Karadzic objected, "I don't need any minder watching what I do."

"Put him with Mladic then."

"And you'll have a troop of Russian soldiers as well." The phone went dead. Karadzic swore and muttered, "They'd better keep out of my way."

In the meantime, Karadzic carried on talking to the Bosnian Presidency, but there was no negotiation:

"Do not think that you will not lead Bosnia Herzegovina into hell, and do not think that you will not perhaps make the Muslim people disappear, because the Muslims cannot defend themselves if there is war. How will you prevent everyone from being killed?"

Djuric was now sending daily reports to Belgrade such was the fast moving nature of the situation. But even he could see that war was inevitable, particularly when he learned from one of his old team whom he had told to get near to the Bosnian Serb 'parliament', that an independence vote was about to be taken. He knew that it would be one hundred percent in favour and, in itself, would activate a non-stop path to war.

He was urgently thinking about some kind of plan to get out of Sarajevo before it all kicked off, when he began to realise that M must be getting all this information from other sources, so what really was his role? Had he been sent to die in this city? Was M cleaning out all those who knew where the skeletons of his activities over the last ten years were buried? He needed a call from Kovac, but his phone remained silent.

The bulk of the Army's weaponry was being withdrawn from Slovenia and Croatia and readied for a move into Bosnia to join the already substantial arms in Bosnian Army barracks. It was a calculated response to the declaration of independence by the Bosnian President who was hoping for EC recognition which might save them from the Serbs. Recognition certainly came but without any intention of that august body stepping in to defend the state they had just recognised.

M wasn't too concerned about EC recognition for he had accurately summed up the Europeans' lack of will to act. He knew they would grasp at any statement by the Serbs to delay having to do anything. Consequently, M was still publicly portraying his activity as a defence of Yugoslavia even though the country had long ceased to exist. Both the EC and the US invited Croatian, Serbian and Bosnian leaders to Lisbon for talks to find a way to avoid war. A noble aim, but doomed to failure.

M continue to talk about peace whilst at the same time preparing for war. General Petar, now in control of what was now the Serbian Army, was called into the Serbian President's office. He was rather surprised that the meeting wasn't at M's apartment with the other members of the team but it seemed that M had dispensed with their input. Petar was surprised that the Russian, Smolov, was already there and, looking at the two empty cups of coffee on the table, had been ensconced with M for some time.

"I had a long conversation with Radavan earlier today," started M looking at Petar. "He wants to make sure we have as many Serb troops on the ground in Bosnia as possible. So I want to transfer all Serb troops in the Army who were born in Bosnia, wherever they are now, to be reposted back there."

"That would be against the internal rulebook," cautioned Petar.

"A rulebook that was developed for a Yugoslavia that doesn't now exist," countered M. "How long will it take?"

"I suppose just a matter of a few days."

"Do it, and without making it too obvious."

Petar left the short meeting thinking that M was surely preparing for war. That, however, was not his immediate goal. Ever the politician, M wanted as much constitutional cover for everything as he could – always one eye on how it would look internationally. Over the next few days, the Serb barracks in Bosnia received hundreds of soldiers from all over what was Yugoslavia. Once this had been achieved, Karadzic arranged for a Bosnian wide referendum which was easily won with the influx of Serbian soldiers. On the basis of the vote, he declared a Republika Srpska within Bosnia.

Meanwhile the Croat and Serb delegates in Lisbon arranged for a secret meeting to be held in Austria after the conference. The agenda: to discuss how to dismember Bosnia to include their own ethnic populations within revised borders. Huge movements of populations were discussed – totally impractical without an overwhelming incentive which, of course, war would provide. Both sides were happy to talk, but neither trusted the other so when a small Croat/Serb conflict happened in Bosanski Brod, no-one was surprised. The rapprochement ended almost as soon as it started.

Djuric meanwhile was having coffee with some people he had met in a bar the previous evening and happened to overhear a conversation at an adjacent table about what was happening at Bosanski Brod. He didn't know the area but apparently there was just one bridge over the river Sava that was open to the Croats, the others either having been destroyed or in the hands of the local Serbs who were blockading them prior to an attack.

He was about to send a report to M when his phone rang. He didn't recognise the number but answered it anyway. It was Kovac.

"Where are you?" Kovac asked.

"Sarajevo," replied Djuric, getting up and walking down the street where he could talk relatively privately. "And it's getting a little hairy."

"You need to get out," Kovac urged.

"But M has sent me here on a mission – one you should be doing." Djuric was being rather defensive. There was silence on the other end of the phone.

"Does M know where I am? asked Kovac.

"I doubt it. I don't know where you are," replied Djuric impatiently, " and no, I didn't tell him you were still alive."

"You need to get out," persisted Kovac.

"Where are you?"

"You don't need to know right now," replied Kovac. "You now have my number. If you call me, I will respond and try to help. But take my advice. You don't want to be in another Zagreb." With that Djuric's phone went dead. Kovac had finished the conversation.

But within a few minutes the device rang again. This time he knew the number. It was M.

"Get over to Zvornik, now"

"But there's stuff happening in Bosanski Brod and I was just mailing you a report."

"That's peanuts. Zvornik. Now!" The conversation ended within seconds of it starting. So what was he going to do? Zvornik was on the bank of the Drina river, north east of Sarajevo nearer Serbia itself so it would certainly get him out of Sarajevo. But it was a majority Muslim city so it could be out of the frying pan and into the fire. He hadn't heard any news from there but clearly something was about to happen. He decided to go.

With his backpack fastened, he thought his traveller credentials were enough to hitch a lift with a truck that was going that way and the truck driver somehow got him through both Bosniak and Serb checkpoints relatively easily. Djuric tried to make conversation with the man who had so easily got him through the checkpoints, but he proved to be a man of few words so Djuric began to replay the conversation with M in his head such as it was, over and over again. He obviously already knew what was going on in Bosanski Brod so didn't need his report and, it was safe to guess, he already knew what was going on in Zvornik. So what was the game?

"Perhaps all I'm actually doing," he thought, "is providing written reports which he'll be using to distance him from what were actually his own orders. It's the only thing that seems to make any sense."

It was quite late in the day when they got within a few miles of the town. "First things first," he thought, "find a place to stay." He had been lucky in Sarajevo for there was a range of cheap places – not that money was a problem but he didn't want to draw attention to himself particularly as he was trying to ask questions as a innocent traveller. He asked his driver about places to stay where they wouldn't ask too many questions not with much hope of getting a meaningful response. But, surprisingly, he received more than the usual grunts. Just a few names came forth, but further enquiries elicited nothing else.

He was let off near the river and Djuric found one of the places mentioned quite quickly. By now it was getting dark and, with a number of armed men patrolling the streets, he decided to get inside and stay there until morning. At dawn, he was rudely awakened by a series of loud bangs. Shelling had begun. He swore. M must have known that an invasion of this place was imminent and here he was – a sitting duck. He cursed M once more and promised he would never doubt Kovac again. Jumping out of bed with no time to wash or shave, he grabbed his backpack and got out to find the roads jammed with hundreds, maybe thousands of people fleeing their homes from advancing Serbs, carrying what few possessions they had managed to grab.

He now had a dilemma. These were almost all Muslims who were fleeing, quite understandably. If he joined them, there would be no mercy from any Serb forces who stopped them. They wouldn't listen to any protestations from him that he was a Serb. He had to find his own way out so that if he was stopped, at least there would be a chance to produce his identity papers.

He began to make his way through relatively empty back alleys whilst the teeming masses of locals desperate to get away were using the main highways. They were making their way south west, further into Bosnia, so he began to go east towards Serbia. But he didn't get far.

"Stop there." The command was clear. Even clearer were the automatic weapons that these six mask-wearing paramilitaries carried. No time for heroics but he took a chance they were Serbs from the language they had spoken, so decided to get his ID out but there was no time to do so. As soon as he put his hand in his pocket, a rifle butt hit him over the head and he found himself in the dust, his ear bleeding profusely. One of them dragged him up onto his feet while another searched his pockets. He had hidden his phone in his backpack as a precaution against muggers but had left it on just in case Kovac called. He was now praying that it wouldn't ring or be found and confiscated before he got released.

"He's a Serb, from Belgrade," the one with his papers said.

"What's a Serb from Belgrade doing here, I wonder?" Djuric started to explain about the travelling before another rifle butt hit him in the stomach. A rough answer came, "I wasn't asking you."

"Take him away."

Djuric found himself on a truck being driven east towards Serbia. Looking out of the back of the truck, he could see station wagons filled with dead bodies and masked militias dragging more corpses out of houses – men, women and children. He was appalled. Further on, he saw the Serb militias going from house to house looting. They were laughing and showing off to each other what they had found. He thought of the thousands of people who he had seen running away and wondered what was going to happen to them, and if they had been caught yet.

As they drove through the town, he saw other units principally the Red

Berets, an elite unit of the Serbian Interior Ministry. Then he knew. This had been a well planned, well executed operation with the blessing of Belgrade and that meant M. He felt sick to his stomach, and not just from the rifle butt. While he felt fairly certain that his release would come when a senior commander knew he was a Serb. The question was, would he live that long? He didn't know.

The next week seemed like an eternity. He was imprisoned with other Croats and Muslims who were in varying stages of confessing to crimes they had probably never committed, but at least a confession stopped the interrogation for a while. He was wondering when it would get round to him and what would he confess to.

"Name?"

"Djuric"

"Nationality?"

"Yugoslav." He was hit across his naked back from behind with a rod of some kind and fell to his knees.

"Nationality?"

"Serb." He was hit again and this time he fell all the way down and stayed. He was hauled up by two guards. The officer in his smart uniform sat unmoved in a chair opposite acting as if he had all the time in the world.

"What are you doing in Zvornik?"

"I'm travelling...." He didn't get a chance to get his story out before a whip lashed his back. He fell to the ground and gasped for breath.

"You're a Muslim who has stolen Serb papers." There was no answer from Djuric who was then kicked viciously in the head. The interrogation continued for a long time or so it seemed to Djuric. Each time he tried to give his story, he was hit. On the last occasion, it was on the back of his legs. This time he couldn't get up and was just left unconscious on the floor. He came to as another pair of guards hauled him up and took him back to the communal cell. His cell mates looked on, some already having the scars to prove their interrogation and others yet to have the pleasure.

Late one evening about two days later, he was called out of the communal cell by a single soldier with a sub-machine gun at the ready. The cell door locked behind him as he was frog-marched away from the camp and he thought, "This is it, the end of the road for me." However, instead of getting a shot in the back of the head and pushed into a mass grave, the soldier handed him his backpack said, "On your way, quickly," then disappeared. Somebody had been looking out for him.

He didn't wait around but set off at a quick limp away from the camp. His first thought was to get back to Belgrade, his second a much better one. Get down to Montenegro to Ivana and take some time to think.

Chapter 29 — Titograd

BOJAN WAS IN Titograd (later to be renamed Podgorice), capital of Montenegro, at the Treasury checking on his colleague, Dragan, who was supposed to be wiring monies into the account set up in Belgrade to finance M's activities. Nothing had arrived for a few months. He knew that the Montenegrin treasury was not particularly flush with funds, but nevertheless he was becoming suspicious and wanted to know what was going on before M noticed. He didn't like to think what M might say to him if he found someone had been siphoning money out of his account. It could be that there was none to send or perhaps something a little more serious. He was going to find out.

Bojan worked his normal day in Belgrade and got the late train to Titograd arriving just in time to check into his hotel and have a simple meal. Bojan was not one to do anything ostentatiously. His upbringing and accountancy background predisposed him to a significant level of meanness when it came to spending money. He rarely did, and when necessity beckoned he might be seen reluctantly counting out his loose change. Perhaps that was also a factor arising from his small stature. At five foot four inches tall, he was usually dwarfed by most, including women which may also have explained why bachelorhood seemed to be a permanent status.

But when it came to business, he had a keen eye and an incredible appetite for detail. He loved it. This was his bread and butter and there was no-one better in the Yugoslav civil service. He knew this account was important and his nose was twitching. When that happened he could almost smell something was not right. Not only was his relationship with M at stake but with that, his entire career. He was determined to examine in detail every possible document he could lay his hands on here and follow the trail wherever it led.

His strategy was to arrive unannounced but be cool and as courteous as he could. Putting Dragan at ease would help him determine if he needed to call in some muscle or not. He already had the necessary ID to gain entry to the building and knew where Dragan's office was. Using the stairs to get to the third floor where the senior bureaucrats had their offices, he headed to the palatially furnished corner office at the far end. Outside the door two secretaries were busy typing. They looked up and, putting his finger to his mouth, quietly opened the door to the main office.

"Good morning Dragan." The man leapt to his feet from behind a very large wooden desk, his eyes looking a little panicky.

"Good morning sir," stuttered the underling. "I wish you had let me know you were coming. I could have sent a car for you."

Bojan, enjoying the man's discomfort, ignored the remark and settled down in the large leather sofa in the corner of the room.

"May I offer you a drink?" Dragan indicated with his hand a well stocked cocktail cabinet.

"Coffee please," replied Bojan. "And while we're waiting can I see your latest summary of tax receipts.

"Of course." Dragan pressed a button on his internal telephone, ordered coffee and the relevant file to be brought in. Bojan didn't like the opulence of the office, nor the well stocked cocktail cabinet. In his experience it was a level of luxury which tended towards complacency. Back in Belgrade, his own office was spartan and deliberately utilitarian, the butt of many jokes – behind his back of course, but he knew them well. In fact, he knew everything that went on in his department both in and out of work. You never knew when information might come in handy, not that he was vengeful or malevolent, he just saw collecting it as how a boss should operate. Standard procedure.

"You have to understand," Dragan began his mitigation, "that the country is virtually bankrupt. Our outgoings are larger than our receipts, and it's getting worse."

"Of course, that could be down to a number of factors." Bojan indicated that he wasn't going to take Dragan's word for anything, or any papers he might have prepared for this eventuality. The requested file was brought in by the Inspector General who was responsible for compiling the data. He was just about to leave when Bojan got up and said to the man, "Let's go to your place." And with that he picked up the file and followed the man out, motioning Dragan himself to stay put.

Once settled in a less plush office, Bojan began to go through the file quickly, asking some detailed questions which indicated to the Montenegrin that Bojan knew what he was talking about and that he would surely find any anomalies if they were there. He didn't expect to find any immediate irregularities. If there existed such inconsistencies, they would be hidden much further down in the accounts. Having covered the summary, he asked to see the tax receipts' breakdown. The Inspector General looked uncomfortable and his comfort didn't improve as the morning progressed. At lunchtime, Dragan put his head round the door and suggested they go out to eat. Bojan declined and waved him away.

Looking at the Inspector General, he took off his glasses to give them a clean and, putting them back on, said, "I would be obliged if you would guide me to where the accounts are not what they should be. I shall find any irregularities be in no doubt about that but it would be to your advantage if you could save me the time."

The red-faced man rummaged around in his desk drawers for a moment and produced another file which he laid on his desk. "I just need to go to another meeting for an hour or so, but you're welcome to sit in my chair at my desk. And I'll have some more coffee sent in, if you would like."

Bojan smiled sardonically and said, "Yes, perhaps your desk would be better. And the coffee would be welcome."

He move across to sit in the Inspector General's chair and it didn't take long to find what looked like the scam he was expecting. However, the details did show that substantial amounts were still outgoing on a monthly basis and had been for a while but didn't show where they were going. Bojan tallied the dates with Dragan's appointment and whistled quietly to himself. The question was what to do about it? Was it Dragan's own initiative or had it been done locally and timed to point the finger at the Serb?

There was no doubt that M needed the funds, although now that he was Serbian President Bojan could legally use Serbian treasury funds for some of M's more transparent activities. Nevertheless, it was a matter of pride to Bojan to get things straight. So he had to confront Dragan. He looked at his watch – just after lunch. Making his way back to Dragan's office he noticed how empty the place was. Discipline was clearly not what it should be. Dragan hadn't returned so Bojan settled himself in Dragan's chair behind his desk with the incriminating documents, and waited.

He didn't have to wait long. Dragan came back to his office at about two thirty. "What time do you call this?" he asked.

"These are normal working hours here. We stay on until six thirty in the evening, so it works out," replied Dragan, sitting on the leather sofa. He wasn't going to insist on having his own chair, but he added, "So you found it then?"

Bojan was a little surprised by his nonchalant attitude and said nothing. Dragan was looking at him carefully, "You really didn't know, did you? I would have told you if I had known. I just assumed you knew."

Bojan was now sitting up straight in the chair, "Knew what?"

"God, you didn't know!" exclaimed Dragan. Bojan, who had been in charge of the conversation was now feeling at a distinct disadvantage.

"Spit it out man," Bojan was getting impatient.

"Well, no sooner had I got here, than I received a message from an impeccable source in Belgrade amending the bank account details that you had given me. I just assumed you knew."

"Whose account is it?"

"I don't know."

"What do you mean you don't know? You have to know the name of the account you're sending monies to."

"Not this one. Just the account number and the bank."

Bojan sat back and stared at his underling who was now looking quite embarrassed. He leaned over the desk, "What bank is it?"

Dragan walked over to his desk, took a file from one of the trays and extracted a sheet of paper. He handed it over to Bojan who paled when he saw it.

"Bloody hell!" he exclaimed. There was not a lot more to say. Bojan picked up all the incriminating evidence and put the documents safely in his briefcase.

Bojan's mind was in a whirl as he walked back to his hotel. It was not a state he usually found himself in and he didn't like it, not one little bit. He needed a strong drink, again not a state he usually found himself in. He was sitting at the bar in the hotel when his phone rang. Such was his disorientation that he didn't even check to see who it was before accepting the call. It was Kovac. "The very man I need at the moment," thought Bojan elatedly. But Kovac had other things on his mind.

"Where are you?" he asked.

"Titograd," replied Bojan. "By the way, everybody thinks you're dead. Where *are* you?"

"Yes, I know, but forget about that. Look, Djuric needs some help quickly."

"Where is he?"

"Don't exactly know, but he's been caught up in the Zvornik invasion. He's managed to get away and is heading into your area. I'll send you his number. Ring him please." With that the line went dead but a solitary ding meant that a text had been received.

Bojan looked at his phone. Yes, he had Djuric's number but he also had another unregistered number which he presumed was from Kovac. "He must have changed his number," he thought. "Perhaps he's in trouble too." As he meticulously put the numbers and their details into his contact page, his mind went back to their last encounter in Belgrade when Kovac was expressing some disquiet about M putting tanks on to the streets of his home city. He himself had also begun to have similar misgivings, though for a different reason.

He decided to call Djuric and once done, he would call Kovac back. Djuric was a mystery to Bojan; they had never met, although he had heard how good an organiser Djuric was and that he had been Tito's adjutant. It didn't take much guessing to assume Djuric was fleeing from someone, maybe some of the armed men he had heard were operating in Bosnia and the civil servant was not a physically brave man. So he procrastinated for a few hours, as civil servants are wont to do, while he got used to the idea of rescuing the man.

He desperately wanted Kovac's advice about the bank accounts and what he should do, and that was not going to come until Djuric's problem was sorted. So he made the call.

"Hello"

"Hello, my name is Bojan. You don't know me, but...."

Djuric interrupted. "Yes, I know who you are."

"Ah. Well, I've just had a call from Kovac."

"Can you help me?"

"Er... well. Where are you?"

"Not entirely sure, but somewhere in Southern Serbia, I think."

"I gather you need a lift to Montenegro?"

" A bit more than that. I haven't eaten for three days. I've nowhere to stay and no money."

"Oh!" This was turning out to be a little beyond Bojan's standard capabilities.

"Look. I could send someone up to you, if I knew where you were."

"OK. The last place I passed was Uzice. I can get back there within a few hours."

" Yes, go there and I'll call you back." Bojan put the phone down and sighed. This was not the sort of thing Bojan did. He called Dragan and explained the problem.

"Leave it with me," he said. He twisted arms and got someone to drive across the border to Uzice that evening. The drive took a few hours by which time darkness had fallen but after a few phone calls back and forth, rescuer and rescued eventually met and the recovery was complete. Djuric flopped in the back of the car, exhausted, hungry, wet and cold.

"Where's Bojan?" he asked shivering.

"Couldn't make it,"

"Where are we going?"

"Titograd," came the answer.

"That's great." And with that Djuric fell asleep.

Chapter 30 — Sarajevo

No need for rumours anymore. The city was terrified. Main thorough-
fares were blocked, other local streets were deserted, traders who were bold
enough to open for business had few customers. Those, and there were some,
who had foreseen conflict had already queued up at their bank to extract as
much of their savings as they could. Most, however, were still naïve enough to
believe no-one would dare to attack this city so didn't bother with the queues.
The banks were now closed and not likely to open any time soon.

Muslim Green Beret snipers were on the high buildings in the centre
attempting to protect the population on the ground, but the attack was
coming from up on the hills surrounding the city. For this encounter, the
Serbian Army had also brought their Yugoslav-produced 105mm M-7 self
propelled guns plus the self-propelled 82mm mortar mounted on an M-60PB
variant of the standard armoured personnel carrier. But they were still heavily
reliant on their old Soviet and US guns. But as with Kijevo, even old artillery
will defeat no artillery at all. The Police Academy of Sarajevo situated up there
had already been attacked and taken over by Serb paramilitaries under the
control of a man not unknown to Sarajevans, Radavan Karadzic.

As a young man, many in the city had dismissed him as just coming from
a peasant family in Montenegro, which was true. Ismet had heard such things
from his father regularly and gathered that it was a regular topic of fun for the
taxi drivers. Well, the fun was about to stop. He may not have been Bosnian
by birth but that didn't matter a jot. He was now a powerful man at the head
of a well armed militia and intent on bringing Sarajevo to heel.

Still thinking they would be safe, a large crowd including Ismet and Ana
carrying the baby followed by his father Nurija Terzic, began to march down
towards the city centre with hundreds of others joining as they went. Ismet's
mother stayed at home thinking the protest was a waste of time. As the leaders
led the crowd up towards Grbavica, the unwitting followers were moving ever
closer to the hidden Serb militias. Suddenly shots began to ring out, then a

hand grenade was thrown. A woman fell. Suada Dilberovic, a twenty year old medical student, was the first to die.

The crowd panicked. Ismet lost sight of Ana who was being pushed by the frightened crowd further and further away still holding Danil. In his anxiety to look backwards towards his wife and baby, Ismet slipped and fell. Before he could get up, he was being trampled by other people all fleeing the gunshots, people who bore him no ill will but were just trying to save themselves. He had no idea where his father was and, to be truthful, it wasn't at the top of his mind.

He had unconsciously curled up into a foetal position to protect himself. Innocent people fell over him and on top of him. Soon he was at the bottom of a pile of bodies, some moving and others not. Gradually those who could move did, and with an enormous effort he managed to wriggle free leaving behind bodies that were never going to get up again. Some stragglers were hobbling, others just crawling, anything to get away from the guns.

Blood seemed to be everywhere. Initially, Ismet thought it was from those who had died but he soon saw his own dripping down his face from a gash on his head. He brushed it away and tried again to look back to where he last saw Ana and Danil. Nothing. The place was now empty except for the dead. He made his way home hoping his wife and child would be there, but they weren't. He rang his mother. No, his father had not come home and no, Ana was not there either. He rang her parents out of desperation knowing they were Serbs.

"Hello, it's Ismet. Have you seen Ana?"

"No, why would we? Isn't she with you?"

"No. We went on the march. We......" He stopped as her mother burst into tears. There was a moments silence until her father came on the phone.

"Where is she?" he demanded.

"There were Serb militias who began to fire on us."

"You are responsible for my daughter and my grandson." His father-in-law was not so much concerned as angry.

Ismet took a moment to process the situation and decided to take the initiative. "Do you know if Stefan is up there with them?"

There was a pause on the other end of the line. "How dare you....." The rest of the tirade showed Ismet better than anything else the divide that was coming. His father-in-law finished with, "I knew Ana shouldn't have married a Muslim. She's coming back to live with us."

Although Ismet was still groggy he determined that he would go back out and look for his wife and son.

Most of the population of Sarajevo went to bed that night in total shock at what had happened and fearful about what might be next. The latter was easily discovered the following morning when all flights from the airport were suspended due to tanks on the runway and its approaches. International civilian connections had been cut making way for a metamorphosis. Sarajevo now had a military airfield instead with the Serb army in total control.

Every taxi driver knew what this meant, at least for them. Nurija Terzic, who had himself staggered back home late the previous evening, got into his taxi and tried in vain to get to the airport. When he was turned around by camouflaged Serb soldiers, he put his middle finger up in the air as a gesture of protest and went back to the city centre, where his cab was hit by a burst of machine gun fire. He survived but the cab didn't. No cab, no work, no money. It was the same for many.

Whilst the Army was occupied at the airport, Serb militia snipers had occupied the top floor of the Holiday Inn, where Karadzic had previously made his HQ. They were carelessly picking off anyone and everyone they could see, causing even the brave who had ventured out to scurry back into the relative safety of their homes. Bosnian troops were hurriedly despatched to silence the guns. They quickly stormed the hotel dragging off every Serb they could find. The sniper fire stopped but they couldn't stop the artillery fire from the surrounding Serbian forces who pounded the city mercilessly, Russian style.

Ana and her baby were nowhere near the centre. They had been taken in by a kindly family who had scolded her for taking a baby on such a dangerous protest. She was desperate to contact Ismet but the phone lines were down, probably deliberately cut. The retired couple persuaded her to stay overnight for the baby's sake and start again in the morning.

She was up early, even before the Danil was awake and got her things together. Not wanting to upset the elderly couple, she wrote a quick note of thanks and quietly closed the front door. The smell of cordite pervaded the air occupying the layer below the mist that hung over the whole valley. Her parents' house was the nearest, so she decided to stop there to clean up before going on to her own rented apartment. It was still early when she arrived and knocked on the door. A delay in answering indicated her parents were still in bed but the door was soon opened after a tentative look through the window at who might be calling at such an unearthly hour.

Her mother flung her arms around her daughter and almost dragged her inside. Her father was just coming down the stairs to see what the commotion was about.

"You're staying here," he announced.

"Let's not have this conversation now," overruled his wife leading her daughter and grandson upstairs. "Call Ismet and say she's safe."

"The lines are still down," said Mr Lukic dismissively. His mind was already turned towards his work. "I suppose no-one will be turning up to the factory today," he added, speaking to no-one but himself. "I wonder how long all this is going to go on?"

Unknown to Mr Lukic, it was to go on, and on, and on. '*Here was a professional army conducting a campaign of unrelenting violence against the inhabitants of a European city so as to reduce them to a state of medieval deprivation in which they were in constant fear of death.*' So ran the eventual War Crimes Indictment. There was nowhere safe for a Sarajevan, not at home, at school or even in a hospital.

Bosnian Serb forces maintained their total blockade of the city including major access roads which cut off supplies of food and medicine as well as the city's utilities. Compared with the besieging force, the Bosnian government forces were very poorly armed almost totally reliant on Bosnian black market criminals to smuggle arms into the city through Serb lines, and raids on Serb-held positions within the city. An international arms embargo declared by the UN ostensibly applied to all parties to the Bosnian conflict and meant well, but had placed the defenders of Sarajevo in an impossible position.

But the population of Sarajevo needed more than arms to survive. Water was available from a well situated at the brewery although that was within reach of Serbian guns but food, medical supplies and fuel were the immediate needs of the population. Rumours were beginning to surface of a tunnel being built underneath the airport runway to link the city with Bosnian territory on the other side of the airport controlled by the UN.

Ismet wanted, needed to do something. "The sooner the siege is ended, the sooner I can reunite my family," he thought. So he signed on to help dig the tunnel. When he arrived the foreman on duty took one look at him and said, "Show me your hands."

Ismet showed his banker's hands and assured the man that he could work. The foreman looked sceptical but said, "Pick up a shovel and fill the wheelbarrows with the debris."

The work was already well underway when he arrived. It looked like a TV set from a WW2 film. Men were toiling away with picks and shovels attacking soil, rock whatever was in their way. Others were assigned to carry the hundreds of cubic meters of debris away in wheelbarrows with yet others constructing timber struts to hold the roof in place as the digging progressed. It was a twenty-four hour operation with men working eight hour shifts, and by the end of his first shift of digging, Ismet's hands were cracked and sore, his arms bruised, his back hurt and his whole body ached. But he refused to give up. When he turned up for his next shift, the same foreman took one look at him.

"Are you OK to work?"

"Sure," answered Ismet putting on the best front he could.

"I'm not sure you are. Show me your hands."

Ismet obliged. "Right," said the foreman, "I'm changing your duty to the wheelbarrows. Grab one over there and get to work."

It was slightly better on his hands and arms, but by the end of the shift his back was giving him some severe pain. He was paid one packet of cigarettes per day and although he did not smoke he knew they were a prized bartering item and didn't want to give up.

The foreman came to the face of the tunnel and saw Ismet working. "Don't bend your back. Keep it straight. Use your arms to lift the barrow."

Ismet tried but by the end of the shift his arms would hardly lift anything let alone a wheelbarrow full of soil and stones. So the wheelbarrow attempt didn't last long either and he was reassigned again, this time to laying pipes through the tunnel for oil and cables for electricity and telephony. As he looked in the mirror each day, he could see his body shape was changing. His shoulders were becoming broader, his chest was deepening and stomach showing signs of a decent 'six pack'. But he was so exhausted at the end of a shift that he could hardly walk let alone source meals and cook for himself. He realised that if he was to continue he would have to give up his independence and go to live with his parents between shifts.

His mother had no idea what he had been doing and was horrified when she saw her son arrive off shift. She immediately took charge, sending him straight to bed where he slept continuously for ten hours just managing to log in for his next shift. Not having to feed himself made an enormous difference to Ismet's mentality. He could concentrate on what he was doing for the city. From this point onwards, he began to recover somewhat and learned to pace himself much better.

His father tried to follow his son to help with the tunnel but was turned away. "We have enough labour for the moment," he was told. Mrs Terzic was glad her husband had not been recruited. "I'm not sure I can deal with two of you working there." Yet he felt he needed to do something to help his city in this time of war, but didn't know what. All he could do was to take the cigarettes that Ismet was receiving and negotiate the best deal he could for whatever they needed. He did enjoy the cut and thrust of bartering but it was not really fulfilling.

One day he returned home with vegetables and some meat, something they had not had for months to find his wife crying. He dumped his goods in the galley kitchen and went over to see what the matter was.

"I go out occasionally to meet my friends if I can, and I see ruins all around." She sobbed. "Every building has been damaged. There's not one which hasn't been hit by something."

The Army backed by Russian expertise and troops were now deploying their 128mm YMRL-32 and M-63 multiple-rocket launchers as well as Soviet FROG-7 surface-to-surface missiles. Still quite old, these had a range of 100 kilometers, ideal for Sarajevo. It didn't matter that they weren't guided, the whole city was down in the valley below. They couldn't miss.

Husband put his arms around his wife. "I know," he said quietly. "But we will get through all this, and we will rebuild every damaged building, if it takes decades."

By the end of the conflict some thirty five thousand buildings in Sarajevo had been completely destroyed and between nine and fourteen thousand people killed during the siege, with Bosnian Serb military casualties numbering just over two thousand killed or missing.

"Today, in the Markale marketplace," she stopped as if she couldn't actually say the words. "The people were shelled, and there were bodies all over the place, some killed, some wounded and crawling away to try and get to safety. A few moments later, and I would have been there. I could have died today." She began weeping. Her husband tried to console her as best he could.

She carried on between sobs, "It was a massacre. I saw doctors and nurses rushing to get there, but they were completely overwhelmed. And yesterday twelve people were killed while they were just waiting in line for water. They just wanted water." Her voice had risen almost to a scream.

He was quiet. What could he say? He was tempted to excuse himself and go, but he knew that was the coward's way out. He would stay in tonight if that's what it took. As he held his wife he realised that he had changed. He had become a listener whereas before he was just a talker. He was taking more notice of his wife than he had ever done and he began to feel ashamed. In the past he had been totally consumed with himself, his mates and his job. Yes, this war had changed him. He went on to think what a selfish father he had been. No wonder his son had wanted to get away.

"When you go out tomorrow," he asked his wife, " will you be able to have a look at the block of flats where Ismet was. See what it looks like, how damaged it is. Don't go too far just in case."

She nodded. That was something she could do.

"The siege affected all sectors of Sarajevo's population. UNICEF reported that of the estimated 65,000 to 80,000 children in the city, at least 40% had been directly shot at by snipers; 51% had seen someone killed; 39% had seen one or more family members killed; 19% had witnessed a massacre; 48% had their home occupied by someone else; 73% had their home attacked or shelled; and 89% had lived in underground shelters. It is probable that the psychological trauma suffered during the siege will bear heavily on the lives of these children in the years to come."

Chapter 31 — Podgorica (formerly Titograd)

IT WAS GONE midnight before Djuric got back to Podgorica and he was tired, very tired. He had asked the driver to take him somewhere near Ivana's apartment rather than risk anyone knowing exactly where he was going to be holed up. The driver just nodded when he was given an approximate address. The car stopped and Djuric stumbled out of the car, mumbling thanks to his rescuer and cautiously made his way through the estate where Ivana lived, then down the pitch black street to where he thought her block was. Yes there it was. Somehow he got up the steps and fell against her door thinking he was making a huge noise that would awaken her and she would let him in. Not so. It took some persistent banging to bring her to the back window to see who was trying to get in. She saw a body but didn't recognise Djuric until he turned his face toward her.

Once the latches and bolts were drawn, the door opened allowing Djuric to tumble in. Ivana gazed at him thinking he was the worse for wear.

"Sorry. I need help."

"It certainly looks like you do," said a sceptical Ivana. She drew a little closer, "You smell, and it's not of drink. Where on earth have you been?"

"Sorry," came the mumble. "Can I stay the night, please? We can talk in the morning."

She stared at him. "Do I have an option? You can sleep on the mattress in the spare room. You know the way." With that she closed the door, left him in the hall and went back to her room and shut her door firmly.

Djuric was in no state to argue or do much else except stumble into the second bedroom and fall down on the mattress. At least it was dry and he was secure. Yes, Ivana would warm up in the morning when he told her the story..... and he must phone Kovac, and of course Bojan, and what was he going to do about M, and what about...... He finally drifted off with his mind still working overtime.

He awoke in the morning to the sound of a vacuum cleaner. He remembered his mother doing the cleaning every morning when she got up at the start of the day. Perhaps it was something every woman did. It seemed safer to lie where he was until the noise finished which gave him time to review the last few days. He was lucky to be alive. Yes he had phone calls to make, but first he needed to talk to Ivana. From what he could recall, she wasn't best pleased to see him last night.

The noise stopped, which was the signal for him to crawl off the mattress and head for the bathroom for a much needed shower. Ivana must have gone into the kitchen for he made it without her seeing him. Thirty minutes later he was clean but his clothes were still dirty and smelly, so he walked into the kitchen in his underwear ready for any sarcastic comments she would make. Nothing from her except surprise and then horror as she gazed at the marks on his body where he had been crudely interrogated.

"Oh my God. Where did you get those bruises?"

"A long story," he said, "in the meantime can I use your washing machine?"

"Give them to me." She took his clothes and said, "there's a dressing gown behind the bathroom door. I suggest you put it on."

She brought out a small medical pack and once he had slipped the gown back down to his waist, she began to gently apply cream to his bruises.

"Perhaps you'd better tell me the story."

Djuric didn't think it was a time for playing any more games, so he just told her everything, from Kosovo to Slovenia, from Croatia to Bosnia.

"Your tone suggests that you're not a fan of M anymore?" She enquired.

"I don't think so," he replied.

"Well, you'd better make up your mind because his maniacs have just kidnapped the Bosnian President and right now they are shelling Sarajevo with everything they've got."

Djuric looked up quickly and winced. This was news to him. But Ivana hadn't finished, "They've also 'cleansed' all Bosnian Muslims from the north of the country, around Brcko and Doboj."

She turned to face him. "This is what you've wrought on the country. You and your thugs. And don't be mistaken, it won't stop here. Mark my words, this is not just ethnic cleansing, it's going to be genocide."

Djuric looked mortified. "I swear I had no idea this was what he planned. Everything we did was political and constitutional with a few demos here and there. We never planned this and I want no part of it."

There. He had said it. He stopped for a moment to replay in his head what he had just said. Did he mean it? Was that the end for him? Had this moment also come for Kovac?

Ivana looked at him. "Is that what you really mean?" she asked.

"I need to phone Kovac," he said not directly replying to her question. He jumped up and walked into the bedroom to rummage around for his phone. Hurriedly he called his boss. Ivana got up and left him. A few moments later he heard the outside door close. She'd gone.

Before he could call Kovac, his phone rang. It was Bojan. "Just calling to check you're safe," he said.

"Yes, thank you. You saved my life," replied Djuric gratefully. "And yes I'm with friends and safe now. Not sure what I'll do next but I'll leave that to Kovac."

"Of course." Bojan changed the subject. "May I ask you a question? You may not be able to answer it, but I can't get through to Kovac at the moment."

"If I can," answered Djuric.

"When M set up his team, my job was to take charge of the Treasuries of the republics we controlled to help finance the activities that M was planning. The odd thing is that someone changed the bank details of where these monies were due to be deposited."

"I'm afraid I can't help you there but I'm sure Kovac could. He and you were part of the inner circle and I wasn't."

Djuric sensed the tension in Bojan's voice. It sounded like a great deal of money had gone missing. "Sorry I can't help." When the call was over, Djuric sat down to think about what Bojan had revealed. Clearly something was not right. He wondered what was going on and who stood to benefit.

His phone rang. It looked as if it was going to be a busy morning.

"Did you get out safely?" asked Kovac as soon as he picked up.

"Yes, thanks to you and Bojan. I owe you both."

"What happened?" Kovac was anxious to see if Djuric had changed his mind as he had done, but didn't want to push him. It had to be his own decision. Djuric was happy to tell the story again with Kovac listening intently without interrupting.

"I'm glad you're safe," said Kovac, "but you know the siege of Sarajevo is not over by a long way." Djuric recalled that Ivana had said something very similar not more than an hour ago. "Karadzic has brought tanks down from the hill where they have been shelling the city centre and they're now trying to cut the city in half."

Djuric paused to take in what Kovac had just said. "You're in Sarajevo?"

"No, but not far away. I'm actually in Travnik which is north of Sarajevo."

"Why didn't you tell me where you were?" Djuric was a little put out that Kovac didn't trust him.

"You were, maybe still are, working for M. Remember," Kovac reminded him.

Djuric paused. "Are you safe?" he asked changing the subject. Kovac smiled down the line.

"I think so, for the moment. I'm in a mainly Muslim city but they are very friendly. I'm not sure they know I'm a Serb so it's a bit unnerving. Sarajevo has it a lot worse."

Djuric was trying to take it all in. From what Kovac was saying, Sarajevo was now a death trap. To think he'd actually been there. He knew it was in a valley surrounded by hills, very easy to blockade especially if Serbs had control of the airport which he assumed they had. It would be what he would have done.

"I'm watching Sarajevo television as we speak," continued Kovac. "It's saying they've occupied the city centre district of Grbavica and a column of armoured vehicles have crossed the Skenderija bridge to get to the Presidency Building."

Djuric was still concerned for his friend's precarious position. "Have you got enough food and water if it turns nasty where you are?"

"Maybe. Depends how long this lasts. I think M just wants Serb populated areas so I think we're safe here in Travnik."

Djuric could now hear rumbles in the background. "That sounds quite near you." he said.

"That's the TV from Sarajevo. Bosnian Muslims are resisting but no match for the Army, or the Serb militias for that matter. They definitely have the weaponry but the Bosnians have the feet on the ground. If they stop one tank on one of the narrow roads, they can block the whole column at least for a day or so."

Djuric was quiet again. It had all changed so fast. One minute he was fully engaged in organising demos, the next he was in an all out war. Finally he said, "I guess you never thought M's plans would end up like this?"

"Well, it was always a possibility. I knew that General Petar and the Russian fellow were looking to beef up the army and its weaponry, so it wasn't much of a leap of faith to see where things could go." He paused for a moment waiting for Djuric to concede the point. But the reference to Smolov had jogged his memory.

"I had a call from Bojan earlier," said Djuric.

"He's a good man," confirmed Kovac.

"He asked me about a change of bank account for monies coming from Montenegro to finance M's work. Sounds like a lot of money has gone missing."

"Really." Kovac sounded surprised. "I was never part of the finance side of things. It was strictly between M, Bojan and General Petar."

Both men were silent for a moment. Djuric spoke first, "When you mentioned Petar and this Smolov character something clicked in my brain. I wonder if that money was really going to the Russian to pay for the weapons that Petar wanted."

"Could be. Financing weapons doesn't come cheap, even Russian ones." commented Kovac.

"But that sounds like black market dealing," said Djuric.

Kovac laughed, but then became serious. "Is that worse than genocide? We've been used, you and I, and Bojan come to that. M always planned to convert the Yugoslavian army to a Serbian one and launch it against his enemies. So if you're asking if I've switched sides, the answer is yes."

More silence. Djuric was not quite ready to say what he had blurted out to Ivana and Kovac was not going to push it. Suddenly there was the sound of smashing glass and a 'woomph' sound.

"I think the Sarajevo TV station had just been hit. The TV has now gone off air."

It was late afternoon when Ivana returned and seemed surprised to find Djuric still there. She smelt food being cooked in the kitchen and noted that the room in which he had slept had been cleaned and a much better aroma was pervading the whole atmosphere. She smiled a little to herself but made no comment as she swept past him going to her own bedroom. Djuric expected nothing less. She was an independent lady and he admired that.

"Please make yourself at home in your room," she said coming out of her bedroom into the kitchen. "By the way," she asked, "I'm Montenegrin and this is my kitchen."

"Just trying to say 'thank you'."

"How long are you planning on staying?" was her riposte.

After hearing about the possibility of missing money, Kovac rang Bojan who proceeded to explain why he was in Montenegro and what he had found whilst examining Treasury documents.

"The issue I have," explained Bojan, "is the bank it went to."

"Which bank is that?" asked Kovac.

"One in the Cayman Islands."

"Oh!" exclaimed Kovac. "You weren't aware of that?"

"Of course not. It's probably to be used to purchase arms and line some-one's pockets into the bargain." Bojan was annoyed about having it hidden from him as the money man, just as much as the probability of it being illegal. He prided himself on being on top of the detail.

"Are you going to challenge M?" asked Kovac.

"I ought to mention it when I get back," said Bojan.

"I would think very carefully about that," cautioned Kovac.

"Why?" Bojan, while being an expert accountant was rather naïve in the ways of the world.

"Well," started Kovac wondering how to put it diplomatically. "If you weren't told, they didn't want you to know. If you confess that you do know......" He tailed off, hoping Bojan would get the message without having to spell it out.

"Oh. Yes. I see." Bojan was hurriedly getting up to speed.

"Watch your step, my friend." Kovac ended the call with Bojan wondering what on earth he should do.

Kovac was sitting back musing on the call and wondering which way the diminutive accountant would go, when the TV came back on air. Pictures were being shown of the UN's General McKenzie, who didn't seem to know which side was which, leading a convoy of weapons and military hardware out of the TO barracks in Sarajevo escorted by Serb militias. Kovac was astonished.

But within minutes the convoy had been attacked by Bosnian militias who were refusing to allow such weaponry to leave their control and go to the very Serbs up on the hill who were bombarding them. In the mêlée, the camera caught pictures of burning vehicles, some dead bodies, a VW Golf crammed full of AK47s, and then the emergence of the released Bosnian President to tumultuous shouts of glee.

It transpired later that a final purge of Army Generals meant that thirty eight of them were relieved of their duties, including General Petar, and the Serbian Army put under the control of one; Ratko Mladic.

Chapter 32 — Croatia

BOJAN HAD LEFT Montenegro and arrived back in Belgrade to resume his normal work routine. He was an habitual man both at work and at home; suits, shirts, shoes all neatly closeted and all worn in the same order; a man who could easily have been kidnapped for his routes never varied.

He had decided to take Kovac's advice and keep his head down as far as M was concerned. Nobody else knew he had been to Montenegro so, once he had sworn Dragan to keep his mouth shut, he would maintain his silence. The situation didn't sit well with him for he was a stickler for detail and, as a good auditor, he didn't like anomalies. But now he was in his office surrounded by things and people he knew with a satisfying pile of papers on his desk. He was trying hard to get back to normal and put Montenegro behind him when his routine was interrupted by a phone call. It was Dragan.

"I thought I ought to let you know," started Dragan.

"Know what?" asked Bojan absent-mindedly, his mind still on the job he was doing.

"I've just had an order from the same person to change the account again."

He suddenly had Bojan's complete attention. "How do you know it was the same man?"

"He used the same code word."

"You never mentioned anything about a code word," Bojan said accusingly.

"Well, if you remember, you were quite short with me. We didn't exactly have very long together." Dragan was a bit defensive.

"Sorry about that," said Bojan, but didn't offer any further explanation. "So, was this code word agreed between you from the beginning?"

"Yes, but I never expected anyone to call me except you. At first, I thought you were in on it."

Bojan was scratching his head. "How did you know the whole thing was authorised by M and not some scam?"

"I'm not totally sure it was, but I knew the voice."

Bojan began to get really frustrated with Dragan, "Whose voice?"

"General Petar. He gave me a code word and said if anyone calls with that word, they would be speaking on his authority."

"And what changes has he, or his sidekick made?"

"Oh. Same bank, just a different account number from now on."

Bojan was thinking back to the conversation he had had with Kovac. This was getting very murky and definitely illegal. He had to distance himself from it somehow.

"You still there?" Dragan was asking. Bojan had been so taken up with his own precarious position that he had forgotten Dragan was still on the line.

"Er, yes. So just carry on, I think. There's not much else you can do is there?"

"Not really. Anyway, I'm glad somebody else knows."

Bojan thought, "I wish I didn't know." The rest of the day went slowly and he didn't get much work done thinking about his options. How could he distance himself from this and still keep his job? After all, he was still paying Kovac and Djuric and others whom Djuric had used to ignite the demonstrations. If he left, he would have to get someone he trusted to keep paying them, and him. As an accountant, money was usually the first and last thing he thought about. He didn't have any family to worry about, no wife or children. No regrets. He had come to terms with who he was and what his skills were. He would admit that on occasion he would have liked some evening company but although he could afford it, he was a shy man when it came to people he didn't know. Thinking about family, he did have a brother.

Yes. Where on earth was he? In Zagreb, he thought. They hadn't spoken in years and never really got on. He was the extrovert whereas Bojan was the introvert. He found himself daydreaming about his childhood with his brother for a few moments and an idea began to grow in his head. The last news he had from Vicktor was that he and a friend had started a night club venture in Zagreb. How long ago was that? Must be all of ten years. He wondered how Vicktor was getting on with all the trouble in Croatia. Perhaps he ought to call, if he could find a number for him.

"Hello, just wondering how you're getting on with all the fighting that's happening."

Vicktor was startled, "Is that you Bojan? I can't believe it."

"Just hoping you are safe and well?"

"Sure," Vicktor was always a glass half full type of guy. "All good. There's no fighting here. All very quiet."

"Excellent." Bojan paused wondering if his brother would invite him down or whether he would have to make the suggestion.

"What are you doing these days?" asked Vicktor.

"Still in Belgrade looking after the Party's money. You know me." Bojan tried to make a joke about his boring life.

"Look, why don't you come over and visit us." Bojan breathed a sigh of relief.

"What a great idea," replied Bojan. "Let me look at the diary and I'll get back to you. That sounds really good." He didn't want to sound desperate.

"You'll have to plan your journey carefully. I think there's a bit of trouble around the Banja Luka area."

Bojan decided to see what Croatian newspapers were saying about Banja Luka. He didn't believe that the Belgrade media was accurate, more like a propaganda machine for M. As he read through the papers, he was shocked.

Refugees were arriving at different Croatian towns and cities in their thousands. Apparently, the stories they carried were so extreme that the national press based in Zagreb didn't believe them at first. Mass killings, villages burnt to the ground, torture of innocent civilians simply because they were Muslims living in the Serb dominated territory of Southern Bosnia. In some villages the men, particularly the community leaders, were separated from the women and children to be carted off and often never heard of again. Even as they fled, the refugees were harassed and robbed of jewellery and money, sometimes a lifetime's savings. Bojan was stunned.

Jakov had been trying to defend his village with the other men and, whilst hiding next to his father's dead body, had overheard Serb militia guards talk about the refugees going to Split. So that's where he headed. It wasn't an easy journey, or a short one but there were plenty of people in a similar positions going in the same direction. Chatting with strangers, even in these circumstances, didn't come naturally to him so he just marched on. Day after day, sleeping rough at night. A man on a mission eventually arriving at the Split camp at the end of yet another long day. He subtly bypassed the UN formalities and immediately started searching for Vesna and the two children. They had to be somewhere here, but it was a vast camp.

Day after day he searched asking everyone if they'd seen a single mum with two children. There were lots of young women with two children, many of whom were also searching for their own men. Without photographs to show anyone, he knew it was a daunting prospect and very rapidly became dispirited. After the first day of ad hoc searching and not getting anywhere, he decided in the small hours of the night when he couldn't sleep, that he needed to be more systematic. But after a further two days and no result, he was becoming frantic. Perhaps he should have registered after all, then he could have asked where his family were. For all he knew, Vesna was also moving around the camp looking for him. He could have missed her by a few hundred yards and neither of them would ever have known. The people he asked were not antagonistic, most were also looking for someone but, understandably, they were interested only in their own family. They just shrugged and he moved on. It seemed hopeless.

On day five his eyes lit up as he saw one of the old men who used to sit with his father outside the village shop. He ran across the narrow space that separated one tent from another trying not to step in the mud.

"Hello, I'm Jakov, Mr Tomic's son."

The old man looked at him closely with his watery eyes and recognition finally dawned.

"Yes, I remember Tomic. We were at school together. He was a fine young man. You know we played football together, in the same team. He was a good friend. Who did you say you were?

Jakov realised that the old man was confused and disorientated but he had no alternative but to try and get something useful. So he kept the conversation going trying to bring the old man's recollections up to date. Jakov remembered someone saying that the memory was like a stack of china. If you pulled a plate from the middle, the whole thing would come crashing down. So the young man allowed the old man to meander through his life with the occasional effort to bring the present to mind.

Where is he?"

Jakov, thinking dementia had taken a real hold for the past was still dominating the old man's memory, said, "Who?"

The old man, suddenly lucid, snapped, "Tomic, of course. Who did you think I meant?"

Jakov's hopes revived somewhat and replied, "I'm afraid he didn't make it. But now I'm looking for my wife and children. Can you help?"

"Who are you again?"

"Jakov, Tomic's son."

"Yes I remember. Where is he?"

"I'm afraid he died on the way."

"Who are you again?"

Jakov realised that the conversation had gone as far as it was going to go, so he thanked the old man and started moving again round the adjacent tents.

"They have to be nearby," he thought. The tents were set out in rows, so it wasn't difficult to go through this area of the camp row by row from where he was. Suddenly he heard a shout, "Daddy, Daddy." It was his daughter Zora. Her calls prompted Vesna to come running with baby Ivan in her arms. There was a great reunion. They had lost their house, their land, their livelihood but at least they were all together, even if it was in a UN refugee camp.

Bojan, still watching television, could hardly believe it. "Surely this can't be the Army, and if it is independent militias, why isn't the Federal Army stopping all this?" he said out loud.

He tuned to Zagreb television to hear more. Reports kept on coming about neighbours killing neighbours, people who had lived alongside each other for years; men forced to commit crimes against each other for the sadistic gratification of their captors. Sometimes those on grave digging duties would themselves being the last victim shot and then pushed into the mass graves they had been forced to dig for their friends.

"Where has all this hatred come from?" he asked himself. "And who has stoked all this?"

Bojan's view of M and the strategies he was pursuing was beginning to change. "This is not what I signed up for," he said firmly to himself. So this is what Kovac meant.

He suddenly felt an urgency to get away. So in the way accountants do things, he began to list what he needed to do to set his affairs in order. It would only take a day or two to make arrangements for salaries to be paid, then he would ring his brother and go. As far as his work was concerned, he decided not to give any notice or resign, merely disappear. If he wanted to come back when it had all settled down, he felt sure he could find some excuse but he might decide to go for a change. "Why not," he asked himself. He could get a job anywhere if he wanted one.

Within a day or so, he was driving through northern Serbia towards Croatia. He wasn't sure about whether as a Serb he would be welcome at the border crossing, so he took his brother's advice and went across at a remote point where there was no official border point. The journey through lanes and even farmyards, was tortuous and frustrating but he knew it was the only safe way. Besides he was in no real hurry. On another occasion he might have enjoyed the countryside and the mountains, but not this time.

He was soon back on the main roads leading to Zagreb. As he reached the city, he began to see miles of refugee camps. "Who are all these people," he asked himself. It was a question he asked Vicktor once he had found where he and his friend lived.

"Those will be Croats who were expelled last year from Serb held areas in Croatia."

"But," protested Bojan, "there are hundreds, maybe thousands of them."

Vicktor raised his eyebrows, "Oh we're not the only place. Muslims from Sarajevo are flooding into Split by the coach load, not to mention those who couldn't get on the buses and are walking over the mountains."

"This is insane." Bojan was still not fully appreciating what was going on.

His brother switched on the TV. "I'm fed up with watching it all, but if you haven't seen any of this, get yourself up to date, because there's a lot more coming and they're now heading our way."

He switched on the Croatian news programme which was running a continuous live service. He saw pictures of Bosnian Muslims herded on to trains, crammed in like cattle and heading to Zagreb. In the northern towns of Bosnia where Serbs, Croats and Muslims lived side by side anyone who wasn't a Serb was fired from their job, harassed in the street, had their home smashed, their business burnt and freedom restricted.

Bojan watched open-mouthed. "This is Nazi-ism. I can hardly believe it."

Vicktor had gone into the kitchen to make some food for his guest. When he returned, he found his brother shell shocked and almost unable to speak.

"Where have you been living?" he asked Bojan. "This has been going on for some time."

"But we don't see anything like this on the Belgrade news."

"Well, that's Belgrade for you."

Vicktor switched the sound down and turned to his brother. "We need to talk," he said. Bojan turned towards his brother wondering what he was going to say.

"Bojan, you're very welcome here but Zagreb is not what it used to be. Firstly, my night clubs can't open anymore because people don't want to come out at night, so any financial contribution from you will be welcome."

Bojan nodded, "No problem. Whatever you need. I'm grateful to be out of Belgrade."

Vicktor looked at him strangely, as of to say that might be a better place than here right now. However, maybe that was a discussion for another day.

"Secondly, Serbs are not exactly flavour of the month here, as you might have guessed so you'll need new ID papers."

Bojan began to object, "But I don't know how or where to do that."

"But I do," reassured Vicktor. "It will cost a little, though."

"Thirdly," Vicktor paused and looked at his brother. "You have probably lived a more.... sheltered... life than I have. True?"

"Yes, I suppose so."

"What I'm trying to say is that I live here with my business partner who is also my 'partner'."

Bojan looked puzzled and then it dawned, "Oh. You mean......"

"Yes. Is that a problem for you?"

Bojan swallowed hard and began to mumble something.

"Because if it is. I'll try to find you another place to live."

"No, no. That's fine. Really. Very kind of you." Bojan stammered out his reply, still trying to get his mind around this revelation.

"Good. He's gone out to get some food and stuff. He'll be back shortly and I'm sure you'll like him."

" I need to get my cases out of the car. I'll do that now." Bojan occupied himself with some practical tasks to take away the thought of meeting his brother's partner.

It was the following morning that they all learnt that Croatia had closed its borders to all refugees.

Chapter 33 — Bosnia

IN THE TIMES Ismet wasn't working or sleeping, he was still trying to get through to Ana. She was on the Serb side of the city whilst he was on the non Serb side, and it was a risky business trying to go from one side to the other. In fact, it was hazardous just going out anywhere in daylight. He was desperately hoping she would understand why he couldn't come and that she would resist her father's anti-Muslim attitudes long enough for him to take her away and re-unite his little family. But he recognised that it wasn't going to happen any time soon.

Ismet was not a mechanically minded man and so couldn't help his father with the taxi, but he knew that the taxi drivers were a close knit group and his father would easily find the help he needed. However, one night he was able to help his father move the stricken cab around an adjacent corner out of the sight of Serb snipers, which they did between them successfully. The following night his father went out on his own to examine the vehicle with his pen torch and concluded there was no quick fix. It was beyond him.

Nurija wasn't so concerned about the bullet holes in the bodywork, rather saw those as a badge of honour. Of more concern was the damage to the engine itself but he knew the community of cabbies was more than a talking shop. They knew their motors and if one couldn't help, another could. He had no trouble in recruiting an older, more knowledgeable cabbie to help. After all he had very little to do either. Under cover of darkness they drained all the fluids out and disconnected the battery and the exhaust. The transmission, however, was a bit more difficult to disengage especially by pen torch but eventually they managed to do it. Both men staggered back to their homes after a long night, happy but tired and aching with the prospect of many more difficult nights to come. That is, if the cab wasn't further vandalised or burnt out by teenage vandals looking for some fun making it beyond repair.

Next night it was still there and unharmed. Now they needed a hoist. There was one available from a garage Nurija had often used but it was about a mile away and there was no possibility of moving the car to the hoist, so the hoist had to come to the car. Together, they planned a route to drag it back to the location of the car. Each night they managed to get it part way and, more importantly, hidden during the day. On the third night they managed to wheel it into place, positioned over the open bonnet. The engine bloc was gradually lifted out allowing them to have a detailed look at the damage. With lots of sighs and grunts, a full diagnosis was made and a repair plan conceived. It took a couple of days more to get parts before they were able to start making what repairs they could.

It took more grunts and groans before they had done all the fixes they could and the engine bloc could be lowered back and secured in the chassis. The hoist was set aside but dawn was breaking and there was no time to do any testing. That would have to await another night when they could recon-nect the various disconnected parts and fill the cab back up with fuel and oil.

The following night came the moment of truth. Nurija turned the key in the ignition. Nothing. The disappointment etched on all their faces was deep. Their energy levels were low and their brains fogged.

"Check the fuel," the older man said. "If a bullet has gone through the tank you may have lost all your fuel."

Nurija said, "I didn't see any leaks and anyway we would have smelt it. It's not fuel."

"What about the battery?"

"Let me put my charger on it and see what charge it's got."

"What does it look like?" asked the older cabbie when Nurija had put the leads on the battery.

"It's dead. Completely gone. I need a new one."

"Right. Let's call it a night. I think I might be able to get one for you tomorrow."

Kovac woke up next morning to find Travnik full of refugees. Fleeing Bosnian Muslims in northern Bosnia had no choice but to go south now that Croatia was closed. It was pitiful. Those who had cars drove them towards Travnik but soon had them stolen at Serb checkpoints on the way. They were forced to join the thousands trekking across the mountains on foot. It was great target practice for the Serbian militiamen who had deliberately positioned themselves for just such sport.

The Bosnian government, such as it was, still had some territory under its control and the line seemed to be just north of the city of Travnik. Thus, this became the go-to place for those in the north who had been forced out of their homes. If they got over the line they were safe, at least for the time being.

Very little of this was getting through to the international community. The western press were kept away as much as possible, but it was Roy Gutman of the New York Times who eventually broke the news. Muslims were being shipped out of majority Serbian areas southward from Banja Luka towards Travnik. He reported that they were being thrown into cattle trucks. One evening he reported there were twenty five wagons leaving crowded with women, the elderly and children. He said it was like the Auschwitz trains all over again. The men were taken to prisoner-of-war camps which were nothing of the kind since all were civilians. His *Newsday* story of August 2nd headlined, 'The Death Camps of Bosnia' and starkly accused the Serbs of organised extermination.

Omarska was one of four such camps: the others were Keraterm, Trnopolje and Manjaca. The Omarska camp held more than a thousand prisoners in metal cages without sanitation, exercise or adequate food. Each cage measured seven hundred square feet and housed three hundred men. Cages were stacked four high and with no toilets, their own excrement dripped through the bars on to the cage below, some eventually reaching the ground.

Penny Marshall of ITN and Ed Vulliamy of the Guardian visited the camp and wrote that the men were, 'at various stages of human decay and affliction, the bones of their elbows and wrists protrude like pieces of jagged stone from the pencil thin stalks to which their arms have been reduced.'

A US Senate Foreign Relations Committee received a report confirming that Serbian ethnic cleansing objectives had been met but with widespread atrocities including 'random and selective killings plus organised massacres' which were 'recreational and sadistic'. The report stated that if the UN and the wider international community had taken the situation more seriously many lives could have been saved. They accused politicians of all western countries and the United Nations of pursuing a policy of 'let's pretend this is not happening.' It's hard to believe that if those being slaughtered had been other than Muslims, there would have been more immediate action.

Kovac wasn't aware of these camps or of the dilatory policies of western governments but what he saw, as these people dragged themselves into a safe haven, was bad enough. He was a different man. Had he been in Sarajevo he would have seen, or been aware of similar horror stories. What was he going to do?

Nurija and his wife sat at the table in their Sarajevo apartment after their lunch of thin vegetable soup and dry bread. Ismet was still in bed after another all night shift. His wife explained they had to ration themselves until more packets of cigarettes arrived. Nurija nodded.

"I hear from Ismet that they're now getting some supplies in from the tunnel," Nurija was letting his wife down gently.

"Are they?" she asked, not realising the import of what her husband was saying. "That must have taken a lot of digging." She was already taking the dirty crockery into the kitchen to wash it.

"Now I've got the taxi working," said Nurija following her into the kitchen. "I think I'm going to offer to help bring supplies from the airport into the city." He waited for the backlash. He knew it was dangerous and on any journey Serbian snipers could take him out. His wife said nothing but kept washing the dishes.

"You've already washed those dishes twice," he said gently.

She sighed and turned to face him. "I knew you had something like this in mind when you got the cab working."

"Do you mind?" he asked.

"Will you be able to take Ismet with you?" she asked praying fervently that the answer would be, yes.

"Yes," he said firmly. "He'll be a lot safer with me, I think. I hope."

She said nothing but nodded and turned back to the sink.

"Do you mind?" he asked again.

"I've lost my daughter-in-law and my grandson. I don't want to lose Ismet or you, but...." her voice tailed off.

"... but you know somebody has to do it, otherwise we starve and they win." Her eyes filled with tears as she said to him, "Go and do it. As much as you can."

The following morning when they came in from their overnight shifts, she cooked both her men the best breakfast she could with what she had, helped by the new cigarette supply Ismet had just brought home. It was now down to her to barter the cigarettes for food. She readily admitted that she was not very good at it, especially dealing with men, so she looked out for women with whom to swap her precious merchandise. Even so, her tender nature got the better of her many times so that she never got the deals that her husband would have secured. She knew it, but didn't everyone need to help each other?

The usual routine was that breakfast was consumed hurriedly, a quick thanks given, a peck on the cheek from her husband and off they went to bed. That was it. They would sleep soundly for eight, maybe ten hours before they readied themselves for the next shift. She also used to be a good sleeper. In fact, the only time she could recall that she hadn't slept well was when she was pregnant with Ismet. Sleep now seemed to be out of the question. Not much, if any last night. In fact, it seemed to her that she hadn't slept for years. She used to be an attractive woman, but not now. As she looked at herself in the mirror each morning she saw rings around her eyes, a pallid complexion and a haggard look, a testament to life in Sarajevo. How much more of this could she endure? Well, she would try for her family's sake. But what if one evening Nurija and Ismet were both killed in the taxi? She had already lost her grandson and daughter-in-law. That would mean they would all be gone and she would be left. What would be the point of carrying on?

"I need to keep my mind on the fact that they are still alive and they will continue to come home," she whispered to herself, over and over again. But the demon on the other shoulder was not so optimistic. It was whispering that one day they would not come home; one day she would be all alone; one day life would no longer be worth living.

She knew she wasn't alone in feeling like this. Most women in the city knew what it felt like but that didn't make it any easier. Many of her friends were now dead. Yes, some were still alive but for how long and when could she see them again in safety? When could she walk out of her house and meet them for coffee or go shopping with them, share details about grandchildren growing up or husbands' total preoccupation with football?

It was turning out to be a lonely as well as a dangerous life. Much of the night she was alone while the men were working, and much of the day she was also alone whilst the men were sleeping. Even when they were about, they were exhausted and didn't want to talk. But she needed to talk, have a conversation, keep relationships established. After all, isn't that what women did? There had to be some normality otherwise she was going to go mad. But at the same time, she had to prepare herself for the morning that they never returned? It would surely come. What would she do then?

Unusually this morning, once breakfast was finished, Ismet disappeared to bed as usual but Nurija stayed up for a while. Man and wife sat together for a while not saying much, just occasionally making some remark or other to let the other know they were still there.

"Do you get cigarettes as well?" She asked.

"No, but I get some fuel for the cab."

They both sat in silence again, thinking how life had suddenly changed, wondering how long this was going to go on and would they all survive it.

"You know," Nurija found something to talk about. "Ismet and I were chatting about the tunnel on the way back. What they're doing is amazing. I believe that tunnel is going to be our saviour. It's not yet completely finished but stuff is already coming through."

"What is left to do then if it's already open?" she asked.

"Well, apparently you can crawl through now and men are doing that and bringing stuff through in backpacks, but they're now building a rail system so more can come through more easily."

"That's amazing. Are there many cabbies helping you?" she asked enquiringly.

"Yes, quite a few but there are all sorts." He had devoured the food she had set before him but now he kissed her on the cheek and collapsed on the sofa. He would wake in a couple of hours then go to bed properly until late afternoon. Another quick meal of something, then a few hours to themselves before he headed back to the airport when it got dark, dodging the Serbian snipers on the way.

A week later and Mrs Terzic found herself desperate to talk to her husband – really talk.

"Nurija." His wife called from the kitchen. It sounded to him as though she had something important to say. He was about to go to the bedroom when she came into the sitting area and sat down opposite her husband.

"I'm not sure how long we can go on like this."

"Nonsense," replied her husband, not really listening to the underlying emotions of his wife. "It's not like before I know, but we can survive. We must survive."

"You're busy, out every night. I'm not. You have a job, a goal, a mission. I don't."

"But we can't do without you. You're crucial to what we are doing."

"Maybe. You're living in a bubble at the moment. It's probably exciting, outwitting the enemy, bringing in supplies. All I see is desolation and destruction and one by one my friends are being killed."

Nurija was silent. What could he say?

Karadzic was playing the international stage. Firstly, there was pressure on him from the UN and its various agencies to evacuate some of the camps and curb excesses. He magnanimously agreed, portraying himself as a moderate. After all, he now had most of the territory M had mapped out for Greater Serbia. Western media was focussed on the siege of Sarajevo, allowing the Serbs to get on with their 'cleansing' of northern Bosnia unperturbed.

Secondly, he pushed Bosnian authorities into a corner by being willing to put the airport under international control, again portraying himself and Serbs as moderates, willing to negotiate. He didn't want Sarajevo to starve completely because that would have increased international pressure for military intervention. Thirdly, he arranged to meet François Mitterrand, on the airport runway after an unexpected visit by the French President organised by General McKenzie, the UN's senior official on the ground.

By an odd coincidence, on the same evening as Karadzic met Mitterrand, the Keraterm camp witnessed a truly sadistic episode. Two hundred Bosnian Muslims were herded into a room and beaten for hours, their screams resonating through the whole camp. When the fun stopped, they were then machine gunned. The following morning other prisoners were forced to bury the bodies.

The international community was now well and truly awake to the revelations of ethnic cleansing and detention camps, thanks to the media reports. Economic sanctions were imposed on Belgrade and an embargo placed on the inward shipment of arms. Some would say, this was all a little too late.

Chapter 34 — United Nations

AFTER RESOLUTION 713 on Yugoslavia was passed which attempted to impose a complete embargo on all deliveries of weapons into Yugoslavia, the debate about what more could the Security Council be persuaded to do continued in the background.

Those members debated the pros and cons of intervention along lines of national interest as they always did. It was they who had the responsibility of decision-making but one might be forgiven for saying that the debate in New York seemed rather theoretical even philosophical, while people in Bosnia were dying.

"It's a civil war between parts of the Yugoslavian nation," said Elias Johnson. He was part of the US delegation and had been given specific responsibility for Yugoslavian matters and for elucidating US policy to anyone who would listen. Johnson was lunching with Ambassador Yildiz from Turkey. "And Article 2 forbids the UN from interfering in domestic matters."

"No. No. No. These are separate nations. They always have been. Then the Iron Curtain came down and Tito managed to keep it all together for his Soviet masters. It was never going to last." The Turk tapped his finger firmly on the table. "And the Bosnian Serbs are acting in conjunction with an outside entity, Serbia. It is clearly not a 'domestic' matter."

Although Turkey was a westward pointing nation, it had a special link with Bosnia Herzegovina from old Ottoman days, a fact which Johnson quickly pounced on with a knowing smile.

" Did the Ottomans really value these groups as separate nations when they were in control?"

Yildiz, ignoring the jibe continued, "If it really was an internal war among groups within a nation unable to agree sharing power, I would agree with you. But Yugoslavia is no longer a nation. In fact, it never was. Just a convenient construct by the Soviets and given to Tito."

Lunch in the UN building or at any of the neighbouring restaurants in

New York was always a good place to discuss issues, promote ideas and pick up the tab on the public purse. You could always find delegates ready to lunch and discuss on their generous expense accounts. Ambassador Ganguly of India came in and Johnson waved him over, insisting he sit with them. He gestured his hand towards Yildiz.

"My friend here is advocating intervention in the Bosnian problem. What is your assessment?" Johnson already knew that India did not favour intervention for it would directly relate to issues at home such as Kashmir.

"Ah! You know intervention can be a very dangerous thing," he began. "Obviously we would like to see the establishment of democratic states," Ganguly always tried to keep both ends of an argument. "But a proliferation of such states here would not necessarily lead to a more stable region, in my view."

Yildiz looked at him with some concern, then addressed the American directly.

"I know what your James Baker's view is," he said, "but surely the peoples of Bosnia Herzegovina are entitled to protection against the unwelcome force of a neighbour? If not the UN, who?"

Ganguly tried to gain some traction with his argument. "But does the UN represent the peoples or the nation states of the world? I believe the latter and as Article 1 says, the UN vision is to secure peace, security, cooperation and friendly relations between nations."

"Good point," agreed Johnson. "So the question is, can Bosnia Herzegovina be classed as a nation when only a section of the community is in jeopardy?"

While Johnson looked on Yildiz tried again. "But what about equal rights and self-determination of peoples? Isn't that an objective of the UN?

"Yes, I believe the UN should be able to send in blue helmet troops to keep the peace, but there has to be a peace to keep." Johnson was not giving up.

"But what if UN blue helmets are at risk from the aggressors in the conflict in their peacekeeping activities, what then?" Yildiz looked triumphant.

Ganguly nodded, "You have a point. India contributes to UN peace keeping and if a battalion of our troops was at risk, yes we would want intervention."

At this point Yildiz had to leave for a meeting and the vacant chair was taken by Bob Jones who, although British, was an employee of the UN and wasn't limited to the UK diplomatic position. Ganguly quickly outlined the issues they were discussing.

"Well, I'm not part of the UN Protection Force (UNPROFOR) team, but as an outside observer I would say that the reason why there is no intervention is that none of the member states of the Security Council see any of their vital interests at stake, except maybe the Soviets who have always supported the Serbs."

Johnson, representing the only power to be part of the Security Council, objected, "I don't think we are always guided by selfish motives. In this case, I suspect the UN itself is substantially to blame."

Ganguly looked at him, "How so?"

"Well, in my experience," explained Johnson, "the UN has always been concerned, maybe over concerned, with its own reputation and future. It doesn't want to be seen as a failure. With such a mindset, concern for its own welfare will inevitably dominate its agreed objectives."

Ganguly countered, "So you're saying that within the UN itself there is a conflict of values."

"Yes," confirmed the American. "The UN can only do what its member states want it to do. If there is a block in the Security Council, nothing can happen. Unfortunately, the result is that it has to sit on the sidelines. Doing nothing inevitably means that the use of force to gain territory becomes acceptable which is, of course, against UN values."

Jones thought about it. "Hence using humanitarian aid as an excuse to avoid direct action."

"Yes, it's called the bureaucratisation of peacekeeping," observed Johnson.

"But surely we need to measure potential UN activities in terms of chances of success?" said Ganguly.

"And that's where the UN does contribute by providing a forum for diplomacy where a peace deal can be thrashed out, thus making way for a peacekeeping force." Jones was trying to salvage some credit for his employer.

On the ground in Bosnia, the UN Commander, French General Phillipe Morillon was in the middle of a mess. He was in charge of a group of Dutch peacekeepers tasked with the job of delivering UNPROFOR's mandate in Bosnia Herzegovina which was to support the delivery of humanitarian aid "so that hundreds of thousands of inhabitants of Bosnia who had taken refuge in enclaves, who were besieged, who had absolutely no means of subsistence would not starve or die of exposure".

Specifically, they had to secure Srebrenica as a UN safe area. Due to belligerent activity mainly from Bosnian Serbs, the UN had moved a little and their mandate had been updated to read: "acting in self-defence, to take the necessary measures, including the use of force, in reply to bombardments against the safe areas by any of the parties or to armed incursion into them or in the event of any deliberate obstruction in or around those areas the freedom of movement of UNPROFOR or of protected humanitarian convoys".

Andries de Ryke was a young soldier, a corporal, seconded from the Dutch army to peacekeeping duties in Bosnia. He was not too pleased, nor were his compatriots but power lay with their politicians who wanted to be playing on the world stage and being seen to make a contribution as did Dutch senior military figures. For him and the rest of the contingent, it was a time to keep their heads down until they were relieved and could go back home. They had gone through the additional training that the UN demanded of the Dutch army and had arrived in Srebrenica albeit with their French commander based in the Holiday Inn, Sarajevo. The politicians and diplomats at the UN probably meant well in giving them the additional authority to use force, but that was no use without adequate men and weaponry.

Corporal de Ryke was part of DutchBat III, so called because it was the third of several Dutch Army contingents to serve as UN peacekeepers in the Srebrenica enclave. He was near the bottom of the food chain and was under no illusion that the task involved a lot of bluster, threats and bluffs if they were to succeed.

"What on earth is this place?" one soldier complained.

"Potocari and be lucky you're not actually in Srebrenica." said his sergeant. They were being billeted in an old battery factory.

"Not exactly the Holiday Inn is it, Sarge?" No immediate answer.

"Get your kit and your bunks sorted tonight. Tomorrow we're out on patrol." With that the Sergeant strode off to the officers area. He looked for his superior but came across Lieutenant Colonel Tom Karremans, the Dutch commander.

"Can I help you Sergeant?" he said pleasantly.

After coming to attention, the Sergeant said, "Sir. I was wondering when we would be getting more supplies?" He added, "The lads are fine, but I think we'll need more in a day or so."

"We're doing our best, Sergeant."

"Of course, sir. Thank you, sir. There's very little petrol, fuel for heating, and not much to eat, just some Canadian and French rations left over. Sir!"

"Thank you Sergeant." With that the commander walked away.

The next morning saw the men move out to take control of their two OPs, (observation posts) Romeo and Quebec. The former was on a nearby mountain and looked out towards Serbia. If it wasn't a war situation it would have been a beautiful scene. Woods, rough hillside, some small meadows in the valley, livestock grazing unaware of what was evolving around them, even some birds daring to sing.

Corporal de Ryke saw them first. He was on the phone.

"Sarge, there are tanks coming in our direction and buses filled with soldiers."

"How many?"

"Well I can see at least ten buses, too much dust and stuff to see exactly how many tanks, but I would estimate twenty or thirty."

The Sergeant reported over the radio the information to be told that the Serbs had been contacted and it was just an exercise and not to worry.

That evening the men were huddled round a pitiful fire.

"You saw them. What does it mean?" asked one soldier.

"An exercise? Not bloody likely," said another.

"There's virtually no food left. There's not been one new delivery of supplies since we've been here," said a third.

De Ryke looked up. "If you ask me, it is clear that the Serbs have all the control here. All we can do is somehow manage the system so that we get supplies in for ourselves."

"But there's only one road in – the one we saw today. Even if our convoy gets close, it could easily be commandeered by the Serbs and we get nothing."

"I'm told that our main task is to observe, and to demilitarise Bosnian soldiers."

"But that's stupid. We haven't got enough manpower or weapons to defend them. If we take away their weapons, they'll be sitting ducks. It'll be slaughter."

The men looked up as their Sergeant and First Lieutenant were coming over. They looked at each other wondering who was going to ask them for some answers. No-one did. The following day the men were ordered to go on what was called a 'social patrol'.

"I've never heard of a 'social patrol'. What the hell is that Sarge?"

"Mind your language, lad. You're just going to walk around the enclave along the main road, to show the people that we're here."

"But I heard from the Canadians that we could be ambushed and taken hostage."

"Don't worry, lad. Just obey orders and you'll be fine."

Chapter 35 — Belgrade

THE TEAM HAD certainly changed. Only Mira remained of the original members M had gathered together. The businessmen had left despairing of any of the promised lucrative ventures in the wake of the revolution which now seemed mired in massacres and 'cleansings'. They did not have armament factories and were not interested in war, but in the quick returns that could only be made in peace time, preferably with Serbia ruling Yugoslavia. That was now a distant memory.

M's trusted lieutenants, Kovac and Bojan, seemed to have disappeared and with them Djuric whom he had high hopes for. He began to wonder whether all three were linked. Perhaps Kovac wasn't dead in Zagreb. Maybe he never went to Croatia. Perhaps it was Djuric he sent – that would make sense. So Djuric gets caught, Kovac feels guilty and can't show his face? It was a theory, but M didn't buy it. He knew Kovac was made of stronger stuff.

"What do you think happened to Kovac and Bojan?" He had turned to his wife for some link he hadn't seen. She was good at that.

"Well, they weren't friends, I could tell that. In fact I don't think that civil servant had many friends. He was creepy – kept taking his glasses off and polishing them. What's all that about?"

"What about Djuric?" M asked.

Mira looked up. "I thought he was a good man. Of course, he may still turn up, but you spoke to him in Sarajevo and told him to get to Zvornik didn't you?"

"Yes." M was beginning to be worried. "If they're dead, they're dead. Not a problem. It's if they're alive that's concerning me." M started thinking of the consequences if they were alive but AWOL from his project. "That could be a problem," he murmured.

"I'm sure you will be able to find them," Mira said, "one way or another."

M called in his man with the grubby overcoat who went by the name of Grgur. "Got a job for you."

Apart from some of the old politicians hanging around, M now spent most of his time in contact with Smolov, Karadzic and Mladic. He needed the Serbian militias supported by the Army to get the territory he had mapped out as quickly as possible before the international community took any military action.

In order to keep up the pretence of negotiation, he was forced to attend conferences and meetings with ambassadors, diplomats and other do-gooders who wanted to be seen by their own populace to be doing something. They cared nothing for Yugoslavia.

"I have to go to London now." M was talking to Mira the following day.

"Will Radavan be going with you?"

"Yes, fortunately. But a load of other hangers-on have been invited too."

"We could do with a lessening of sanctions," Mira pressed him. "People can't get foreign goods anymore."

"We'll see." M was not very hopeful. It looked as if they would have to make more concessions.

"You know they want you to resign?" Mira didn't look up from her book.

"Who wants me to resign?" asked M combatively.

"The Orthodox Church, the University and even some factories." They both looked at each other and laughed.

"No backbone, that's the trouble with these wets. No. We're the winners. That's why we're at the table."

M had looked around for civilian help to negotiate time with the do-gooders allowing the military men time to get on and finish the job at home. He had chosen a Belgrade-born millionaire from California, Milan Panic, to be Yugoslav Prime Minister and Dobrica Cosic to be President. However, when they got to the latest conference in London, Panic showed himself incapable of following M's script but he talked a good talk to the international leaders gaining their respect with expansive words about co-existence, without them having the slightest knowledge of what was continuing to happen on the ground.

"I want to speak," announced M during one of the sessions.

"SHUT UP" read a piece of paper which Panic held up in front of the

Serbian President. From that point on they disagreed about most things, particularly when Panic offered to have UN monitors at the borders of Serbia and Bosnia. After threatening to punch Panic, M declared he was leaving.

"We need to get rid of Panic." M was relaying some of the details of the conference to Mira a week later.

"Why? I thought you chose him."

"He's eccentric, independent and can't be trusted."

"But I thought the international leaders liked him." Mira was not giving up.

"Well I don't and he's going to have to go."

Grgur was a disgraced ex-secret policeman, a captain no less. M used him for work which no-one else would do, sometimes wet work. He was expensive, but it gave M total deniability. Who would believe such low life if they said they worked for the President of Serbia? Everyone hated the secret police, especially those who went above and beyond their duties to line their own pockets which he had successfully done over a number of years.

A quick call to a previous informant at the phone company established to Grgur's satisfaction, that both Djuric's and Bojan's phones were active. Kovac's wasn't. "That doesn't mean he hasn't got a new one," surmised Grgur. And it didn't stop him from getting started with the others. It would take a little more time to get any actual data from their phones, but he knew it would come.

"Then, I've got you," he licked his lips thinking this could be a very easy increase in his bank balance.

Bojan, he decided, was the easiest target. The man would be easy to frighten and Grgur could do that quite well. He found his office quite easily. It was empty and those around him said he had been gone for two weeks now. No, he didn't have family, but was a confirmed bachelor who lived for his work and, by all accounts, was good at it. Which is why M had chosen him, of course.

"I need to see his expense account," he announced holding up his old police badge. It was brought to him. Immediately he saw something; a claim for a return train ticket to Titograd not long ago.

"That wasn't difficult, was it?" he said to himself. M had briefed him on what Bojan's role was, so Grgur knew exactly where to go.

Panic was relatively simple to fix. M controlled the Serbian media and all he had to do was to smear his opponent, casting him as a CIA stooge responsible for the economic sanctions people were suffering from. With an election coming up, M intensified his campaign as Panic decided to stand against him. The population of Serbia now believed that Panic was Washington's boy, that the Serbs in Bosnia were fighting for survival and that 'Muslim fundamentalists' and 'Croatian fascists' were waging war against Serbs. Fake news, but hey, it worked.

M was re-elected by a large majority.

Chapter 36 — Istanbul

SMOLOV HAD REPORTED back to his bosses that M was the only candidate in Yugoslavia who might be able to fulfil their requirements but that he was soft and would have to be hardened up. He reported that his military leaders, Mladic and Karadzic were capable as long as their political master had the bottle to let them loose. After making his report, he was called back to Moscow to learn that those he reported to, and would make the decisions on military supplies to Yugoslavia, were no longer in power. The younger men had taken over the Kremlin with their '*glasnost*' and '*perestroika*'.

Gorbachev had declined to intervene militarily when various Eastern European Soviet bloc countries began to express nationalistic sensibilities even though it threatened the very existence of the Soviet Union. The hard-liners were aghast and plans were afoot to quash this unwanted liberalisation. At all costs the Mother Russia had to be saved. Smolov was relegated to waiting while the power struggle worked itself out. He had no idea how long this would be or indeed whether those plans would succeed, but having promised M some heavy machinery, he knew he was now impotent to fulfil his promises. Having already received the cash in the original Cayman Islands account, his only strategy was to play for time and not admit his real situation.

Back in Belgrade, the situation was causing M some angst and after an ill-tempered phone call to the Russian, M was invited to meet Smolov in Istanbul again. His play was to give M a good time in Istanbul and get any bad news out while they were on his turf rather than in Belgrade. M was certainly not averse to having a good time on someone else's tab, but was determined to push for what he wanted as hard as he could. The same plane was made available and a car at the other end. This time there was no tour of the city. The driver took him straight to the Russian consulate where Smolov clearly still had some pulling power.

"What the hell is going on?" M did not hold back once he had been shown into exactly the same room as before. Smolov put his finger to his lips and led M out of the room and through some double doors at the back and into the garden.

M waited for the Russian to explain. "It is true that currently we are in some turmoil," began Smolov once they were clear of the room. It was now obvious that the room was bugged and every meeting had in that room had been recorded. M wondered who else had been subject to the unwanted listening devices. If Smolov didn't want anyone to overhear their conversation, maybe he was going to hear something important. "A change from last time," muttered M.

"We are presently going through what you might call, a transitional period in our government," continued the Russian. M stared at him as if to say, "Tell me something I don't know." Smolov shrugged, "Policies may change, but....." He saw M's reaction and wanted to cut him off. "...but I can assure you that we have the equipment you need."

"That we have already paid for." reminded M curtly. He was determined that he was not going to take any rubbish from the Russian. He wanted answers this time so had decided to go on the offensive.

"Of course." Smolov's tone was smooth and emollient.

"Why do you not want our conversation to be recorded?" pressed M looking at the Russian straight in the eye. "I believe last time it was not a problem?" M was rather enjoying this change in the relationship. He wanted to force Smolov to admit Soviet weaknesses and to ascertain the truth about what was really going on in Moscow.

Smolov took his time to answer, then leaned into M as they walked, as if he was sharing something really secret. "It's difficult to know who supports our new liberal President we have just inherited, and who supports the old ways. I have to be careful our plans are not scuppered by those who want to see Yugoslavia break up and begin to westernise."

M pushed his advantage, "So when can I expect some hardware?"

"There are already plans afoot to replace Gorbachev with Vice President Yanayev who understands what we need to do."

"Plans, what plans?"

"Look." The Russian was getting rather uncomfortable. "I understand the urgency of your situation in Yugoslavia, but I cannot divulge this information."

"Are we not on the same side? Are we not comrades?"

Smolov pursed his lips and looked around as if someone might be listening. "Yes, we are of course." He paused as the inner struggle finally resolved itself. "All I can say is that it will happen next month, August."

"What will happen?"

Smolov began to whisper so quietly that M, who was standing right next to him, had trouble hearing him. "Gorbachev and his family will be at their holiday dacha in Crimea. A group of senior comrades calling themselves the Committee on the State of Emergency will arrive at the dacha and if Gorbachev doesn't declare a state of emergency, he will be kept under house arrest and not allowed to leave. They will go back to Moscow, say that Gorbachev is ill and take control."

"Then you can ship my machinery to Belgrade?"

"Yes."

"And what happens if the coup d'etat fails?"

"It's not a coup d'etat, merely bringing back the order that existed before. Gorbachev was a mistake."

M was quiet. It sounded possible. He knew how the Soviets worked, but he also knew that it was not just Yugoslavia that was seeking to change the nature of its relationship with the USSR. If the whole of the Eastern bloc broke free, the old order would become the obsolete order and he would never get his product for which he had paid.

As if understanding M's thought processes, Smolov proffered some information about himself and made an offer which he hoped might ameliorate him.

"You will have guessed that I'm a military man. I was a colonel in the Red Army until General Varennikov spotted me and transferred me to military intelligence. I understand warfare and will happily come to Yugoslavia and personally liaise with Mladic and Karadzic whom I admire. They are excellent leaders."

"I'm sure that will be welcomed. As you say they know exactly what we need to achieve."

"Excellent." Smolov smiled for the first time.

"But I want the key to the account we have already paid into, just in case."

"Of course." Smolov smiled again. "Now I'm afraid I have to leave you in the company of my colleague. He has specific instructions to show you the delights of Istanbul at my expense. I promise to join you later."

M was gently shepherded out to the car where another man waited to greet him. He was whisked off to the Old City Bosphorus Hotel where a room was already reserved for him and a sumptuous evening awaited him.

Nothing was off the table, it seemed. M surprised himself by rather enjoying the evening and its various entertainments. On the way back home though he began thinking more seriously about these Russians. They seemed to have no conscience whatsoever, no capacity for delicacy or regret. He knew they would knife him, either physically or metaphorically, if it was in their interests to do so. He smiled.

"We seem to be so much alike," he murmured to himself. "But I will certainly need to watch my back."

Chapter 37 — Srebrenica

STEFAN, BROTHER OF Ana and son of the Lukic family in Sarajevo, was enjoying officer life in the Army and, following his basic training, had cut his teeth in Croatia working alongside the Serb militias to defend the Serbs living in Croatia and establish a land corridor into Serbia itself. That corridor also necessitated operations in northern Bosnia around Banja Luka. It was good to be on a winning side. There was no doubt that he was a natural, both in physique and in temperament which had caught the eye of the Army commander there, Ratko Mladic, who promoted him to Lieutenant.

He did manage to send messages home every now and again with glowing reports of his experiences. Although his father was disappointed that Stefan didn't want to take over the management of the furniture-making business, he was proud of his son and gradually begun to understand the mission that the Serbs were on. Whilst his wife distanced herself from the views her husband was now espousing, she also was proud of her son who was carving out the future he wanted and not just following his father's footsteps.

As Mladic had been transferred to the Sarajevo operation, he took Stefan with him and promoted the boy again, this time to Captain. Mladic didn't know this was the boy's home town and even if he had, it would have made no difference which is why Stefan never told him or anyone else. He had seen a glimpse of Ismet and his sister Ana on the fateful march, but his men had a job to do and he was there to see that they completed it. They did.

However, it filled him with anger. Firstly, that Ismet would put his sister at risk on such a mass demonstration and secondly and most importantly, that Ana would betray her nation, her culture, her family and marry a Muslim man. He knew where the young couple lived and began to use his binoculars to try and pin point their apartment block. Yes, there it was. He found the coordinates on the map and resolved to attack the block. He didn't know the exact floor on which they lived but nevertheless, gave instructions to his Lieutenant to unleash a barrage of shells to those co-ordinates with his artillery.

Srebrenica was a couple of hours east of Sarajevo and by 1993 it had been surrounded by Serb forces for almost a year – a similar strategy to that being executed in Sarajevo. The ring of Serbian forces was getting ever closer and the Bosnians' ammunition supplies were running low. They were losing. True, at the beginning of the siege, the Bosnians had defeated the initial Serb advance, one of the few setbacks in their mission to create a Greater Serbia, but it came at a tremendous cost to lives.

Srebrenica was an enclave, which meant that it was surrounded by land that the Serbs needed and was ripe for 'cleansing'. Nearby Bosniak villages, some two hundred and ninety six of them, had already been destroyed, forcibly uprooting some seventy thousand people from their homes and systematically massacring over three thousand, including women, children and the elderly. The lucky ones escaped to the local town of Srebrenica so that it became swollen with refugees, now living and sleeping wherever they could, mostly in the open air. Occasional aid convoys were allowed in by the Serbs to keep on the good side of UNPROFOR, but even these had now been halted by the militias. It was 'ethnic cleansing by starvation.'

The militias were getting frustrated with the time it was taking to complete the mission and, on Smolov's recommendation, asked Mladic and Karadzic to provide more troops and heavy weaponry.

"Lukic?" Mladic shouted his name in the officers' mess.

"Sir?"

"Take another company of men to Srebrenica and assume overall control of all the troops there."

"Sir." The order was clear, but there was more.

"Your orders are to finish them off. I want that place levelled."

"Sir."

The French UNPROFOR commander in Sarajevo tried to remain neutral as his mission was supposed to be. As well as struggling with Serb attacks on Bosniaks, he reported that attacks by Bosniak forces under the command of Naser Oric on Serb villages had:

"created a degree of hatred that was quite extraordinary in the region, causing the entire Serb population in the area to rebel against the very idea that through humanitarian aid

one might help the population".

There was hatred on all sides which, to the UN peacekeepers, seemed to come from nowhere but which everyone else knew came from multiple generations of deep suspicion.

Jusuf and Munira Petrovic were among the older residents of Srebrenica and were considered to be part of a well off family. Jusuf had started a building firm in his early thirties. Although he had trained as a carpenter, he was good at his job and reliable so had been asked to do lots of other building and property jobs as well and thus the building business was born. Munira stayed at home to bring up their two sons and look after elderly parents until they passed away. They had felt themselves very blessed. Jusuf had been a community leader for some years and, although Muslim, had good relations with the Serb population within the town and did work for all the different communities.

Their family had now grown up and although the sons were married, they still all lived in their multi generational house not far from the mosque where Jusuf was a prominent leader. Tarik had his family on the first floor, with Armin's family on the top floor whilst Jusuf and Munira had their bedroom on the ground floor. The other rooms on the ground floor such as the kitchen, dining and living rooms were communal areas but mostly strewn with toys.

Tarik was a slim man taking after his mother with his black hair combed straight back. He was the youngest at twenty years of age, married two years ago to Emina and they had just had their first baby. Everyone was delighted. Possibly the brightest of the four sons, Tarik was studying to be a doctor whilst Armin was much the more physically strong man taking after his father, had gone straight into the family business and taken over responsibility for it five years ago. The enterprise had done well and now employed six other men, that is, until the blockade began. He was now thirty, had married Sajra and they had a son, Adem, seven years old who loved football, and a toddler, Zaim, aged three who idolised his older brother and followed him everywhere.

This year was a significant one; Jusuf and Munira had been married for forty years but it wasn't a time for celebration. Now in their early sixties there was no guarantee they would live to see their fiftieth anniversary. In fact, if things went on as they were, they might not see the current year out but that was nothing to do with their health issues. Munira really needed a hip replacement and could barely walk without severe pain whilst her husband had fits of coughing, indicating a lung issue probably related to the asbestos he used years ago. There was little chance of anything being done for them. In fact, these issues were the last thing on their mind. Obtaining enough food and warmth from day to day provided the biggest challenge.

The town's mosque was the centre of the resident Muslim's life, the minaret of which was an obvious target for the encircling Serb forces and one which every artillery man wanted to get. It was a miracle it hadn't been hit so far although several nearby houses had, but it was just a matter of time.

"Where do we go if our house is hit?" Munira asked her husband one night in bed.

"Don't worry. We'll find somewhere," was the stoic answer.

"There's no room even on the streets anymore. People are sleeping anywhere and everywhere."

"I know. It's a desperate situation. I'm going to talk with the UNHCR man again tomorrow to see if any further aid might be coming." Jusuf tried to be upbeat, but his wife was inconsolable.

"I'm afraid that the Serbs will break through and take our young men away and we'll never see them again," confessed Munira. She could hear a baby in another room beginning to cry and they knew that once one started, the other three would start and even the toddlers might join in. Another sleepless night to go with all the other hardships.

Another aid convoy was approaching. Lieutenant Stefan Lukic ordered his men to stop it and turn it around.

"Sir, there's a detachment of UN soldiers with them." His Captain wanted to check his orders.

"Hold the line. No-one is to get through." Stefan was adamant.

"Apparently, some PR person in Belgrade has said that General Mladic had expressed his "support for and cooperation with" the UN in their task."

"Over my dead body and those of my family," roared Stefan Lukic imitating his idol, Mladic. He had his orders and the UN did not figure in them. "I want an intense artillery discharge on Srebrenica in six ten minute bursts now. We'll show them who's in charge here."

The Serbs quickly recalculated the bearing and distance of their guns to the centre of Srebrenica re-setting the sights of each gun. Each gun was loaded and fired when ready. It was deafening. Everyone who could dashed to a shelter of some sort. No-one could hear anyone else speak, as they all covered their ears. Then it stopped.

It was Munira who first heard some high pitched screams once the sound of the barrage had ended. "Where are the children?" she shouted.

"I thought they were with you," shouted back her daughter who's ears were still ringing. The men were in another part of town shoring up defences.

"I bet they went out to play football." Sajra dashed out towards the school playing area amid a dozen other mothers with the same sinking feelings, with Munira hobbling after as fast as she could. They converged on the playing area to be met with the gruesome and harrowing sight of what had been their children, Adem and Zaim.

The screams morphed into unrelenting cries of anguish, torment and despair. Everyone in the vicinity ran towards the wailing echoing round the buildings. That hour saw the killing of fifty-six people, among them fourteen children playing on a school football pitch.

Louis Gentile, a UNHCR official recorded:

Fourteen dead bodies were in the school yard. Body parts and human flesh clung to the school fence. The ground was literally soaked with blood. One child about six years of age had been decapitated.

It was the final straw and the Srebrenican authorities asked the remaining UN official to smuggle out a message to Belgrade, conveying a surrender notice.

Chapter 37 — Belgrade

Bojan was not a man to make friends. He kept himself to himself both at work and at home. But there was a lady at work who had carried some hope that Bojan might ask her out. Branka was a middle aged lady, never married and slightly overweight. It was possible that Bojan may have inadvertently given her some expectation which had never been fulfilled. Instead of becoming angry and resentful, she still looked out for him and was concerned when the secret police came asking questions. She knew mobile numbers had to be registered just in case of emergency so she planned to stay on that evening and, after personnel staff had gone, try to obtain his.

It was not an easy task. She didn't normally stay a minute longer than she needed at her desk, so it had been necessary to dream up some work which had to be completed that day. By seven o'clock, everyone had gone and the office where such records were kept was empty. She knew security would be along soon, but cleaners might be around before that. Anyone passing on information about suspicious activity might receive some benefit so she couldn't risk anyone seeing her. This was planned as an initial foray with a view to another attempt tomorrow if she couldn't get the phone number immediately.

She was in luck. The keys to the metal cabinets which held personnel data were still in the drawers of the supervisor.

"That was slack," she thought. The cabinets were four drawers high and each labelled A-C, D-F and so on. She found the right drawer easily. "Ah. This is the one. Quickly, find the correct key without too much fumbling." She talked aloud through the exercise to try to stop herself from trembling.

"Got it." She withdrew his folder and found his number. "Easy!" She wrote it down and replaced everything just as security was entering the floor. She swept out of the office and the building as if she owned it and made her way home. Not having a mobile phone herself she decided to wait and use an office phone the next morning.

"Hello, this is Branka."

There was silence from Bojan on the other end of the line who was almost having an out-of-body experience. He knew who Branka was but she was in Belgrade, now a world away. Why was she phoning his mobile?

"Branka?" Bojan was disbelieving.

"Where are you?" asked the lady.

"Umm. Why are you phoning? Is something wrong at the office?"

Branka noted the non-reply.

"Something like that," she replied.

"Branka, what is it?" Bojan's curiosity was now getting the better of him.

"Have you done something wrong?" She wanted to milk this moment.

"Branka, I really don't understand what this is all about."

She giggled, not like the serious side of her that she showed at the office. "Apparently, you've a secret admirer in the 'special' police."

"A secret admirer? The 'special' police? What are you talking about?" Bojan couldn't keep the frustration out of his voice.

"Well, the secret police visited the office yesterday looking for you, asking lots of questions about where you might be, where you had been. She paused to let the enormity of it sink in. Bojan was completely silent, not knowing what to say.

She went on. "He also looked at your expense account. What have you been up to?"

"Nothing." Bojan tried to answer in a neutral voice while his heart was racing. "You know me. Anyway thanks for the call. See you shortly."

Bojan tried to indicate that he wasn't far away. He put his phone down and tried to think straight. He knew what his expense account would show – a visit to Titograd. For a sedate accountant, he managed to conjure up such a stream of curses that his brother came in to ask what on earth was going on.

Bojan waved him away. She had obviously got his number from somewhere. "How on earth did she get hold of that?" he wondered. But that was not the most pressing matter. Titograd. Dragan didn't know where he was, but Bojan didn't want to get him into trouble. He called him.

"Hi Dragan. I'm taking a few days holiday but apparently somebody has been sneaking round my office asking questions. It could be nothing, but it could be about those money transfers."

"Whoah." Dragan already saw the implications.

"No need to panic, but you might want to tidy up the paperwork your end and say that my visit was just routine. Nothing out of the ordinary."

"Yes, of course. Thanks for the tip." Dragan put his phone down and went to talk to the Inspector General.

Bojan was worried. If it was M who was hunting them down, Kovac would also be on the list and possibly Djuric. He should call Kovac.

"You remember the conversation we had in Belgrade after the tanks had been sent in?" Kovac was surprised to get a call from Bojan and had already been looking to get out of Travnik. After the brief conversation with him, Kovac was convinced that M had engaged someone to eliminate each of them and now was surely the time to move.

"Bojan, listen. You must get rid of your phone and SIM card, deleting everything on it."

That didn't sit well with the thrifty accountant who didn't like waste, wherever he saw it. So he objected.

"That's a waste. I need it."

"They will be able to trace you through it."

"Oh. Of course. I'll do it right away."

"Good," said Kovac. "I'll delete everything from my phone and get Djuric to do the same and then get rid of them. If data can be gathered from our phones, they will be able to read all our phone numbers, so I think we're on our own from here on in."

"Yes. I understand. Good luck. Perhaps see you back in Belgrade some day."

Kovac didn't answer. Indeed he had already cut the line and was finding Djuric's number. He knew Djuric was in Montenegro, at least he was last time they were in touch. It was probably a good place to be. Maybe he could get there from Travnik.

"Djuric. We have a problem." Kovac got straight to the point. He wanted to get this message over and dispose of all the mobiles as soon as possible.

"Bojan has just told me that the secret police are tracking him."

Djuric was used to Kovac's abruptness. "So?" he asked.

"M is trying to find us. We know where the skeletons of the last ten years are."

"Oh!"

"We must both delete all records from our phones, then take out the SIM cards and destroy them."

"Why?"

"Because they can not only trace us but retrieve all the data on them."

"OK."

Kovac paused longer than he would have liked. "Are you all right?"

"Yes. I'm fine and I don't intend to move."

"I agree. I think your place is just as safe as anywhere. I might try to get there myself." Kovac waited for a reply to tell him whether he might be welcome or not.

"Sure. That's a hell of a journey though."

"Give me two weeks from today and I'll meet you at the monument in the centre." He had to keep the name of the city out of the conversation just in case.

"OK. Two weeks from today."

Both men proceeded to delete everything they could from their phones and destroy the SIM cards. Neither of them was an expert in these matters and had no way of knowing whether this would keep them safe or not.

Chapter 38 — Srebrenica

THE DECISION OF the Srebrenica leaders not to surrender directly to the local militias was understandable fearing it would initiate an all out assault on the town killing thousands. The news of the capitulation however, leaked out via the press and proceeded to shock everyone since international politicians and the UN had been talking up the possibility of a ceasefire which, in reality, had not the slightest prospect of happening. Mladic had never given any indication that this was an acceptable outcome. There was now a rush by the UN, US and the West in general to reposition themselves. They began calling it a 'disarmament agreement' though no-one suggested that the Serbs were going to disarm.

Jusuf was one of the local community leaders who agreed that surrender was the only course open to them, knowing that their homes and businesses would be demolished and they themselves would join those sleeping on the streets as refugees.

"Where will we go?" Munira was crying. She hadn't got over the death of two of their grandchildren. Perhaps she would never get over it.

"If only you had agreed this earlier, maybe we would still have them." She shouted at him as if it was all his fault. Jusuf looked a beaten man. His head sagged and his voice trembled as he tried to reply.

"I'm sorry." It was all he could say. He retreated away from his wife to the relative safety of his own company and wept as only grown men can.

Mladic dictated the terms and the UN had little leverage except to declare Srebrenica a 'safe area'. The term 'safe haven' was not used precisely because it carried the legal import that all who entered would be safe. That meant that the UN would need to enforce it and thus renounce their much loved neutrality policy. A ceasefire was agreed and a 'disarmament' agreement was signed at Sarajevo airport. General Lars-Eric Wahlgren announced that Srebrenica was now "protected by the blue flag of the United Nations" as he and his Dutch blue helmet troops took charge of the town. What in normal times was a town of eight thousand souls, was now home to some forty thousand people, ruled not by community leaders now but by gangs and black market traders who pilfered UN supplies on a large scale.

"I want to go," said Munira to Jusuf. "I can't stand another day here."

"But what happens to our sons and all the other young men?" asked Jusuf. Munira was quiet. If she lost her sons as well as her grandchildren, would she want to go on living? She didn't know.

"We must trust that the United Nations will uphold their word and keep them all safe." It was said with a tired desperation. "Who else can we trust?"

Jusuf called the whole family together, at least what was left of it. He announced, "Whether we like it or not, we will be leaving tomorrow for another Muslim area, where we will be safer."

"Where will that be?"

"I don't know."

"Can we take anything with us?"

"No. Even if we tried, it will probably be stolen from us."

Their sons saw the sense in the decision and prepared their families as best they could. Later, when grandfather and grandmother were alone, Munira moved towards her husband and hugged him. "Sorry," she whispered. They sat down in their living room whilst the other families were gathering their most precious belongings together.

"So this is the last night in our own home," said Munira wiping the tears away from her eyes. It was a mixture of fondness and regret. She looked at Jusuf, "How has it all come to this?"

Jusuf was silent. What was there to say. Then he had an idea. "Let's eat everything we've got and share it with the family. It'll be our celebration of nearly forty years in this house."

Munira looked up with a determination in her eyes, and said, "Yes, lets." She went into the kitchen and began to take out everything she had and prepared the banquet. Jusuf went to the other floors in the house to tell the rest of the household what his wife was going to do. This was possibly the last thing she could do for her family.

It was July 6th. A fateful day. Bosnian military leaders in Srebrenica had been spirited away through the Serb lines ostensibly for new orders but it had been a ploy by their commanders in Tuzla. They believed that Srebrenica was now indefensible and they did not want to lose key personnel. Thus the town was left with no military leadership.

Karadzic intervened and sent a directive, known as Directive 7, to Mladic. "By planned and well-thought-out combat operations, create an unbearable situation of total insecurity with no hope of further survival or life for the inhabitants of Srebrenica." Those orders were passed on to Lukic who would proceed with a vengeance.

Corporal Andries de Ryke and the rest of his cohort were at the Romeo OP just expecting another tiring day. They had no idea what orders Captain Stefan Lukic had received from General Mladic the previous day, but would soon find out. It was early morning and the Dutch lads were on duty but still yawning when an almighty barrage began from the Serbs going straight into central Srebrenica.

De Ryke grabbed the phone. In his fear and haste he dropped it, cursed, picked it up and shouted into it.

"Sarge, a major offensive looks like its started. It looks like they're going to go all out."

"Keep calm lad. I can hear it."

"Also, there's a contingent of Serbs heading for us with heavy weapons. There's no way we can fight them."

"Do not, repeat, do not engage them."

"But what do we do?" It was not difficult for the Sergeant to hear the panic in the Corporal's voice.

"Try to hold the line. If it comes to it, you will need to retreat."

"Retreat?" Through the noise, de Ryke thought he hadn't heard correctly. "Please repeat."

"Retreat," came the reply.

By the end of the day all Observation Posts manned by Dutch peacekeepers were overrun. Later they were to admit that in hindsight perhaps they could have sensed something was coming, but they could have done little about it. At the time, nobody thought that the Serbs would put two fingers up to the UN and just barge past, daring the blue helmets to stop them attacking the enclave. In any event, they had nothing that could compete with the heavy armoury of the Serbs. Denied the tools to do the job by the UNPROFOR Commander in Sarajevo, the Dutch soldiers could do nothing except retreat to their base and wait for new orders which were to help evacuate women, children and the elderly on Serb buses, probably the same ones that brought in the soldiers.

"God Almighty," said one Dutch soldier to another. "It's like 'Schindler's List' and we're just helping ethnic cleansing."

"Poor buggers," said another. "The height of summer and they've nothing to eat, no privacy and no toilets."

De Ryke had an idea. "Let's go with the buses and protect them as best we can. After all, we're supposed to be the UN peacekeepers."

Six soldiers went with Corporal de Ryke and it all went well until they got out of sight of the town. Then the cavalcade stopped and the accompanying Serbs approached the Dutch and relieved them of their cars, weapons, helmets and flak jackets. The peacekeepers trudged back to their base on foot and empty-handed. They were helpless.

Other Dutch peacekeepers had gone within Srebrenica itself to try to help the inhabitants but had totally given up. They just watched as the Serbs did what they wanted, with whom they wanted; with women, with men, with possessions, with anything they fancied. After all, Captain Lukic had given the go-ahead. Once the militias had had their pleasure, Bosnian Serb civilians entered the enclave stealing whatever was left including cattle, horses, TVs and fridges.

" This is nuts," said one of the Dutch peacekeepers. "They're just waving at us. They have no fear of us whatsoever. It is humiliating."

"That's because we have no power except bluff, and they've called it."

"What do we say when we get back home?" continued the first soldier.

"As little as possible," advised the second.

Chapter 39 — Lujbovija

KOVAC WAS NOW desperate to get out of Travnik. It was crammed full of Bosnian refugees with nowhere to go. He had driven out of Belgrade some time ago not having anywhere particularly in mind except out of Serbia, and had ended up in Travnik which he quite liked. He had found a nice place to stay with a garage to put his car in. Now though everything had changed. It was a sad affliction of war that it provided gang lords with lots of opportunity to steal, intimidate and racketeer, and he didn't want his car to be either damaged or stolen by any mobsters who might be operating. It was his ticket out of the city.

He knew he had to avoid Sarajevo which was still being blockaded and blasted by the Serbian Army artillery. Everyday he would hear of new horror stories of inhabitants without food, shelter and safety. It was a dire situation. He looked at a map he kept in the car and determined that the only way was eastwards over the mountains and through towns such as Doboj, Vares, Turalici and Lujbovija. He would then reach a reasonable road southwards towards Montenegro.

The next morning, he tentatively looked around as he exited the building. In the faint light he could see a little eddy of dead leaves and cigarette stubs outside the door but looking left and right, the coast looked clear of any jeopardy. He was determined to set off early before the sun rose, so quickly ran to the garage where his car was kept. Within a few minutes, he was in his car and moving through the town trying not to run over people sleeping in the streets at the same time as accelerating out of the place as quickly as possible. Unfortunately for them, but fortunately for him, the weather was atrocious which meant that as he drove through the only checkpoint he came across, those on duty were more interested in keeping themselves dry rather than dashing out and stopping his car. The first ten miles was easy going but the next ten became slower and slower not because of the condition of the road, but rather the growing number of refugees that were moving out of the town having started their journey. There were whole families, three generations sometimes, all pushing their wheelbarrows, old prams or anything that helped them save the precious possessions they had been able to grab quickly. He felt sorry for them but knew he had to push past as safely and quickly as he could. They must have been annoyed at the spray he was kicking up but their will was broken. They just allowed the rain to soak them and they trudged on, heads down. There was no alternative.

As Kovac was making his way through the melee, he began to realise how he had changed in the last six months or so. Past intelligence colleagues would hardly recognise the man he now was. He had gone from a rational, skilful intelligence operative oblivious to people's individual situations to a man who had discovered his emotions and humanity. He wasn't sure which man he really liked. The former he knew inside out and had served him well. That man had earned him respect and access to the most powerful people in the country. Yet he knew that underneath all that, it hadn't really satisfied him. That man was always on edge because he never knew when things would turn against him and he might find himself on the wrong side, with all that could mean. He would always be on the lookout for the next powerful individual.

"That life was exhausting," he admitted to himself. "Maybe I need to get away from all the misery and settle down."

Woah! Where did that come from? He had never before had the desire to 'settle down' whatever that meant and besides, he had no-one to 'settle down' with. Was he having a mid-life crisis in his thirties? Djuric had obviously found someone; Bojan would probably never find anyone but someone might find him.

His attention was taken away from himself as he began to notice the fleeing refugees becoming more spread out. He was past the three generations going at the pace of the slowest, now he was seeing young families with their children and the occasional dog. He looked at the children. They didn't deserve this but neither did their parents and all because someone else wanted their homes and land. He was ashamed of his part in this but what could he do? Nothing if he was dead, so he'd better keep on driving. The skies had cleared, the road was emptying and the driving became easier for the next hour or so.

Just as he was about twenty miles away from Lujbovija, he began to hear artillery firing to the south of him. "Must be Srebrenica," he thought. He had heard there was trouble there .... and here it was. Trouble. A Serb checkpoint.

"Stop." A man in military fatigues stepped forward with his hand up in front of the barrier, with about six other men sheltering under the trees on the side of the road. The sub-machine guns slung around their necks clearly weren't there for show. Kovac stopped the car and got his papers out ready to show. He was hoping to get through easily.

"Papers," ordered the soldier. Kovac proffered the papers only for them to be promptly taken away, which was a bit concerning. Ten minutes later, nothing was happening. He decided to get out of the car and lean against the bonnet, hoping this might remind them he was waiting. Bad move.

An hour later, after Kovac had got back into the car, another soldier came over and began questioning him.

"Where have you come from?"

"What were you doing there?"

"Where are you going?"

"What business do you have there?"

And so it went on and on. Kovac had spent his time in the car preparing for such an eventuality which he knew would come at some point. He explained to the soldier a story about a dead relative, a funeral, a burial and being asked to go to Serbia to inform other relatives. The soldier didn't seem very interested in his answers but had loads of questions. When Kovac started asking questions himself about what was happening in Srebrenica, the questions stopped. The barrier was lifted and he was on his way, his only concern being that his name might have been logged and that information might trickle through to someone who knew exactly who he was.... and that he was alive.

Kovac knew all too well what the Serbs were up to. Srebrenica and the surrounding region were strategically vital to Mladic and the Bosnian Serbs. It was the connecting area to two currently disconnected parts of the Serbian state they wanted to create. A useful by-product was that Srebrenica's capture would weaken the practicality of any future Bosnian Muslim state. A double whammy!

It was slow going on the mountain roads through tracks and trails which had probably never seen a car before. He drove through the day and for as long as he could in the dusk hardly ever getting out of second gear. The dashboard lights, such as they were, glowed dully in front of him as he bent forward struggling to see the way ahead, not helped by regular torrential rain as can only happen in the mountains. It whipped into the car blinding him to the seemingly invisible ditches and potholes which even the headlights were not strong enough to enable him to avoid. More than once he had to stop, get out to survey the damage as the car lurched into some god-awful hole, then try to reverse out before continuing. He prayed there might be no permanent damage to engine or tyres, for he was no mechanic and didn't want to risk engaging with locals.

There was no going back so for three days he crawled forward, sometimes down dead ends and other times seemingly in the opposite direction to where he wanted to go. There were no signposts to guide him so he could only judge his direction from sun and moon. One night spent in some hay barn in the middle of nowhere, the other two in the car meant he had hardly slept and ached all over. It wasn't that he was short of money – he had plenty but he didn't want to broadcast his presence or get into any conversations.

Determined to have a reasonable night's sleep, he resolved to find an hotel of some sort – any sort – when he arrived in Lujbovija. He found a four storey hostel in the centre of the town and persuaded the manager with a little incentive to give him a four bunk room to himself. The town was just over the border in Serbia so he felt quite at ease to sleep which he did for twelve hours solid, before venturing out for some breakfast and to fill up the car with fuel.

The day's rest comprised a short walk around the centre of town and lunch at a bar where he sat next to a table where a group of men were discussing some recent events in Bosnia. The conversation he overheard didn't endear him to his own countrymen who, in graphic language, loudly publicised their approval of the 'cleansing' of Srebrenica. A year ago, long after Tito's death, the different ethnicities were still living in relative harmony although always conscious of their differences. But whether Orthodox, Catholic, Jewish or Muslim they somehow got along. Now it was different. Ordinary Serbs could have dismissed M's vision of a Greater Serbia to be brought about by demon-strations, ethnic cleansing and now genocide, but they hadn't. They could have seen through the propaganda and ignored the biased media, but they didn't. Rather they had embraced it all and wallowed in its darkest depths, and so had he.

Such was the metamorphosis that he had undergone that Kovac left the bar quite angry. Women and girls raped, men and teenage boys shot en masse and dumped into mass graves. It was as if Satan himself and his devilish hordes had invaded their minds and souls, taking their greatest pleasure in the desecration of human beings supposedly born, 'in the image of God'.

Stumbling along the roadside a little further along the road, he came across a beggar who looked as if he had been well off at one time; his shoes were good quality but worn out, clothes neat but tattered and hair unwashed. He held himself erect rather than sitting in the gutter. Instead of eyes down, he looked at passers-by full in the eyes, asking for nothing yet asking for everything. Kovac stopped. He briefly wondered why on earth he had done so but out of his mouth, almost before he had consciously thought about it came, "Can I help you in some way?"

"That's very kind of you." It was a rich baritone voice that sounded as if it's natural context would be the stage or a choir. The men looked at each other, both wondering whether each could trust the other. That's what it had all come to.

"I've managed to escape from Srebrenica." He paused as if to see whether Kovac would stay or take that confession as the excuse to walk away. Kovac felt his feet were glued to the pavement.

"Actually, I would like to help you," he said.

"Well, my name is Armin," and he held out his hand. Kovac shook it and felt them to be hard and calloused. "This man doesn't look like a labourer so he must be a craftsman of some sort, maybe a builder," he thought. At the same time he noticed other people giving them a wide berth. Strangers were suspicious, and here were two of them together.

"Come with me," said Kovac and the two of them walked back to the hostel. Even if the manager had been there to see them come in, it would have made no difference for Kovac was on a mission.

"The bathroom is just down the corridor. Take these items," said Kovac handing the man his wash bag, "and tidy up whilst I do a bit of shopping. By the way, what's your waist, chest and leg sizes?"

The other man stared at him and gave him the required dimensions. An hour later, the scene had changed and they were sitting at another café bar he had noticed, where he hoped the clientèle might be a little more human. Money wasn't an issue for Kovac until Belgrade stopped paying him which, he knew might happen any day now. All it would take was a call from M's office, but hopefully he had other things on his mind. They ate together while Armin told his story.

" My father, Josif, started a building business which I inherited a while ago. My younger brother, Tarik, wanted to be a doctor and I think he would have been a good one."

"Would have been?" Kovac asked.

"We were taken away by the Serb militias," Armin said looking at Kovac intently. He had recognised his friend as a Serb and didn't want to upset him. Kovac shook his head as if to say 'no matter'.

"I managed to fall off the truck that was taking us away and escaped into the woods. Unfortunately Tarik was loaded on first so he was at the front. I was at the back." He stopped for a moment as if he was re-living the events. Kovac gave him space to collect himself.

When Armin recovered he looked at Kovac. "I saw terrible things, terrible things. My wife...... my wife was gang raped in front of me while I was being held back by two soldiers." He collapsed into tears, sobbing so much that Kovac saw the manager looking across at them. Kovac nodded to him and suggested to Armin that they go now that they had finished their meal. He left some notes on the table and both exited.

Armin was wanting to tell someone all that had happened. "This was occurring all the time, even to teenage girls. Terrible. I don't understand it."

"Neither do I," said Kovac sympathetically.

"There was a baby that was crying. The mother couldn't stop it. One soldier ordered the mother to stop it. If she couldn't, he would. He knifed that baby."

Both men were silent as they meandered around the town going nowhere in particular. There were no more tears to shed. Kovac was almost as discomforted as his companion. He recalled some of the things he had asked Djuric to do in Kosovo to whip up enmity between communities which he now bitterly regretted.

Armin hadn't finished though. "There was a place called the White House. That's where they took the men and boys, just shooting them in front of each other and pushing them into mass graves."

They kept on walking around the town, the long silences between them almost palpable out of respect for the dead. Kovac glanced over at Armin, wondering if he had anymore to unload. He did.

"A witness recounted how three brothers, one merely a child and the others in their teens, were taken out in the night. When the boys' mother went looking for them, she found them with their throats slit."

Armin stopped, looked up and breathed a huge sigh. "If there is a God, He must really believe in man's free will otherwise......" his voice trailed off. He looked at Kovac. "I'm a Muslim, I guess you're Orthodox or Catholic?"

"I don't think I can claim to be anything right now," responded Kovac. "I knew what I was once, but now it doesn't seem to matter any more."

They shook hands; Armin firm in his conviction that he would find other members of his family somewhere if only a grave, and Kovac to continue his journey to Podgorica.

Chapter 40 — Podgorica

THE REST OF Kovac's journey through Serbia and Montenegro to Podgorica was without incident for which he was very grateful. He felt emotionally drained after listening to everything that Armin had had to say but it reinforced his decision to step away from what M was doing. He wondered how long this kind of warfare could go on before someone called a halt. The UN seemed ineffective if not complicit in it all. There was a lot to think about.

Such was his gloomy thinking that several times on the drive south he had to stop and check where he was for he couldn't remember whether or not he had passed this or that town. Montenegro as a whole seemed calm and peaceful, probably because M already had a puppet government in place but he was grateful for some tranquillity.

Bioce was a town just north of Podgorica itself and he decided to stop for the night to give himself time to think about what he was doing. What was he going to do in Titograd besides have a reunion with Djuric? He had no other reason to be there, no family, no partner, no job. So where did he go from there? What was he going to do with his life now? He had chosen a side and halfway through had decided he couldn't live with it. He didn't want to suddenly re-appear at his Belgrade office, at least not in the present climate. More than that, he now thought he wanted to work to stop it somehow, but how? He sighed; too many questions and no answers at all.

Yes, Bioce was a nice place. He liked it. So he booked himself into a bed and breakfast since he had a couple of days in hand before he had agreed to meet Djuric. Perhaps he could settle here, perhaps meet a girl and settle down. Those words again! But do what? The perennial question would not go away. He decided that he could now only live one day at a time. Enjoy what he could today, for tomorrow the secret police might find him.

He drove into Podgorica on the date arranged, making his way to the monument in the centre of the city to wait. It was early, 9am. He didn't want to miss Djuric. Time waiting allowed more time for thinking; about the journey he'd been on, what he'd seen and heard but mostly about himself. He had always been a loner. It was the life of an intelligence officer and he admitted to himself that it suited him. Or was it that he had suited himself to it?

But now he had a great desire to see his friend. He had never had 'friends' before, partly because he could never reveal who he really was and partly because, yes he could admit it now, he was afraid he might be rejected. Now he had a friend called Djuric and he really wanted to see him, talk to him, be friends, find out how he was thinking about M and what they had been doing for him.

"Perhaps," he thought to himself, "I need someone else to corroborate what I'm thinking and feeling. That's the second time!" He smiled grimly as he waited. He had spotted a café bar across the street in full view of the monument and at 10.45 am decided to take a coffee break. There were many government buildings nearby and the café clearly prospered on business from civil servants so he decided it would avoid a queue if he went now. Not for long though, for he wanted to meet Djuric outside at the monument where they had agreed. He took the coffee proffered by a pleasant looking girl, paid and selected a seat at the back where he could view everyone. Just habit.

Just before 11am, a man stepped out of the Treasury building also wanting to beat the mid morning rush and walked into the same café for coffee. He didn't look like a civil servant in his rather shabby coat but his sharp eyes scanned the customers and immediately recognised one of them sitting in the corner, the table he would have chosen for it had a clear view of the whole place including the door. Kovac! His face broke into a smile and his heart began to beat a little faster thinking of the little matter of a substantial bonus coming his way shortly. Queuing up for coffee still allowed him to see his quarry in the mirror behind the counter and once served, Grgur took a table at the opposite side of the café where he could easily see the intelligence man.

After about fifteen minutes, Kovac made a move to go outside. Grgur didn't, but watched him all the way to the monument where he stopped and sat down. The ex UDBA man waited in the café watching Kovac as long as he could, but after three coffees and some sandwiches, he couldn't stay any longer. All thoughts about going back into the Treasury to see Dragan again were put on hold as he walked around the square looking for a suitable place to continue his surveillance.

"What is he waiting for?" Grgur asked himself. He didn't look as if he was doing any intelligence work. In fact, he appeared very relaxed as if he was on holiday. Then the penny dropped. "The question is rather WHO is he waiting for?" Grgur's smile broadened. "It's got to be," he thought. It was noon when Grgur spotted Djuric coming towards Kovac.

"Well, well, well," the ex UDBA man said out loud. This was a pleasant surprise, a double bonus. "I wonder what on earth they're cooking up."

Both men were smiling and after a moment hugged each other.

"Really didn't think you would make it," remarked Djuric as they walked away.

"I nearly didn't," returned Kovac.

"You can stay with us if you like, at least for a while until Ivana turfs you out." He smiled.

"She must be quite a lady."

"She is."

"Are you two...... an item?"

"Working on it."

Kovac explained that he had a car nearby with all his stuff in it, so they walked together for about five minutes with a man in a shabby-looking coat following at a distance. As they got into the car and pulled away, Grgur took a note of the number plate and made a call to Belgrade.

"Do you have any friends in the police in Podgorica?" he asked an old acquaintance who owed him.

"Why?"

"I have a car I want to locate here."

"Shouldn't be difficult. Give me the number."

Grgur gave the number and added, "I just want a BOLO put out and its location, nothing else."

"OK. What's your number?"

Grgur gave his number. He knew it could be days before they located it, so time to grill Dragan again. The man must know how to contact Bojan. Maybe have some fun this time.

Kovac parked the car next to Djuric's and both men hauled Kovac's belongings up the concrete steps to the top floor and in through Ivana's front door.

"The spare bedroom is this way and you can put all your stuff there while I get some lunch together." Djuric was pleased that Kovac was here, not just because he was a friend, but when he had mentioned Kovac was coming, Ivana had promoted him to her bedroom as long as Kovac stayed. He hoped maybe a little longer, as the sofa didn't look that comfortable.

They spent the afternoon talking about M, the Serb militias, the Federal Army and the extent of Russian involvement. Their own complicity in it all was not forgotten. Both men were now of a similar mind but was it possible to absolve themselves of their personal responsibility for the deaths they had caused? It was the unspoken question at the back of each of their minds. The urgent business of UDBA interest enabled them to neatly skirt the question; each had their own future to sort out.

At about 4pm the outside door opened and Ivana walked in. Both men got to their feet and before Djuric could introduce their guest, she exclaimed, "So this is the famous Kovac."

Kovac responded with an eye on Djuric. "I want to express my deep thanks for allowing me to stay a while in your apartment."

"Polite, isn't he?" Ivana said to Djuric. Both men stayed standing as she hung up her coat.

"Please, don't stand on ceremony because of me," she said striding into the kitchen. "Djuric, I'm assuming you're doing the evening meal while I get to know Kovac a little." It wasn't said as a question. Djuric stood rather open-mouthed, "But you always do the cooking," he said staying in the living room almost as protector of his friend.

"It might be good if you got started," she looked at Djuric enquiringly.

"....of course." Djuric stuttered and he disappeared into the kitchen and the sounds of rummaging indicated that he was trying to get to grips with the kitchen again and put something together. In the meantime, Ivana sat herself down opposite Kovac and began interrogating him as to his situation, where he'd come from and what was going on in the rest of Yugoslavia.

"So you live alone?"

"Yes. Living with someone hasn't been very compatible with my job."

"So you have chosen to be alone?"

"I suppose so," said Kovac wondering where she was going with this questioning. He began to tell his story and as the tale unfolded, it was clear that Ivana was becoming very troubled.

"I suppose Djuric has told you how we met?"

"Er, no he hasn't," Kovac replied.

"Well, I was housekeeper to Tito up and until he died and thereafter that served the next Yugoslavian President in the same capacity," she said, looking him straight in the eye.

"I had no idea," Kovac replied.

"Djuric was, of course, Tito's adjutant," she explained, "and we kept an eye on each other, if you get my drift." Kovac nodded in a manner that neither said he did or he didn't.

"He made a number of promises to me when Tito died that he was finished with the army and with politics, promises he then proceeded to break." Ivana still fixed Kovac with her eye.

Kovac shifted a little on the sofa. "Ah. That was entirely my fault, I'm afraid."

"How so?" asked Ivana. Kovac sighed. He could see she was going to extract payment from him for his stay, but not in monetary terms.

"I was Tito's inside intelligence man tasked with keeping an eye on the big beasts of the Party, which I did. To cut a long story short..."

"Oh please don't. We have all evening," interrupted Ivana. Djuric put his head around the kitchen door to see how things were going, then ducked back inside as he heard Ivana's sarcasm still in full flight.

Kovac relayed everything they had done together for M, emphasising that it was mostly political and constitutional until the Federal Army, purged of non Serbs, became a Serbian Army which then proceeded to support various Serb militias both in Croatia and Bosnia in a quest for the creation of a Greater Serbia.

"The ordering of tanks on to the streets of Belgrade was the beginning of my change of heart," Kovac explained. "Since then I have seen unutterable things perpetrated by my own people that I never wish to see again."

"Who do you mean by 'my own people'?" asked Ivana, clearly wanting every fact she could wrest from the intelligence man.

"Principally the Army, although Serbian militias as well," replied Kovac, squirming a little.

"The Army that Tito had was never like this."

"I believe M was in hock to the Russians. He had a permanent Russian adviser next to him and I believe he flew out of the country more than once to meet with them." Kovac was almost using this interview as his confessional.

"The Russians?" exclaimed Ivana. "How did the Russians get their dirty hands on us?"

"General Petar thought we needed more tanks and artillery."

"So that's why the Army has been demolishing everything in their way. They've adopted the Russian style." Ivana spoke quietly as if to herself. As if to educate a mere intelligence man, she turned to Kovac and proceeded to summarise the tactics of the Russian military.

"The Russian approach to fighting is to cause the maximum damage to civilians and civilian infrastructure as a way to break resistance and remove any semblance of control of the inhabitants. It's just extraordinarily brutal."

She went on, "In my limited experience, they have no sense of kindness or generosity of spirit. They, or at least those in power, are completely heartless, pitiless, totally lacking in humanity."

"And what is your experience?" Kovac asked, trying to turn the tables a little.

Ivana looked up sharply. "I'm not just a pretty face, Kovac."

Kovac looked as if he was expecting further amplification, but was disappointed.

"That's all you're going to get," she said with an air of finality. "So," she took the reins of the interview once more. "So, what are you going to do about it?"

Kovac was quiet. "To be quite honest, I don't know. I suspect that M has put a price on both our heads since we have 'disappeared'. He sent both of us into war situations so my hope is that he thinks we are dead. But it's not wise to assume that."

"So you need to stay indefinitely?" It was a direct question and Kovac thought it deserved a direct answer. "No but until I can put together a plan, if possible. I'm still being paid by the Party but the man responsible for both our salaries has also had to go on the run so I don't know how long funds will still go into my bank account. But I can pay for my keep," he hastily added.

"I should hope so." Ivana was giving nothing away. "But surely M will be monitoring your account and will notice if it is being used?"

"Some time ago, I put in place a mechanism to transfer all monies into another numbered account as soon as it comes in and advised Djuric to do the same. I don't know if he did."

"Well, as both of you have renounced this Greater Serbia nonsense, you can stay as long as you like." With that she got up and went into the kitchen to critique Djuric's cooking with Kovac thinking he had passed the first test. Djuric was right; she was an independent lady and he liked her.

Grgur got the information he requested after four days and decided to take a taxi to the street where Kovac's car had been spotted. He had to assume that the men were staying nearby. The taxi driver was asked to drive up the street to check that the car was still there and it was, next to another which he thought might be Djuric's. He had no idea which block they were in let alone which apartment they were in, so concluded he would have to come back another day and stake out the street, hoping to see either of them entering or leaving.

It happened one Sunday lunchtime. Grgur had been there all day Saturday and had prepared for another all day surveillance. He had correctly thought that a weekend might be the best time to see either of the men emerge. He was in an old car that Dragan had been blackmailed into giving to him. It was a car that suited the street so didn't look out of place. He was yawning when suddenly he saw them come down some concrete steps not twenty meters away. Both men got into one of the cars and drove away. He watched them go.

At last, he had found them and was about to call M when he decided to wait to see if there was anything in the flat that might be useful to him. So having given his quarry five minutes to clear the area, up he went and knocked on the door to make sure the place was empty. The door opened and Grgur came face to face with Ivana.

"You!" She almost spat out the word as she stared at him.

Grgur took a surprised step back. "Well, if it isn't Tito's whore."

Ivana went to slam the door but Grgur had a foot in the corner and although it must have hurt, he showed no sign of harm as his smile grew wider. He moved in and shut the door behind him.

"Shacked up with Djuric, are we?" He couldn't stop grinning. "Haven't come very far from Tito's apartment have we?"

"What do you want?" She went to slap him across the face, but he grabbed her arm and squeezed it until she cried. After a few moments, seeing she was not about to repeat the manoeuvre, he let her go.

"Guess," he invited her as she turned, walked straight into her bedroom and shut the door. It didn't have a lock and she knew there was no way she could prevent him doing whatever he wanted to do. Grgur made no attempt to follow her but busied himself looking around the apartment.

"Not quite what you're used to, is it? He mocked. There was no answer from the bedroom. He helped himself to a drink before taking his pistol out from his inner jacket pocket and placing it carefully on the coffee table. He called M.

"I trust you have good news." M was straight to the point as usual.

"Oh yes. I have found Djuric and Kovac alive and well."

"Where?"

"Podgorica."

M snorted. "I want a clean house. Do you understand?"

"Of course. It shall be done."

Chapter 41 — Croatia

WHILE BOSNIAN SERB militias were concentrating on 'cleansing' the eastern part of Bosnia, Croats decided to launch an offensive to take back areas of western Bosnia around Krajina which the Serb militias had taken. Franjo Tudjman, the Croatian leader, let it be known publicly that they just wanted to release Bihac, still in Serb hands and occupying a strategic position. In reality, the plan was to go much further. To ensure he got a strong foothold in Bosnia, he offered all Croats living in Bosnia, Croatian citizenship. It rather backfired as many were leaving to relocate to Croatia itself.

News about such events always travels fast and as soon as Jakov and Vesna heard, they set about planning how they could leave the pitiful refugee camp in Split and go home. All those who had left Kijevo village, at least those who had survived, constituted a little community in the camp and Jakov began talking to the others to see who would join them. The elders were sceptical.

"Jakov, you've got two young children and a wife. It's too dangerous."

Jakov could only see the benefits. "How long are we going to stay here in this wretched camp? All the thieving, the gangs. I've had enough of it. It's no place to bring up children."

There was no consensus. Opinion was split along age lines with the younger men wanting to go and the older, they said wiser, men warning caution.

The Croatian army made fast progress up the Livno valley now that Serb militias were concentrating their focus on Sarajevo. Some Serb villages were retaken with ease, then came to the Krajina capital, Knin. The Croat forces had the high ground and, after some intense fighting finally took the city. Now a large swathe of territory had been re-conquered. A huge victory. Western Slavonia then fell causing tens of thousands of Serbs to flee to Serbia in anything they could lay their hands on; tractors, cars, horse-drawn wagons, you name it.

The news was being trumpeted by the Croatian leadership everywhere. Jakov was jubilant. "Now is the time," he said "We've got to go in case other people take our homes and land. If we don't, we're doomed to stay here for years."

His words now carried weight. Nobody wanted to stay. "At least let's take a week or so to build up supplies for the journey. We're going to have to walk and we'll need carts or wheelbarrows, or something to carry our stuff." The elders' voices were heard this time and so plans were made.

No sooner had agreement been made than they heard there had been two enormous explosions in the centre of Zagreb. The Serbs had fired two Orkan rockets in retaliation. The news was that seven people were killed, forty wounded and Split might also be targeted. It caused a degree of caution amongst Jakov and his people but also increased the pressure and the determination to leave.

A few days later they were all on the road trying to stay together, so offers of help were not accepted as no one offer could take them all. It was a long journey but not quite as long as the fleeing Serbs. The population of Knin fell from forty thousand to about six hundred in less than twenty four hours. The Serbs knew the Croats were coming for them. The UN could do nothing as a large Croatian army tank had been parked right outside the gate of their compound blocking any exit until the victors had secured the town.

Motley refugees from all over Croatia were arriving back to see the Croatian army taking revenge on the Serbs.

"You can't blame them," said one old man. "Remember how they treated us."

"But they're throwing stones at women and children, the old and the vulnerable," complained a woman. "It wasn't them who killed and tried to destroy us. We should be better than them."

Jakov agreed, but said, "I guess they were caught up in the Greater Serbia myth. They certainly did nothing to help us but at least we allowed them some escape routes."

As they got nearer to their village, they began to meet others whom they recognised, all savouring a joyful reunion. They explored their village together taking note of what had changed and what had remained. As evening fell, each returned to their home if they could. If it had been demolished they simply occupied an empty one nearby. Normal it was not and it was a long time before Jakov, Vesna, Zora and Ivan were able to relax.

There were nightly meetings together to exchange news about what was happening elsewhere. Gradually news emerged of the gruesome killings of elderly Serb men and women who couldn't flee and so had to stay in their houses. It was reported that "one lady was tied up with a fish net and a tyre put around her neck before being set on fire."

Vesna wasn't at that meeting but putting the children to bed. When Jakov came home he was quiet, even disturbed.

"You know that old Serb woman in the next village who waved at the children each time they passed?

"Yes," said Vesna rather distracted.

"Well, she's been murdered."

"What?" Vesna turned to face her husband. "I know she was Serb, but she was a lovely lady. She wouldn't hurt a fly."

"I know," said Jakov. "Some terrible things are still going on." He had determined he wouldn't tell his wife how she died.

"Why don't they stop? We've got our homes back." Vesna felt tears in her eyes. "What is wrong with the world?" They went to bed that evening in silence and regret. This homecoming was not how it was supposed to be. They didn't know if they could ever feel at home again.

When the morning came, Jakov carried on getting his land back to some sort of order. There was no chance of any produce this year and, unless he cleared the ground ready for planting, they'd not have anything next year either. Vesna spent the day coaching Zora because there were no schools open as yet and also looking after toddler Ivan. But she was thinking.

"How did the Croats manage to rout the Bosnian Serbs, when only a short time ago it was the other way round?" It was a question she raised when she was sitting on the village bench watching her children play.

"That," declared an old man sitting besides her, "is a very good question. Tudjman couldn't have done this himself."

At that moment two war planes went overhead towards Serbia deafening them. Zora looked up at them out of fear but noticed the insignia on them. "Mummy, They're American planes. Look at the markings." By this time the planes had vanished, but the old man smiled.

"They must be NATO planes," he said and turning to Zora he said, "They're here to protect us. We have nothing to worry about." The family was assured and parents were happy for the children to carry on playing where they always had. A dull thud, rising smoke and screams from a dozen small children brought parents, including Vesna, rushing over to find Ivan lying on the ground with blood pouring from his leg. While she was picking up her son, the old man had followed her and shouted for all the children to come away from the playing area.

It was a land mine. They didn't know it but in Croatia alone there were seven thousand land mines, some put down by the Bosnian Croats as a defence against the incoming Serbs and some put down by the fleeing Serbs against the incoming Croats. None had been formally documented so it was down to those who planted the mines against the Serbs to try and remember where they had put them. That still left many lying in wait for unsuspecting men, women and children.

Zora was dispatched to get her father while Vesna rushed home with the toddler trying to stop the blood flow as best she could. There was no hospital within reach and no pharmacy either. They could only do the best with their limited knowledge. It was ten minutes before Jakov rushed in to find Vesna in a terrible state, not making much sense but wrapping Ivan's leg in what bandages she had. Zora followed in a few minutes later but was immediately dispatched by her father to get one of the old ladies in the village who had more knowledge that he had.

Ivan was going in and out of consciousness and they both felt totally helpless. Jakov removed the bandages now completely soaked in blood so he could look at the damage. He could see severe damage to the foot and leg but was more concerned about any shrapnel embedded in the flesh which might cause secondary infections. That would mean amputation. Also it was clear the toddler had lost a lot of blood so he quickly bound up the gaping wounds again and tried to comfort his son.

The old lady arrived with a bag in which she had some medication. It only took one look and she said,

"We must take him to Knin immediately. He lost too much blood and we need to prevent him becoming unconscious if we can. There's a hospital there."

"But how are we going to get there? I don't have a car nor even any horses."

The old woman's son had a tractor and trailer so Zora was dispatched once again.

"I'm sorry, but it'll have to do," she said.

Vesna had managed to recover herself and immediately set about gathering together cushions and blankets to ensure that the journey minimised any additional aggravation of Ivan's condition. She went off with him while Jakov stayed with Zora. All they could do was pray and hope.

They had only been gone ten minutes when Vesna let out a loud scream and the tractor ground to a halt. The young man driving came round to the back to see what was happening to find the mother sobbing loudly with her limp son in her arms. He knew instantly what had happened. The only thing he knew how to do was take a pulse which he did, just to prove to himself that the lad had died. He turned the tractor and trailer round and headed back to the house, dreading the reception he would receive.

Just another death to add to the thousands upon thousands of others. Unbeknown to Jakov, Vesna, Zora and the villagers of Kijevo, the end of it all was approaching.

National leaders inside and outside Yugoslavia were beginning to realise the same thing. Even M realised that the game was up and had sacrificed the Krajina Serbs in the vain hope that he might be seen as a peace-maker. Karadzic launched a tirade of vitriol at M accusing him of "turning your back on Serbs. You have relented under foreign pressure to an extent which could be compared to treason." M needed the sanctions imposed against him lifted. Yes, sanctions had worked, but at what price? Hundreds of hostages taken including UN peacekeepers, thousands of young men slaughtered, hundreds of thousands of men, women and children displaced, millions of people traumatised and generations of lives ruined.

Chapter 42 — Dayton, Ohio

ALTHOUGH POLITICIANS AND diplomats in the West were talking about what to do, Sarajevo was still under siege and being shelled. The Bosnian Serbs were not giving up easily. But finally, the humiliation of UN peacekeepers being chained to lamp-posts, the defeat of Srebrenica, the fall of Krajina and evidence of the mass murder of Bosniaks began to make up minds. Either the West was going to leave the parties to fight it out or someone was going to have to threaten some muscle.

Inevitably, it had to be American muscle under the guise of NATO, in parallel with some tough talking by Richard Holbrooke, the American Assistant Secretary of State. Success was by no means certain. M, the master negotiator, was weighing up the situation.

"We've lost control of the Bosnian Serbs," he was talking to Mira striding up and down his apartment living room. "Smolov has disappeared and that bastard Mladic continues to ignore us."

Mira noted the 'we' and 'us', but knew it was M they had ignored and M who had lost control.

"Surely they're still continuing with the Greater Serbia objective which you started?" questioned his wife. Nobody else could speak to M like that.

"But the situation has changed," M's voice was rising. "The Americans are now in the game and they're not going to accept anything less than success. Mladic must compromise or he'll lose and we'll lose."

"So," Mira was always pragmatic, "we have to negotiate. But from a position of strength. We just have to find that position."

"So.... ," M was now analysing the situation with a calmer head. "As a minimum, we must secure Serbia itself. We've lost most of the Croatian territory and if Mladic carries on we'll lose the Bosnian territory. The Americans will bomb them out of existence."

"What are you going to do?"

On August 28 1995, a mortar launched by Bosnian Serbs under Mladic's direction, landed near Sarajevo's marketplace killing thirty-seven people. M went ballistic.

"That's just what the Americans were looking for as an excuse to bomb him."

There was no-one else to turn to except Mira. M had either sacked or dispensed with all his original team. Or they with him.

"Perhaps," Mira again. "You need to get the Serb leaders together and get them to agree that you will negotiate with the Americans on their behalf. If Mladic thinks he can negotiate, he'll bring us all down."

"I agree and it will also reinforce my credentials as a peacemaker, whereas Mladic and Karadzic will probably be extradited as war criminals." M was always looking to change his colours if the situation called for it.

It was a meeting where the heat outweighed the light, until Patriarch Pavle whom M had invited, made his intervention. He had previously supported the Bosnian Serbs against M so his view counted with Mladic. But M had spoken to him and outlined the international political situation. The Patriarch was not a military man, but politics was second nature and he agreed to support M this time. On his recommendation, they all agreed to let M take charge of any negotiations.

Mladic was, however, a military man and still refused to withdraw his heavy weapons. So on August 31, three days of NATO air attacks against Bosnian Serbs started. M had agreed that the Bosnian Serbs should withdraw their heavy weapons but when Mladic heard about it, he was incandescent.

"You've just capitulated. That's your way of negotiating?" Mladic would have none of it. "The war isn't over and you want us to withdraw? No. Never."

Karadzic backed him, "We will lose everything we've fought for including Sarajevo. We would be open to savage Muslim hordes attacking Bosnian Serbs. No."

"So," M taunted them, "You want your Bosnian Serbs to be bombed to death by American weapons rather than by Muslim weapons? It's one or the other. Wake up. The situation has changed."

Eventually, the Bosnian Serbs removed their guns only with a guarantee that the Bosniaks would do the same. After three years and four months of Serb shelling, Sarajevo had some peace but was still besieged. M had achieved his personal goal. He was now the lynch pin of any negotiated peace in the region and was quite satisfied.

"Congratulations." His ever loyal wife was pleased that, even though hard won Serbian territory would be lost to both Croatia and Bosnia -Serbia itself was secure and M's international status was enhanced. "Let the Bosnian Serbs stew in their own juice. You owe them nothing."

"It won't be long before they lose even more of what they have gained." said M.

"How so?"

"Their forces are stretched so thin and so depleted that I predict that Croatia and Bosnia will take the opportunity to grab back as much territory as they can, particularly in the north west of Bosnia, at least until the Americans stop them."

"Do you want that to happen?"

"O yes!" said M rubbing his hands with glee. "That'll cut them down to size. As long as I've got Serbia itself, I've got the only Serb platform."

The leaders of the warring Yugoslav republics were gradually coming to the international table albeit reluctantly, each wanting to grab whatever territory they could before the Americans called time. M had the Serbs in line now and Holbrooke had cautioned Tudjman to cease activity and withdraw their troops from western Bosnia. The Bosnian President, Izetbegovic, was holding out as his generals believed they could gain more territory with a little more time.

"So Mr Izetbegovic, will you sign the ceasefire document?" Holbrooke looked him sternly in the eye.

"Mr Holbrooke," replied Izetbegovic, "I congratulate you on your powerful negotiation with the Serbs and the Croats, but we know that any lasting peace must inevitably mean that each ethnic group has borders it can defend. Otherwise, it will all happen again with more genocide and ethnic cleansing."

Izetbegovic was using every argument, rational and emotional, at his disposal to ensure that a new Bosnia was not neutered from the start and to gain time. His generals were certain they could gain more territory which would stand them in good stead when it came to their negotiating position. The 'facts on the ground' always represented high value cards at the negotiating table. Eventually, when pressed hard, he agreed to sign but only once Sarajevo had its utilities restored. That bought his generals a little more time, but the political settlement was always more important to him than the military one.

Even when detailed talks began Sarajevo continued to be at the centre of everyone's attention. The Serbs wanted to split the city in two but the Bosnian government refused absolutely. The Americans backed them saying, "We shall not create another Berlin Wall at the end of the twentieth century, so there will be no division of Sarajevo."

Dayton talks went on for days before an uneasy agreement was reached which saw Bosnian Muslims sandwiched between Serb and Croat populations. Map drawing was the key and the fall of Srebrenica and other such enclaves made drawing new boundaries much easier for the American negotiators who deliberately turned blind eyes to war crimes, Srebrenica, Sarajevo, ethnic cleansing and genocide. It was not their concern, for the American election was coming up fast and a deal was absolutely vital to get Bill Clinton re-elected.

War crimes were left for another day and another institution. Meanwhile.....

Chapter 43 — Podgorica

KOVAC AND DJURIC were happy in each other's company. They had been through much as part of M's team and since each had come to the same conclusion about M's desire to lead a Greater Serbia, the relationship had changed. They had spent the evening going over the past few years, the highs and the lows, each charting their feelings about it all. Although both expressed their repugnance at the senseless killings and ethnic cleansings it was Kovac who seemed to need someone to hear his confession.

Djuric was more sanguine confining himself to letting his friend confess away. He had seen it more as a job and hadn't particularly been caught up in the idealism of it all. He did wonder if Kovac might need some counselling at some point and as he wasn't a religious man, a priest probably wasn't going to do. But he was not the one to suggest it. Maybe time would sort it out. He had Ivana to confess to if he felt the need to, which he didn't.

As they approached the apartment they were chatting seemingly without a care in the world until Djuric saw Ivana's bedroom window. He grabbed Kovac's arm and stopped.

"Look. A Montenegrin flag."

"She's seems very patriotic."

"No, she's not. It's upside down."

Kovac looked again. They looked at each other and without another word, Djuric indicated to get into his car. They knew it was a warning, but what about?

"They must have found you," said Kovac.

"Who?"

"The secret police, sent by M to track us down." Djuric looked sceptical. "It must have been our phones," Kovac continued.

"I got rid of mine as soon as you alerted me," said Djuric.

"Yes, but they could have got our history from the phone company."

Djuric wasn't totally convinced. "Well, whoever it is must be up there or," he paused, "perhaps around here somewhere keeping the place under surveillance," analysed Djuric. "But I don't see anyone out here."

"If they're in the apartment, we have to assume they're waiting for us," said Kovac.

"What about Ivana?" Djuric suddenly woke up to the fact that his girl might be in danger. "We have to go up."

"And get her and us killed? We don't know how many there are." Kovac tried to calm Djuric down. "The likelihood is that she's a hostage for you, or us both. M doesn't want her, just us."

The conversation lapsed for two or three minutes whilst each used their differing experiences to size up the situation, preparing to make their suggestions on how to resolve the situation.

"Have you got a key?" whispered Kovac, not quite sure why he was whispering.

"Yes," replied Djuric.

"OK. This is what I suggest," started Kovac. "Let's wait here until the early hours when at least one of them will be asleep. Then let ourselves in quietly and take them by surprise."

"I suppose there's no way of contacting Ivana beforehand?" asked Djuric, still anxious about his girl.

"Can't see one," replied Kovac. So that was the plan.

They both tried to settle down in the car, but it was uncomfortable and cold. Djuric was thinking of Ivana and how she was coping. She hadn't asked for this. It was all his fault. Kovac, on the other hand, was wondering how to capitalise on their advantage of surprise.

"What rooms are on the other side of the outside door?" he asked Djuric.

"The kitchen and bathroom."

"Why not do a quiet recci of the back?" said Kovac, "I'm getting stiff here,"

Djuric was glad to do something so they both left the car and quietly made their way up the concrete steps, Djuric hoping that the lady below Ivana didn't have insomnia and hear them. They reached the top. So far, so good. The kitchen light was on and its glow illuminated the far side of the balcony.

Djuric felt his way along the wall with Kovac right behind him. The first window was the frosted one of the bathroom which was dark. The second was the door which did have a small window at the top but was too high for them to look through and the third was the light of the kitchen.

Djuric peered round the corner of the window hoping that Ivana might be in there on her own. She wasn't but the light suggested she might be soon and he could see a kettle heating up on the gas hob.

Djuric turned to Kovac. "I think she'll be coming into the kitchen soon."

"Get her attention and find out how many are in there, where they are situated and if they are armed."

It wasn't long before Ivana appeared, nervous and stressed. Even the gentlest of knocks on the window startled her. Once she looked up and saw Djuric, her shoulders visibly relaxed. He put his finger to his lips, then pointed to the lounge. She looked back and saw Grgur relaxing, feet up, drinking and watching the television. So she came closer to the window and opened it slightly. Djuric was able to get all the information he wanted signalling that he would be back up in ten minutes and blew a kiss to his girl.

Both men crept back down to the car to work out their plan in more detail.

"I know this guy," said Djuric. "He's ex UDBA. Tito used him and now M's using him. He was sacked for lining his own pockets from criminal gangs. A nasty piece of work, but he's now in his fifties and lazy. He has a gun laid out on the coffee table, so we will need to get to him somehow before he can grab it."

"If we could pass a gun to Ivana through the window, could she kill him?"

"No. Too risky. As far as I know she's never handled a gun."

"Has he got a straight line of sight to the door from where he is?"

"No, but he only has to turn his head to see us."

"What if we asked Ivana to 'occupy' him?" Kovac was hesitant to suggest this but it was a viable way forward. The answer was immediate, "No." Djuric added, "even if she tried, he would see straight through it."

"The only way then is for Ivana to create another sort of diversion and gives us that split second advantage," murmured Kovac thoughtfully. "It's got to be believable, though."

"Wait," exclaimed Djuric, "he probably doesn't even know you're here. Why don't I just go in through the door as normal, you slip in behind me and into the bathroom. If we don't put the hall light on, he'll never see you."

"Then you get him focussed on you and Ivana and I do the business. That just might do it."

Their ten minutes was nearly up. Djuric ascended the concrete steps once again and got to the kitchen window. A few minutes later Ivana appeared and a brief conversation ensued. Ivana appeared not to be convinced at the plan but conceded she had nothing better. Operation Grgur would start at precisely midnight and she was to make herself scarce in her bedroom.

It was three minutes to midnight and both men were waiting at the front door. On time, Djuric opened the door using his key as quietly as he could but, nevertheless, it prompted Grgur to snatch up his weapon and point it at the incoming Djuric. Kovac came behind and easily slipped into the bathroom through the door which Ivana had left open.

"Welcome home, Djuric. Where's your pal?" sneered Grgur.

"Pal. What pal?" Djuric started sweating now their fundamental assumption had been wrong. But it could still work, he thought.

"Why Kovac of course," answered Grgur waving the gun towards Djuric. I know you went out together so you will have come back together."

"Kovac. Hardly a pal. He's been trying to make me come back to Belgrade with him. Says I'm a traitor." Djuric was furiously inventing something which would put Grgur off his guard and at the same time walking around the room so that the gun was pointing away from the hall from where Kovac should make his entrance..... any time now.

"Oh please. Let's not be silly. Kovac is on the run with you, but I'm afraid this is the end." He then addressed himself to the bathroom door and challenged Kovac to come out or Djuric would be shot. "It's that simple," said the ex UDBA man. Kovac appeared in the hallway with his hands away from his body.

" Put your weapon on the floor and kick it towards me," he ordered Kovac. The intelligence man did as he was ordered. As Grgur was screwing the silencer on his gun, he said pointedly, "You've both been naughty boys. M was rather miffed that you went away with not so much as a goodbye."

They looked at each other as he ordered them over to the other side of the room near the kitchen. Grgur was obviously not going to waste any time.

"Sorry I can't spend more time with you, but I need to be going." He raised his weapon only to stiffen and fall forward with a large kitchen knife in his back revealing Ivana right behind him with almost a crazed look on her face. She had taken a knife back to the bedroom concealed underneath her clothing and had been listening with the door ajar. She was not going to let this creature ruin everything. Once Kovac had been forced to drop his weapon, she knew it was down to her. She had crept out of the bedroom unseen and plunged the knife deep into Grgur's back. He fell forward, gurgled and twitched for a few seconds then went quiet. The men looked at her then at each other, not quite believing what she'd managed to do. They had thought it was the end for them.

"So much for your wonderful planning," she said with her standard sarcasm. "Now I suggest you get this animal out of my flat while I try to clean up."

Grgur was rolled up where he fell. His blood was still oozing out all over the rug that was on the living room floor.

"I'll buy a new one," offered Kovac.

"That would be the right thing to do," answered Ivana going into the kitchen to wash her knife.

"Give me the knife," ordered Djuric. "I'll get rid of it."

As the men struggled down the concrete steps as silently as they could, Djuric had an idea. "Put him in my car on the back seat and we'll take the road to the coast. I know just where to put him."

Back in the apartment, the minute the men left Ivana started trembling all over, so much so that she had to sit down. Her legs were wobbly and tears were forming in her eyes. She had never done anything like that before even with the anger and vitriol she felt towards Grgur. Now the adrenalin rush was receding, she felt weak. She wanted to be strong in front of Djuric and Kovac; in reality, she wasn't. The clean up would have to wait until the morning. She left a note on her bedroom door not to be disturbed.

Djuric drove out of the city on the road to the coast for about twenty miles with Kovac in the passenger seat. He then turned off up a mountain track. A further ten minutes of bumpy riding led them to a ridge where the car stopped.

"Let's get him out," said Djuric. Both men strained to pull the overweight secret policeman out of the back seat and drag him to the edge of the channel.

"Where's the knife?" asked Kovac suddenly, concerned that if it was found with the body, Ivana's fingerprints might be a clear giveaway.

"I gave it a clean and threw it out on the journey." Kovac raised his eyebrows, thinking that might not have been a brilliant move. Djuric shrugged. A minute later over went the body with the rug. They couldn't see where it had landed but heard the undergrowth in the ravine make way its new occupant. Both men leaned back on the bonnet of the car still breathing quite heavily, neither saying anything; Djuric thinking how Ivana had saved them and what an amazing woman she was, Kovac wondering if there was anything else they should do to minimise any chance of a blow back. Finally, both men got back in the car. Djuric started the engine, reversed and they began making their way back to the main road. Not a lot more was said on the return journey.

"I think I ought to leave," said Kovac as they were travelling back. "Ivana will need you to herself for a while. That was a brave and amazing thing to have done and she will not get over it quickly."

Djuric looked sceptical. "She's a strong lady."

"Not always on the inside," guessed Kovac. "Look. Here's the money for a new rug. Once we get back, I'll go off in my car and you go and comfort her."

Djuric looked concerned for his friend. "Where will you go at this time of night?"

"I'll get a hotel tonight then decide in the morning."

Djuric pondered as he drove back through the city and as he was parking the car, said, "My family has a studio flat at a place called Igalo near the coast. You could stay there awhile, if you like. You know, until you decide what you're going to do."

"Really?" said Kovac.

"As long as you like. It's a great holiday area." He dug his keys out and gave one to Kovac. When you leave just post it back here." said Djuric, his eyes twinkling a little as he looked at his friend in the passenger seat. He realised that both of them were now free of their past as they ever could be. The men got out of the car, said their final goodbyes to each other and went their separate ways, with no promises to keep in touch.

Kovac decided to travel through the night and arrived in Igalo in the early morning. He found the apartment relatively quickly and settled in. Both mind and body needed rest, and lots of it. He didn't wake until 4pm later that day and lay in bed for a while thinking about his past life and what might be to come. He felt he had aged years, but for the first time in his life had a blank canvas for the years to come. He reported to no-one and no-one reported to him. There was no mission except to stay alive and find his future.

He could hear the world outside going about the business of living and he wanted to join them. For the first time in many years, he stopped thinking just to listen; a barking dog wanting to be let out, a few shouts of greeting from one friend to another, the odd car backfiring and the smell of salt from the Bay of Kotor. He smiled. He was free.

Djuric made his way up the concrete steps wondering how Ivana was after what she had done. She had saved them single-handedly when their plans had failed at the first hurdle. He crept in through the front door, saw the note and understood Ivana's wish to be on her own. So he settled down in the spare room which had been Kovac's. He didn't know what would happen in the morning. Ivana could be unpredictable.

They sat opposite each other over breakfast saying nothing. Djuric was tempted to repeat his "Sorry", but knew somehow that was not going to cut it. Either she was going to send him on his way or invite him to stay. As it happened she did neither. Suddenly she got up.

"Let's go."

Djuric was taken by surprise. "Where are we going?"

"Take me to where you dumped his body."

Djuric's mouth was open. There were things he could have said such as, "You don't want to go there," or "I don't think that's a good idea," or even, "Why?" But he said none of these things innately knowing that questioning her decision would provoke a flash of anger and some kind of retribution. That he didn't want. Rather, he wanted to smooth over this situation until regular service could resume. He obediently followed her out of the apartment and into his car.

"Where has Kovac gone?" she asked tightly.

"To Igalo."

She turned to look at him, but said nothing immediately.

"He's not coming back?"

"He's not coming back," confirmed Djuric.

"Ever?"

"Ever, but he's given me money for a new rug."

They resumed their respective silence on the journey until they came to the ravine. She looked down to where Grgur's last resting place was. Djuric looked at her, wondering what was going on in her mind. Her face was a blank. Then it changed and she picked up a large rock and flung it at the body. It missed. She tried again with the same result. She started to shake with tears in her eyes. Djuric took her gently by the shoulders and tried to encourage her back to the car. She acquiesced allowing him to guide her back but not before she had spat at the body.

Nothing of consequence was said on the return journey. Djuric noticed in her face that whatever distress she had been feeling had now morphed into a look of determination. Her chin was set firm, her eyes clear, her head steady. Out of nowhere, she said simply,

"He raped me."

Djuric was used to her unpredictability but even he was taken aback. He stared across at her and in doing so, nearly drove off the road.

"Don't crash the car on my account," Ivana said, her sarcasm returning.

"I'm so sorry," stuttered Djuric, not knowing what else to say. What do you say? He decided to wait until Ivana offered any more, indicating she wanted to talk about it. For while she said nothing.

"It was in Tito's apartment," she started. "Tito had gone and I was cleaning up. I didn't notice that he had come in...." she shuddered again.

Djuric put his spare hand on her knee, wondering whether to say anything. He knew he could say the wrong thing but he could also easily be criticised for saying nothing, so even if it brought a sarcastic comment he decide to risk it. "He got what he deserved."

Ivana looked across at him on the verge of saying something but checked herself.

"Let's go home."

Chapter 44 — Netherlands 2022

"WHAT DO YOU mean, 'you tried'? asked Erik, taking no notice of his father's pronouncement that his previous question was definitely the last. The studious twelve year old was still anxious to finish his homework and was not going to let go until he got what he needed. He didn't want to be shown up in class on Monday, rather he expected to be at the top. There were stars at stake.

Ex Corporal Andries de Ryke put his paper down and breathed a heavy sigh, not of frustration this time, but of acquiescence. His wife looked at him with enquiring eyes thinking he was at last going to talk about his war experience in Bosnia.

"Andries. Even I don't really know what happened. You've never spoken of it. I've heard what the newspapers have said and what the government's enquiry said, but you've never trusted us with the truth."

"Yes, Daddy. What is the truth?" asked Erik echoing his mother, but still concentrating on trying to slurp more spaghetti into his mouth. He could clearly do more than once thing at a time.

"Erik. That's no way to eat at the table," his mother scolded. "And don't pressure Daddy. When he's ready, he'll tell us." It was a comment which had the subtext of, 'but it had better be now.' De Ryke had that faraway look in his eyes, not saying anything in response to the pressure that was building, but re-living something in the past. His wife coughed a cough which meant 'we're still here,' which had the desired effect of suddenly bringing him back to the present. He looked at her, then at his son.

"Let's clear away the meal, then we can sit down and I'll try to explain what I can." With that, he got up from the table and disappeared upstairs. His wife and son watched him go, then looked at each other before Mrs de Ryke told her son to quickly finish eating. She began to clear away the dirty dishes and load the dishwasher. Erik, still oblivious about what was about to happen, went back to his homework book and carried on writing another part of his assignment that weekend.

After fifteen minutes or so, Andries de Ryke reappeared with a box which he set down on a clear dining table except for Erik and his homework book. His wife noticed he was back sitting at the table and came out of the kitchen to join them. When she saw the box, she lifting her eyebrows in surprise.

"Andries, what's that?"

"It's a box containing bits and pieces of when I was in the army."

"I've never seen it before. Where was it?"

"Up in the loft."

"You've never shown it to me in all the time we've been married." It wasn't an accusation, more a statement of disappointment that she felt he didn't trust her with what was in it. Her husband looked embarrassed and struggled to regain some rationale as to why he had hidden the box.

"Don't forget all this happened well before we got married and," he added smoothly "I haven't looked at it in years," he replied. Too smoothly, thought his wife. She said nothing but just looked at him waiting for a real answer.

"The truth is," he started, "the truth is, that I wanted to forget about it all. It wasn't exactly the most distinguished episode of my army career or any of the other guys who were with me." Without any more explanation he took the lid off and began to lift documents and clippings out of the box holding them close in his hands as if he didn't want anyone else to see them. Erik was glancing backwards and forwards to his mother and father sensing something was not quite right. All he had wanted was a page of his father's recollections of the war for his homework. Instead, he was seeing his father hesitant and secretive as he had never seen before, and his mother being quite assertive, pushing and probing his father for some secrets that he had clearly kept hidden for years.

After a few minutes of silence at the table, Erik's mother suggested to her husband that he give Erik what he wanted now and they talk further later on. Mr de Ryke nodded, put the contents of the box back with the lid on and turned to Erik,

"OK Erik, ask me any question you need to do your homework." An hour later Erik's father called time. "That's the lot. You've got enough now to finish it and its bedtime in half an hour. If you haven't finished it, you can come back to it tomorrow."

Mrs de Ryke was not messing about when she insisted that Erik go to bed on time. She firmly refused all his usual delaying tactics and only ten minutes late, which was a record, Erik was in bed and she was with her husband sitting together downstairs expectantly.

"So?" questioned his wife.

"I don't know where to start," said a hesitant husband.

"OK. You mentioned the Serbs. Who are they? Where do they come from? They sound as if they're straight out of Lord of the Rings."

"A bit of background first. Yugoslavia was made up of a number of different countries which have never really got on and been constantly invaded by other empires. Before the Communists, it was the Ottomans and before that probably someone else. Tito was the President put in by the Soviets and when he died the whole aggregation that was Yugoslavia began to fall apart as different ethnic groups began to compete for territory." He paused.

Elka jumped in. "So, you're saying that Yugoslavia didn't exist before the Soviet Union took it over and installed Tito?"

"No. I think it was created after WW1 in 1918 as a kingdom of Serbs, Croats and Slovenes. I'm not an historian, but I think that's right."

"So what were these ethnic groups?"

"Well, there was Slovenia in the north, Croatia in the west, Serbia in the east, then came Bosnia in the centre with Montenegro, Kosovo and Macedonia in the south."

"That's an awful lot of countries and they all started fighting each other?"

"No. The capital of Serbia happened to be Belgrade which was the former capital of Yugoslavia, so I suppose they felt pre-eminent. Anyway, there were lots of Serbs living not only in Serbia itself, but in enclaves within Croatia and Bosnia and a guy called Milosevic began manoeuvring to try to create a Greater Serbia which would encompass all these extra areas of population."

"So why did you have to get involved?" Elka now had her hands in the box and was looking at the various bits of paper and photographs.

"I don't exactly know what started it, but the Serbs began to invade these other areas trying to annex them to the homeland. Obviously, Croatia and

Bosnia didn't like that and began to fight back." De Ryke paused, as if trying to remember the history.

"What about Montenegro and Kosovo?"

"I think Milosevic had successfully installed puppet governments there so I don't think there was a lot of fighting. I'm not sure."

"So again why did you have to get involved? We have no connection with this area of the world."

"The Balkans."

"What?"

"The area we are talking about is called the Balkans. You remember the Winter Olympics held in a place called Sarajevo?"

"Yes. That's where that British couple, what were their names?"

"Torvill and Dean."

"That's right. They got all 10s in the ice skating, didn't they?"

"I think it was ice dancing."

"OK. Same thing."

De Ryke didn't want to get into an argument over the difference between ice skating and ice dancing so he moved on.

"Where was I?"

"The Serbs were fighting everyone."

"Well, there were lots of really horrible things going on...." His wife interrupted, "Yes I remember the television reports: civilian killings, mass graves, women raped, homes demolished." She shuddered as she selected some gruesome photos out of the box. "What are those people about? It's just what the Nazis did in the Second World War. I thought all that was past us."

He nodded. "Well, we saw things that I really don't want to mention, inhuman things that were done purely for the entertainment of soldiers, and people packed in small cages stacked on top of one another with no privacy, no sanitation..." His voice trailed off.

"So again why did you have to get involved?"

"Everyone was reluctant to get involved. I think politicians of all sorts just wanted it to go away. But the horrendous human rights violations forced the UN (United Nations) to do something. So they asked different nations for troops to go in and keep the peace." He snorted in derision.

"What a joke! There was no peace but the Dutch government and generals put their hand up and said, "We'll do it." They had no idea what they were doing. We were the third Dutch force to go in – DutchBat III. Our task was to keep the Bosnians safe from the Serbs in a place called Srebrenica."

He paused again, shaking his head. "Not a cat in hell's chance." He looked as if he was now talking to himself. His wife kept silent still sifting through various documents in the box waiting for his next revelation,

"The UN said they had to be neutral, so that meant treating each side the same. But the sides were never the same." His voice was now rising with emotion. "One side was looking to exterminate the other and had vastly superior weapons, some supplied by Russia."

"Russia?" echoed his wife.

"We reckoned they had military advisers and special forces on the ground with the Serbs, not that this took anything away from the behaviour of the Serbs. They were animals."

"But surely you had your own weapons stop the Serbs?"

De Ryke laughed harshly. " In comparison, we had nothing. Nothing." That faraway look came back into his eyes. "They just walked right by and laughed at us. All we could do was watch them kill, rape and 'cleanse' the place."

"What does 'cleanse' mean?" asked Elka hesitantly.

"It meant killing everyone in a town or village that they wanted, by whatever means."

"But surely you had commanders who knew this was going on?"

De Ryke laughed a hollow laugh. "Our so-called commander was a Frenchie and he was living it up in Sarajevo at the bloody Holiday Inn and refused to give us any weapons even to defend ourselves."

"But that's terrible."

"Anyway, eventually we got taken out." He was shaking his head. "What an absolute farce!"

They both sunk into silence. She put her hand on his knee. "Sorry," she said. He turned to her and smiled weakly. "It was a long time ago. Not sure anyone has learnt anything judging by what's happening in Ukraine right now."

The following morning, De Ryke was sitting in his chair reading the Sunday paper when he suddenly stopped.

"I don't believe it," he exclaimed. He called urgently to his wife. "Look at this." She sensed something more important than the performance of the Dutch national football team was catching her husband's attention.

"Do you remember that veterans invitation I had several weeks ago? Well this is what it was all about apparently. He folded the paper up and passed it over to his wife.

Prime Minister Mark Rutte has said the troops had been under-equipped to stop the massacre and were asked to perform an "impossible task".
June 2022

In July 1995, some 8,000 Muslim men were massacred after Dutch forces were overrun by Bosnian Serb troops. Previously, Dutch governments have insisted fault lay with the UN for failing to provide air support.

But speaking to veterans at a military base in central Netherlands on Saturday, Mr Rutte accepted troops of the DutchBat III peacekeeping force had struggled because "your mandate, your equipment and the military support you received during your mission were all inadequate" for a mission "that ultimately proved impossible to carry out".

"Today, I apologise on behalf of the Dutch government to all the women and men of DutchBat III. To all of you here, and to those who are not with us today," Mr Rutte told veterans.

"With the greatest possible appreciation and respect for the way in which DutchBat III kept on trying to do the right thing, under very difficult circum-stances, even when that was really no longer possible."

In addition to the apology, soldiers deployed to Srebrenica were also given the Bronze Medal of Honour from Defence Minister Kajsa Ollongren.

She stopped reading and exclaimed excitedly, "You're going to get a medal. Wow. Erik will love that."

De Ryke wasn't so excited. "I'm not sure I want one."

"Why not?"

"It's nearly twenty five years after the fact." He paused. "And look at this." He brought out a picture from the box still on the dining room table. It was of his platoon in Bosnia.

"Do you know that some men never returned home. This guy here," he stabbed at a soldier in the picture. "This guy served alongside me and was killed by those animals." He was quiet again as his eye wandered over the soldiers in the photo.

"Some have got PTSD, some can't hold down a job, others turned to drugs, still others had their marriages collapse. And now they want to give us a medal?"

She was quiet and resumed her reading of the paper.

In July 1995, amid a campaign of genocide by Bosnian Serb forces, thousands of Muslims fled to a UN safe zone in Srebrenica. They were protected by lightly equipped Dutch troops who were quickly overrun during a Bosnian Serb advance.

After securing the surrender of the Dutch forces, Bosnian Serb troops under General Ratko Mladic took aside men and boys aged between 12 and 77 for what they said would be an "interrogation".

Over the next five days, the men were executed and buried in mass graves by Mladic's troops. Serbia has always denied the killings formed part of a campaign of genocide, but accepts it was a crime.

Mr Rutte's apology comes a year after a report made a series of recommendations into how to support the 850 troops of DutchBat III, many of whom suffered from post-traumatic stress disorder after their experiences of the war.

And in 2019 the Dutch Supreme Court ruled that the Netherlands was partially liable for the deaths of some 350 men in the massacre, ruling that they had removed the men from a Dutch base despite knowing they "were in serious jeopardy of being abused and murdered" by Bosnian Serb forces.

"What happened to the Serbs?"

"NATO (North Atlantic Treaty Organisation) came in to provide air cover, much too late of course, but the Serbs got a lot of what they wanted in Bosnia from the Dayton Agreement, brokered by the Americans."

"What about the people who gave the orders?"

"Milosevic, Mladic and a guy called Karadzic eventually got tried in the Hague and went to prison."

"Yes, I remember that. It went on for years." She took a folder of press reports out of the box and pulled the cuttings out. "You were following the trial!" she exclaimed as she began reading.

The indictees ranged from common soldiers to generals and police commanders all the way to prime ministers. Slobodan Milosevic was the first sitting head of state indicted for war. Other "high level" indictees included Milan Babic, former President of the Republika Srpska Krajina; Radovan Karadzic, former President of the Republika Srpska; Ratko Mladic, former Commander of the Bosnian Serb Army; and Ante Gotovina, former General of the Croatian Army.

De Ryke admitted that he had. "I owed it to the men I lost, to track those indited and record they got what they deserved."

"But what about the men underneath them, those who actually carried out the rapes and killings?" asked Elka.

"If people managed to identify them and catch them, yes, some got indited. But just like many of the lower ranking SS men after the Second World War, too many just slipped away probably reinvented themselves and are still free, maybe still in positions of power and perhaps still hankering after a Greater Serbia."

"But that's terrible." exclaimed Elka.

"I expect someone knows who they are," continued de Ryke. "But it's all too late now. No-one had got any appetite to capture them. Besides, any evidence would be non existent or at least easily refuted."

He began to collect all his bits and pieces together and put them back in the box. He put the lid on and sat back.

"You know, it seems certain nations or ethnic groups have some in-built tendency for aggressive talk and violent behaviour and Serbs seem to be one of them."

"Surely you can't impugn a whole nation. There must be some great humanitarians who are Serbs?"

"Possibly, but not that I've seen." He paused.

He looked at his wife. "Are you happy now you've seen all this?" he asked.

"Happy is probably not the right word, but I'm glad I can now share in that part of your life." replied Elka.

"Well, I'm going to put this back in the loft and never going to get it down again. If Erik wants to do so when I'm gone, that's fine. But while I'm living, I don't want to think about it again."

Acknowledgements

AS WELL AS a considerable amount of desk/internet research, there is nothing like visiting such places as Sarajevo, looking at the airport tunnel remains, seeing where the Bosnian Serb army were positioned to shell the city and so on. Thank you Sarajevo.

If I was to highlight one tome which tracks the detailed history of the events, it would be:

'Yugoslavia, the death of a nation' by Laura Silber and Allan Little published by Penguin. Laura was Balkan correspondent for the Financial Times and Allan Little an award-winning BBC journalist.

Also, thanks to my daughter-in-law, Melida Hadzovic Daplyn for numerous corrections in the edit and other friends, Phil Everest, Simon Porter and Liz Crozier for their help and encouragement.

www.ingramcontent.com/pod-product-compliance
Lightning Source LLC
Chambersburg PA
CBHW061559170626
46811CB00001B/251